Smoke

Kaye George

An Imogene Duckworthy Mystery
Book 2

White City

Press

Also by Kaye George

A People of the Wind Mystery

Book 1
Death in the Time of Ice

Book 2
Death on the Trek

Book 3
Death in the New Land

Imogene Duckworthy Mysteries
Book 1
Choke

Book 2
Smoke

Book 3
Broke

Book 4
Stroke

PRAISE FOR BROKE

"I loved it. The series gets better and better."
—E. B. Davis, Short Story Writer, Avid Reader and Beach Bum

PRAISE FOR CHOKE

"A total delight! Laugh-out-loud dialogue, adorable characters, and a truly original voice. Fresh, feisty and hilarious. More, please."
—Hank Phillippi Ryan Anthony, Agatha and Macavity winning author

PRAISE FOR SMOKE

"A Texas-sized slice of murder and mayhem, makes for a fun, fast-paced read."
—Rhys Bowen, Agatha and Anthony-winning author of the Molly Murphy and Royal Spyness series.

"Kaye George knows how to write a fun mystery! She will make you laugh. Don't miss Smoke.
—Sasscer Hill, Agatha and Macavity Finalist

Smoke

Kaye George

Copyright © Kaye George 2023
White City Press Edition: 2024
White City Press is a division of Misti Media LLC
https://whitecitypress.com
Cover © 2023 Karen Phillips and White City Press
Cover Design by Karen Phillips
Available in both Paperback and eBook Editions
1 2 3 4 5 6 7 8 9 10
Paperback ISBN: 9781963479485
eBook ISBN: 9781963479478

Dedication

To the Austin Mystery Writers, especially Kathy Waller, Gale Albright and Mary Jo Powell

Acknowledgements

I owe much to my cover designer, Karen Phillips. This text is as good as it is because of the editing of Ramona DeFelice Long. If you see editing problems, that's probably stuff that she corrected and I chose to ignore. As always, I'll thank the Guppies for helping me stay with mystery writing and the Plothatchers, Krista Davis, Janet Bolin, Marilyn Levinson, Peg Louden, Janet Koch, and Daryl Wood Gerber in no particular order.

I modeled the physical plant of Jerry's Jerky after that of Texas Best Meats near Wichita Falls, Texas, but every character in the book is entirely fictitious and none are based on any of the wonderful people in the Wichita Falls and Holliday areas. Thanks to the Wichita Falls Police Department for letting me participate in the ride-along program, especially Karl Lillie. Also to the Austin Citizen's Police Academy, of which I am a graduate and where I learned so much about policing. Any mistakes in that area are mine and no fault of my teachers. Jim Jackson, Cher'ley Grogg, Kristi Blank Makansi, Cathy Sonnenberg, Jackie Vick, Judy Daily, and Dr. Lyle gave me help with parts of the plot early on. Thanks for some of my ideas from the Brainstorming Gups, and from classes with Mary Buckham, Kris Neri, the Writing PIs, and Laurie Schnebly.

One

Imogene Duckworthy did not like pigs. She was fairly fond of cattle, having grown up surrounded by them. She hadn't been around pigs much. In fact, this was the first time she'd ever driven toward a pig farm.

Immy drove the ancient Dodge van out of Saltlick, a small Texas town with at least one foot planted firmly in the last century, and down the highway where cattle ranches, thickets of mesquite, and a few old oil wells stretched to the horizon. Cowboy country, not pig country. Not a pig in sight.

Her daughter, Nancy Drew Duckworthy, three-years-old-going-on-four, was squealing like a pig in her car seat. Drew adored swine. She had recently transferred her passion from Barbie dolls to pigs (with a brief interlude of worshipping hippopotamuses—because she liked saying the word). Since Immy loathed the fixation on Barbies, she was trying really hard to like pigs.

In fact, she was on her way to pick one out for Drew's upcoming birthday.

"Pig, pig, pig!" squealed Drew. "I'm getting a big, big pig!"

Immy cringed. Not *too* big, she hoped.

Immy would do anything for her daughter, anything in the world, but she wondered if this was the right thing.

Her mother, Hortense Duckworthy, thought Drew should have a pig. Drew certainly wanted a pig. But the money to pay for it was making a dent, a ravine—no, a crater—in the pile Immy had saved to buy herself a car. A nice, clean, used car that had shiny paint and no rattles. Or maybe less rattles than the van.

After the dent made by the payment for her online PI course, her pile of savings was more like an ant hill. Not a big fire ant hill, either, a puny mound made by those Yankee red ants.

Ralph Sandoval, who had come along to help handle the animal, shifted his weight to look back at Drew. "Yes. A big, big pig."

Immy glanced over to see both of them grinning like maniacs.

Ralph sure hung around a lot lately. Ever since that first electrifying kiss in the spring. Immy wasn't stopping him in case there might be more of those.

"They're miniature potbellied pigs, y'all," Immy said. "Not big ones."

Her statement didn't dampen their enthusiasm at all. They kept up a chant of "Big, big pig," until she spotted a wooden sign swinging from a post: AMY'S SWINE. She turned the van up the dirt road that led to the pig breeder's place, just outside the town of Cowtail. The van bumped along the dry dirt ruts, raising even more glee from Drew.

The bilious green van belonged to Immy's mother and was their only family vehicle. But it was a trusty old thing and kept bouncing down the road.

Road dust blew in the windows and Immy reluctantly rolled them up. The van had no AC and Texas, this close to the Fourth of July, was damn hot. Immy didn't like the windows closed. Confinement made her feel like she couldn't breathe. Maybe that came from living in a small single-wide with her mother and daughter. Or maybe that time she locked herself in a closet for three hours when she was five had scarred her for life. Whatever caused the fear, her breathing became shallow and quick with the windows up.

By the time she negotiated the ruts and arrived at the house and outbuildings, Immy was drenched in sweat. She took a moment to mop perspiration off her face and hands with the paper towels she kept on the floor behind the passenger seat, then climbed out and unbuckled Drew from her seat in the back.

Drew, growing shy now that she was free to run to the pigs in the nearby pens, clutched her mother's jeans with the hand that didn't hold a small rubber pig.

Ralph came around to stand beside them. They almost looked like a little family, Immy thought. Well, except that Ralph wasn't little. The sole underling to the police chief of Saltlick, he was ex-high-school-football-player large. Out of uniform, as he was now, he was only slightly less intimidating. He hoisted Drew to his shoulder. Immy worried that her daughter was so awfully far from the ground. Drew didn't look scared at all.

Immy surveyed Amy's farm as they walked toward the smell. A neat white ranch house with a storm cellar off to one side, a sparkling clean, white pickup parked at other side. A red barn and tractor shed twenty yards or so to the right. A few large live oaks dotting the front yard. She glimpsed more trees hanging over the pens in the rear. The scene was serene, idyllic. The stench was not.

As they reached the backyard, a short woman came out of one of the pens. "I heard you coming. I'm Amy JoBeth." She wiped her hands on her overalls and looked down at them. "Maybe I'd better not shake hands. I have your piggy dumpling ready." She squatted down to Drew's level. "So. You're going to be four years old?"

Drew gave an enthusiastic nod, setting her glossy chestnut curls bobbing in the strong afternoon sunlight.

"Your piggy is right here." Amy JoBeth stood and waved for Drew to follow her toward the pens. "Come see him."

Immy wondered if it was true that people came to resemble their pets. Amy JoBeth was pig shaped, with a nice round middle and skinny arms and legs. Her nose even turned up. Her short, brown, wiry hair, if it were thinner, might look like coarse pig hair. Her overalls were practical, Immy supposed, for a pig person.

Immy had gotten the name of the pig farm from Ophelia Jenkins, a

Saltlick resident who sold leather harnesses to breeders of miniature pigs. According to Ophelia, Amy JoBeth had started raising the smallish porkers after her recent divorce.

Amy JoBeth started walking and Drew took her hand saying, "I wanna walk wif the pig lady."

Immy followed. When they rounded the corner of the house, she was stopped in her tracks by the sight of the pigs. Three pens of spacious, woven-wire-fenced dirt plots held neat rows of pig houses lined up under the trees. Each pen also had a soft-sided pool of muddy water. Several animals lay in each. They were the size of, and kind of resembled, Immy decided, Basset hounds, with their thick bodies and stubby legs.

In the second and third pens, some pigs lay outside their door flaps, their eyes closed in contentment. The wooden houses looked like backyard playhouses minus windows, with mansard roofs and wildflowers painted on the sides. The fourth pen was smaller and held a single small pig. Amy JoBeth headed for that one.

On the other side of a substantial fence, a mean-looking bull regarded them with bad intent.

"Is that your bull?" asked Immy.

Amy JoBeth made a face. "No. I don't keep cattle. That bull belongs to the rancher across the road. I wish he didn't have it right there."

The incessant west Texas wind ruffled the tall grass outside the pens and rustled the tough leaves of the live oaks. Immy lifted her straight reddish brown hair to try to dry the nape of her neck. She hoped her hair and clothes wouldn't be soaked in pig stink after she left.

The baby pig in the enclosure trotted over to the fence.

"This guy is the friendliest of Gretchen's babies," Amy JoBeth said, sticking a finger through the fence to scratch the pig's head. "Gretchen was one of my favorites. I hated to let her go, but they wanted her so badly." Amy JoBeth gave a sniff and blinked her eyes. "I just sold Gretchen to the Buckets a few days ago. You know, Rusty and Tinnie, the people with the beef jerky place?"

Yes, Immy knew who the Buckets were. Her mother, Hortense, consumed great quantities of Jerry's Jerky.

Amy JoBeth opened the gate, took Drew's hand, and led her toward the pure white pig. Immy's breath caught. The little guy looked at her with clear, china blue eyes.

He was just about the cutest animal Immy had ever seen.

"What's his name?" asked Drew, looking up at Amy JoBeth.

"That's a good question. I don't think he has a name. Would you like to give him one?"

The piglet was the height of Drew's knees. That would be a good sized pet for her. Immy hoped he wouldn't grow too much more.

Drew tilted her head, considering the piglet. It bumped its nose against her leg and she giggled. She reached a tentative hand to scratch its head, as Amy JoBeth had. "I think his name is Marshmallow."

"I think you're right," said Amy JoBeth, beaming at Drew.

"How big will he get?" Immy asked.

Amy JoBeth waved her hand at the other pens. "You can see. A couple feet tall, most likely. But he'll probably weigh about a hundred pounds when he's full grown. You have to be careful not to overfeed him. I'll give you a booklet to take home."

Marshmallow seemed to like Drew's ministrations. He closed his eyes and grunted while she continued to scratch the same spot on the top of his head.

Amy JoBeth grinned at Immy and Ralph. "Looks like they've bonded already." She fished a piece of paper from the pocket of her overalls and held it out to Immy.

It was the bill for Marshmallow. Immy made out the check, mentally kissing the money, her precious, hard-earned dollars, goodbye. She'd done a lot of filing and typing for that dough. As she wrote she saw Amy JoBeth's name printed at the top of the invoice. "Amy JoBeth *Anderson*? You're *that* Amy JoBeth?"

"How many Amy JoBeths do you know?" said Ralph.

That Amy JoBeth bent down and snapped a piglet-sized harness on

Marshmallow, led him from the pen, and handed the leash to Drew.

"Did you used to work for Mike Mallett?" Immy asked her. "The Mike Mallett who's a PI in Wymee Falls?"

Amy JoBeth nodded as she took the check. "Yes." She chuckled. "I am *that* Amy JoBeth. And I worked for that Mike Mallett."

"Maybe you don't know that I now work—"

Amy JoBeth's cell phone trilled and she wandered away for a private conversation. Immy would like to talk to her some time about some clippings she'd found in the desk. She'd assumed they'd been collected by her predecessor and wondered why they'd been left behind.

Ralph and Drew started for the van. Marshmallow trotted alongside on his leash, like he'd always known them.

Immy started to follow but Amy JoBeth finished her conversation and called after them. "You have a cage in the car?"

Ralph nodded. "Yep. I'm loaning out my dog crate. I built a pen in Drew's yard, too."

"Wonderful!" Amy JoBeth rubbed her hands together. "He'll do fine in the house, but he needs to be outside sometimes, too. Let me run in the house and get the booklet."

Ralph picked up Marshmallow and carried him to the crate in the back of the van. He cradled the tiny animal like a baby. The pig looked even smaller in his huge hands, hands more suited for holding a football, or taking down a drunken arrestee.

Amy JoBeth came running out the front door waving the booklet, which proved to be three pieces of paper stapled together. She peeked through the rear side window and Immy saw tears in her eyes.

"He's a very special pig, you know. The son of Gretchen." She stood on tiptoe to see the crate. "Gretchen is the best pig I ever had. I hated to let her go, but Tinnie Bucket wouldn't have any other. Just fell in love with Gretchen." She stepped back to the driver's window. "He's been neutered, but he'll need a shot and a de-worming. I called Dr. Fox in Cowtail before you came and you can stop there on your way home if you'd like."

"I think Drew loves him already." Immy turned to Ralph. "Do you mind if we stop at the vet's? Could you help us get him out?"

"No problem, Immy," said Ralph. "I'm off until tomorrow."

"Okay," said Immy, buckling Drew and climbing into the van. She started it up, waved to Amy JoBeth, calling "Thanks!" and drove away, thinking out loud. "I'll go to the vet's first, then head home. Is that all right, Ralph?"

He turned and gave her that heartwarming smile of his. "I told you. I'm all yours tonight."

She realized she hadn't gotten a chance to talk to Amy JoBeth about those papers in her desk at Mike Mallett's office. But she could do it another time. Now she wanted to get the pig home to meet Hortense.

Immy had begun to favor Ralph with a few dinner dates and he seemed satisfied with that for now, but how long would that last? It had taken awhile to be able to let her defenses down this far. Immy had a history of bad choices in men and knew she should probably give up on them. It was hard though. She was only twenty-two and she liked them. And Ralph made it clear he liked her a lot.

Immy didn't know if she liked Ralph as much as Ralph liked her and she thought she ought to keep him at arm's length more than she had lately. She was afraid she might be leading him on, as they used to say in school. He'd been over every night for two weeks building the pig pen, fixing up a shelter for it and lining it with straw. Next, he said, he would dig a hole and pour a cement pond for the pig. Immy felt like she needed to help, or at least entertain him.

But she had studying to do. She'd signed up for her online PI course three months ago and was already getting behind in the homework. There was so much to learn.

Ralph leafed through the sheets on pig care. "Hey, it says they can be trained to a litter box. I'd better get one set up in the pen. And one in the house, too, I guess. Do you need a pet door?"

"I don't think that would work, Ralph." The doors out of the single-wide, both the front and back doors, led to small wooden porches with steps to the ground. The pig would probably have to be carried in and out until it got bigger. "I need to study tonight."

"That's what you say every night. Why do you want a PI license anyway?"

Immy sighed. "It's hard to explain."

"Try me."

But they had reached the vet's parking lot. "Later, Ralph. Let's go get Marshmallow de-wormed, whatever that means."

Ralph grinned. "It means the vet reaches down his throat and pulls slimy, stringy worms out."

"Ew, gross!" called Drew. She giggled louder than Ralph.

"He does not. Don't tell her that." Immy frowned at Ralph. "He'll just give Marshmallow some medicine, sweetheart. I think."

Ralph fetched the pig while Immy unbuckled Drew. As soon as she set her daughter on the pavement, Drew ran around to the back of the van to see her new pet. An orange truck careened around the corner from behind the vet's building and barreled toward her.

While Immy screamed her daughter's name, Ralph, pig in one hand, grabbed Drew with the other and flattened both of them against the side of the van. Although Ralph didn't get very flat.

"Son of a bitch," yelled Immy after the careless speed demon, but the driver was out of hearing by the time she recovered enough speech for the curse.

Ralph hurled a few choice words of his own in lieu of the finger, since his hands were full. "Damn, I didn't even get the license number with all that dirt on the plate. The sorry, fuckin'…." He shook his head, then his whole body, like a wet dog, and seemed to remember Drew. He gave Immy a sheepish look. "Sorry about that, ladies. Drew, Uncle Ralph should not have said that word."

Drew ignored both the grownups and gave Marshmallow a kiss on his snout. "He has a big nose!" She giggled and stuck a finger up one of his large nostrils.

"Drew!" said Immy. "We don't—."

"I think he likes me." Sure enough, the pig's eyes were closed and he was grunting softly, sounding almost like a purring cat.

Immy wiped off Drew's hand in case of lingering pig snot and held it tight, crossing the parking lot to the door, her hands trembling from the close encounter with the maniac driver. Inside, Ralph lowered Marshmallow to the green tile floor and handed Drew the end of the leash.

No one was behind the high counter, but a young woman soon showed up and gave them a high watt smile, which made her face seem mostly teeth. "HELL-o there. I'M Betsy Wiggins. Dr. Fox's assistant. And YOU must be the people Ms. Anderson called about. How's the little piggy doing?"

She looked at Immy as she said the last bit, which disconcerted Immy for a second. She thought Betsy had called her a little piggy. The toothsome smile, baring her glistening white teeth, and the shiny blonde helmet of hair above almost hurt Immy's eyes.

"I think that's what we're here for, for you to tell us how he is," said Immy. "Ms. Anderson says he needs a shot and de-worming, but I'd like Dr. Fox to give him a once-over." After all, if you should get a car examined when you buy it, you probably should get a pig looked at, too.

"Sure thing. O-key DO-key." Betsy sat to type at the computer. Her long, red fingernails clicked against the keys and Immy wondered what on earth she could be typing at such length.

"Well, all righty then," Betsy said, straightening up when she finished her treatise, or whatever. "Y'all can wait in Room Two." She flipped a wrist toward a door.

Immy saw two rooms, so deduced that the one Betsy hadn't waved at must be Room One. Yipping exploded from it as they passed, but the puppy grew quiet as they entered their examination room. They could hear the departing dog owner talking to the doctor. Dr. Fox came in shortly afterward.

He was a tall, stringy man with carrot top hair and light blue eyes. "This is Gretchen's little boy, isn't it? He has her coloring."

Marshmallow seemed to like Dr. Fox, too. Maybe he liked everyone. Friendly piglet, Immy thought. That might make being a pig owner easier.

Dr. Fox peered into the pig's mouth, eyes, and ears, then took a look at the other end and felt the soft, droopy tummy. He assured them that the pig was healthy and that the one shot and the de-worming was the only thing he needed that day, then stuck his head out the door and yelled, "Vern! Pig Inoculation! Wormer!"

"Vern and Betsy will take care of you," he said to them as he left.

Immy knew Vern Linder from his brief stint as a dishwasher in the diner when she used to wait tables. He always seemed to have a job in Saltlick or Cowtail, sometimes in the much bigger town of Wymee Falls, but didn't stick with any of them for long. Vern could be charming when he wanted, and kept himself in shape, except that he usually needed a haircut. He came into the room bearing a tray with a vial and syringe and threw Immy a smile that brought an answering grin. My, those dimples were cute.

She glanced at Ralph and wondered why he was frowning so hard. His eyes had that steely glint they got sometimes. Vern, Immy noted, still dressed like he was one step up from homeless.

Betsy followed Vern into the room and shut the door. "All righty, then. Ready for your shots, little guy?" she chirped. She fluttered her hands toward Marshmallow, just as Vern moved toward the counter with his tray.

The tray flew into the air.

The vial smashed on the tile floor.

When Vern hollered, Immy realized the needle had landed in Vern's biceps.

Two

"Oh, I am so sorry," simpered Betsy. She snatched the syringe from Vern's upper arm. Twisted it and yanked it out. Blood dripped from his arm and a drop spattered onto the floor.

"What in the HELL are you DOIN', bitch?" Vern grabbed his arm, which prevented him from striking Betsy. Immy thought he looked like he wanted to.

Betsy's eyes turned almost as hard as Ralph's. "What did you call me?" Her ugly sneer threatened to crack her makeup.

"Never mind." Vern opened the door, smearing blood on the doorknob and started out the door, running into Dr. Fox.

"I just came to tell you someth—What happened here?"

Vern threw Betsy a sour look and she glared back, her lips pursed tight.

Betsy spoke first. "Vern dropped some things and—"

"Your wonderful assistant, the one who sleeps around with married men, knocked the tray out of my hands, then she—"

"You were in my way or I wouldn't have—"

"—then she stabbed me with a needle." Vern parted his fingers to show Dr. Fox the blood, still oozing from the jab.

A shadow of bewilderment flitted across Dr. Fox's narrow face. "Vern, wait in my office and I'll bandage your arm. Betsy, bring a new syringe and dose for the patient. I saw the note you left."

He turned to Immy and pulled his face into serious doctor mode. "About that note I just mentioned? I came in to tell you what I've just learned. The Buckets' new pig, Gretchen, the sow who farrowed this little guy…." Dr. Fox gave Drew a worried glance. "Could I speak with you outside, Ms. Duckworthy?"

Immy threw Ralph a perplexed look and he lobbed it back. "I'll stay here with Drew and Marshmallow," he said.

The vet paused on his way out the door. "Marshmallow?"

Immy didn't like his incredulous tone. She stuck her chin out, daring him to make fun of Drew. "Yes. My daughter named the pig Marshmallow."

His face eased into a gentle smile. "What a wonderful name, Drew."

Immy relaxed and followed him out of the examining room.

He kept his voice low so it wouldn't carry into Drew. "Gretchen got out of her fence at the Buckets' place." Immy didn't like the direction this was going. "I told them chicken wire wouldn't hold a potbelly. Tinnie, Mrs. Bucket, thinks a drunken hunter killed her by accident, since she found Gretchen, dead, after she heard a shot outside her house."

"Dead?"

"Tinnie wants me to do an autopsy. She had Rusty drop the pig off a short time ago. But all I can tell her is that a bullet killed Gretchen. I don't do necropsies on pigs."

"Thank you for sparing Drew. She doesn't need to hear this right before her birthday, not when she just got Marshmallow."

"I don't want you to lose your pig the same way. Don't make the mistake of thinking that chicken wire will make an adequate fence."

"Oh, Ralph built us a nice wooden fence already."

He frowned. "Be careful she doesn't chew through it. If he could reinforce it with woven wire it might be better."

This would mean more nights with Ralph over to the house. Less time for studying. "I'm sure he could."

"I'll take care of Marshmallow's shot and de-worming today. Then I'll go talk to Vernon and Betsy about professional behavior." This last was added in an undertone.

As soon as Immy and Ralph got Drew and Marshmallow loaded into the van, Immy's cell phone rang. She glanced at caller ID as she picked it out of her purse. "It's Mother."

"Geemaw!" called Drew to her grandmother. "Tell Geemaw 'bout my new pig."

"Yes, sweetheart, I will." Immy answered the summons, which turned out to be an urgent request for beef jerky from Jerry's Jerky Shoppe.

"I guess I can," Immy said into her cell. "What kind do you want?"

"My usual, I think," her mother, Hortense, answered. "Oh, wait, I heard Rusty was going to begin processing porcine jerky. See if he will confer a free sample on you. If not, please purchase a modicum so I can examine and taste it."

"Sure thing," answered Immy, cutting the connection. "We're going to Jerry's Jerky first. For Mother."

She glanced at Ralph to see if the detour would be okay. But he smiled and nodded. "Fine. I'll get some, too."

Ralph and her mother got along surprisingly well. Hortense was fond of demonstrating the full breadth and depth of her extensive vocabulary and, although Ralph could be slow on the uptake at times, he seemed to understand most of what she said. Hortense also had turned into darn good cook ever since the chief had started coming to supper, and Ralph loved to eat.

Jerry's Jerky Shoppe was down the road a short piece from the vet's clinic. The hot sun of the long summer day baked the hardtop road and wilted the grass in the ranch pastures stretching to the horizon. To her left, invasive mesquite shrubs clogged the pastureland, but the land to the right of the road was kept clear. That land belonged to the Buckets and was where they grazed some of their cattle. They had to burn the mesquite off every few years to keep it from choking out the sparse grass that managed to survive the hot summers and harsh winters on the high plains.

Near the door to the small wooden shop behind the Buckets' modern brick ranch house, Immy nosed the van into a slot between two pickups, one orange and one white. There weren't that many orange pickups around this far from Austin. And one had almost run them down at the vet's today. This one's license plate was as muddy as the one on the reckless driver's truck. Ralph gave it a good look.

The buildings where the jerky was processed ranged behind and beside the shop, with the smokehouse standing on its own about a hundred feet from where she waited for Ralph to lift Drew from the van.

Immy glanced around the spread. Drew tried to convince Ralph to take Marshmallow into the jerky shop with them, but Ralph resisted. Immy took another look at the smokehouse. A woman with hard, glossy blonde hair disappeared behind the smokehouse, dragging a heavy-looking plastic bag. She didn't appear to be a professional meat handler. She did appear, though, to be the annoying Betsy, the assistant from the vet's clinic. How did Betsy get here so fast, if that's who she was? And what in the heck was she doing?

Ralph held the door, so Immy broke off her mental questions. When Immy, Ralph, and Drew entered the shop, Tinnie Bucket was standing behind the counter with a man's arm around her shoulder.

"Sweetheart, I know this is hard, but…." The man gave Tinnie's shoulder a squeeze, picked up the well-worn cowboy hat from the counter, and slapped it on his head. Immy realized he was Sonny Squire, Tinnie's filthy rich rancher-banker father. She hadn't recognized the crusty old cowboy without his hat. He left a trail of eau de Old Crow as he passed them, nodding, on his way out.

"Bye, Daddy," said Tinnie softly, just before the door clicked shut. She turned red-rimmed eyes toward them, greeted them with a limp howdy, climbed onto her stool, and began frowning at the computer screen in front of her. She would have been quite pretty, Immy thought, if she didn't have such a deep vertical furrow between her eyebrows. And today, those red eyes. Her hair was naturally light blond, rather wispy in an appealing way, and her features were regular in her small face.

Her crying was probably due to losing the pig she had so recently gotten from Amy JoBeth, but that furrow was a more permanent feature. It must be stressful to own a jerky shop, thought Immy.

Tinnie's stool stood behind the counter that topped a display case of combination packages they offered. In addition to jerky, the Buckets sold sausage, salsa, candies, and nuts that they purchased locally for sale. These were displayed, along with the two dozen or so varieties of jerky, on shelves lining the room. A large glass window behind Tinnie gave a view of the room where the meat was cut when it first arrived. That room was usually empty when Immy was there, but once she had been able to see Rusty and an employee, aproned in white, wielding large knives and hacking through a carcass. Both Rusty and the employee had the brawn to do it.

"I just heard about Gretchen," said Immy. "I'm so sorry."

"Thank you," murmured Tinnie without taking her gaze away from the screen.

Immy mentally shrugged and got busy gathering Hortense's favorites—teriyaki, hot 'n' spicy, and black pepper. Ralph picked up some plain beef jerky for himself and paid for it.

A thin young woman, maybe late teens or early twenties, came into the shop from an inner door and started replenishing the shelves from a rolling cart she pulled behind her. Her long neck, along with eyes that threatened to bulge from their sockets, gave her a frightened rabbit look. Those features pegged her as Poppy Jenkins, Ophelia's daughter. Ophelia, the maker of pig leashes, had the same neck and eyes.

Tinnie pursed her lips and squinted a malevolent glower at the young woman. Poppy stared back a moment, but her bulging eyes couldn't compete with Tinnie's hard ones. Poppy finished her task, then retreated through the same door without speaking a word.

As Immy inspected the shelves at the rear of the showroom, trying to ignore the interaction she'd witnessed, she heard two voices arguing behind the door Poppy had used. A female was throwing accusations at someone, berating him for "fooling around" on her with that something-something. Immy inched closer to the door.

"We haven't been together for over a week," the woman continued.

"I don't even like her," the man said. "She's just…tell you what, we'll go somewhere next weekend." The man sounded like Rusty.

The voices grew quiet and Immy finished her shopping. As she took her selections to the counter to pay, Rusty, trailed by the silent Poppy, came in through the door that Immy could now see led to the packaging room. Rusty hoisted a pile of boxes in his impressive arms.

"Hi, hon," he said to his wife, as relaxed and good-natured as if he hadn't just been in a fierce battle.

"Poppy," said Tinnie. "You're not needed in the shop."

Poppy left and Tinnie whirled on her husband. "What's she doing here today? I thought she was going to part-time."

"Aw, hon—"

The furrow between her eyes deepened. "Don't you 'hon' me, you son of a—"

Their small tow-headed son, Zack, followed his father into the retail space. He was small-boned and delicate, like his mother.

Zack was a pre-school classmate of Drew. He'd been the first friend Drew wanted to invite to her upcoming birthday party. He ran to her and she started babbling about her new pig.

Tinnie lowered her voice, but Immy could make out every word.

"You just want her here for the quick, occasional blow job, don't tell me you don't. Are you now taking our son with you when you go to see your other whore?"

Rusty's face froze mid-grin. He threw a nervous glance at his customers.

Immy had wanted to ask him if that was his orange truck that almost ran them over at the vet's, but this didn't seem like the right time.

"I'll just take these," Immy said, trying to deflect Tinnie's attention to business.

It didn't work.

Tinnie slid off her stool and stood, tall and willowy, facing her square, hard, cowboy-garbed husband. The air in the place seemed to stand still. Immy had no desire to see another face-off.

"Tinnie, I want to pay for these."

"Wait on the lady, hon." Rusty's voice cracked. "We'll talk later."

"No, we will not. We'll talk now. I saw that whore out there at the smokehouse. What the hell is she—"

"Zack, go outside and play," said Rusty, giving his son a shove toward the door.

He was a little late with that, Immy thought. "Drew, go with Zack." She was late, too. She could kick herself for not shooing Drew out earlier, before she had heard all the ugly language. Maybe the children hadn't noticed through their chatter.

The two children ran out the door and the tension in the room seemed to let up a bit. Immy felt her shoulders relax a notch.

Tinnie waited on Immy, taking her money and sacking her purchases without looking her in the eye.

"I was goin' to tell you a shipment of pork just came in," said Rusty, coming to stand beside his wife.

Tinnie whirled on him again. "Pork! How can you talk about pork at a time like this?"

Rusty blew out a breath. "You're right, hon. I forgot about Gretchen."

It was Immy's turn to whirl on him, in disbelief. "You forgot about Gretchen? Your wife's pet has just been killed and you forgot about it?"

"Are you through here?" asked Rusty, giving Immy a cold look.

"Yes, I'm leaving." Immy gathered her package and her purse and she and Ralph fled the quarrelsome scene.

"How rude," she said to Ralph when they were outside.

The white truck was gone. It must have been Sonny Squire's. The orange one was still there.

Drew and Zack knelt in the dirt at the edge of the parking lot, drawing pigs with sticks they'd found on the ground under the scrub oaks there.

Drew looked up and spotted them, then said goodbye to Zack and ran to them.

"Hi, Unca Ralph." Drew wrapped her arms around his legs and he nearly fell over. "I wanna see Marshmallow."

He opened the back and she got a reassuring glimpse of her new pig before he buckled her in.

This was a development Immy wasn't ready for, Drew calling Ralph her Uncle. It could have permanent, fixed connotations she wasn't prepared to face.

Vern Linder pulled into a parking space and said "Howdy" to Immy before he entered the jerky shop. He didn't give her a chance to "Howdy" him back. Popular place, thought Immy. Everyone comes here, seems like.

"Damn," she said to Ralph before she took the driver's seat. "I forgot to ask for a sample of pork jerky."

"The timing wasn't good for that, Immy," said Ralph.

"You're right. Bad timing all around, today."

*****

While Ralph and Drew took Marshmallow around to his pen behind the singlewide, Immy mounted the wooden steps to her front door. The smell of Hortense's incredible brownies greeted her nose and she let out a whoop.

"Brownies! Exactly what I need."

"They're fresh out of the oven, dear," called her mother. "Come give Louise your salutations. Where's the animal?"

Immy entered the kitchen to find her mother's recent friend, Louise Cotter, at the kitchen table, making quick work of a gooey-looking, chocolaty-smelling lump of goodness. Two months ago the women had met in Wymee Falls at a meeting of the Association for Retired Librarians. Louise had moved to Wymee Falls about a year ago, after retiring from the library in Bootstrap, way out west, she'd said.

Louise could probably stand to lose a few pounds, but not a hundred, like Hortense, whose apron ties had been augmented with string to stretch around her girth.

"Mmm. Let me at 'em." Immy washed her hands and poured herself a glass of milk. "Ralph and Drew are showing Marshmallow his new home."

Hortense went to the window to watch the pig get acquainted with the yard.

"Marshmallow?" Louise's cackle could probably be heard outside by Ralph and Drew. And Marshmallow. "Does Amy JoBeth know you named him that? She'll love it."

"You know Amy JoBeth?"

Louise's bright gray eyes lit up. "She's my daughter, silly goose. I'm glad we're living so close now."

"She's your daughter? Small world. I have the job she used to have, PI assistant for Mike Mallett. She acted like she approved of the pig's name," answered Immy around a mouthful of brownie. Ralph was going to be extra glad he came with them today. Hortense only baked brownies when she was moved by some mysterious spirit.

Immy handed her mother the bag of jerky as she came back to the table. "I got all your favorites."

Hortense took the bag and plopped into a chair. "Did you procure the pork?" Her thinly penciled eyebrows rose high above her many chins, and Immy felt chastised. She hated the way her mother could make her feel like a small child.

"Well, I couldn't, really. There was, there were…things going on." She didn't want to mention the dead Gretchen in front of Louise. She might have been attached to the pig. Her daughter sure was. "But Rusty did say a shipment of pork had just arrived, so maybe next time."

"I suppose it would be rude to eat pork jerky in front of Drew's new porcine pet." Hortense laughed at what she perceived as a joke, wobbling her topmost chins.

Louise snorted, not a happy snort, and her gray eyes darkened. Immy concluded that, with Amy JoBeth for a daughter, she probably took pigs seriously. Louise raised her nose into the air to signify her disapproval and spotted the crepe paper Immy had strung across the room for Drew's party tomorrow.

"I nearly forgot to mention the piñatas to y'all," Louise said to Immy. "Amy JoBeth makes the most marvelous pig-shaped piñatas. Would you like one for the children?"

"Most definitely," said Immy. "They would get a kick out of that."

Louise hauled her cell phone from her saddlebag-sized purse and called her daughter. "You do?" she said after asking if she had any available. To Immy she said, "She made a bunch last weekend. You can pick one up tonight it you want."

"Too bad we didn't know about them when we were there just now," said Immy.

"Yes," agreed Hortense. "Legal tender for gasoline doesn't spring fully formed from large botanical vegetation."

Immy mentally rolled her eyes. Louise did the same physically.

"I'll pick it up after supper," said Immy. Not that anyone would be hungry for a meal after scarfing down Hortense's wonderful baking. "Tell her I'll be by around six."

"Will do. Well, I'd better get going." Louise rose from her chair and hefted her purse onto her rounded shoulder. "Amy JoBeth and I are going to a movie later tonight. She's been so awful upset about having to sell Gretchen. Her business started out good, but it's been slow. She needed the money bad and those Buckets gave her a pile of it. I thought I'd take her out tonight and cheer her up some."

"Oh." Immy's quiet syllable drew the attention of both women. "Maybe I should tell you. Amy JoBeth doesn't know yet, I'll bet, since this is brand new news."

Louise and Hortense both leaned toward Immy.

"Gretchen's dead. A drunk hunter shot her."

It was a good thing Louise was standing next to her chair. Otherwise Immy could not have managed to shove her onto it as she fainted.

Three

Hortense could move surprisingly fast for a large woman. By the time Immy had propped up the fainting Louise Cotter in the kitchen chair, Hortense was there, swabbing Louise's face with wet kitchen towels.

She gave her daughter a disappointed look. "Imogene, you could have used more sensitivity in revealing that distressing communication to Louise."

Immy nodded, still holding Louise as upright as she could. "I realize that. How was I to know she'd faint at the thought of a dead pig, though?" Maybe it would be better to lay Louise out on the floor.

"Not jus'…a pig." Louise was coming around, although her words slurred and slid from her plump lips. "Amy… JoBeff…pig." Louise batted a dripping towel away from her cheek. Her words solidified into a long wail. "Amy! Her prize, her pet, her most beloved pig. What will she do without Gretchen?"

"She was already sold to the Buckets," said Immy.

"Yes, but she wasn't *dead*," said Louise. "She was only down the road a piece. They also had an agreement for farrowing future litters. Amy JoBeth was supposed to get the pick of Gretchen's next litter, with a special boar that Amy JoBeth chose. That litter pick was part of their price negotiations."

Immy was glad Marshmallow was a neutered boy pig. No litters to worry about.

"I'd better go break the news to her before someone else does." Louise pushed herself up from of the chair and wobbled out the door.

"I wonder if she should be driving," said Hortense.

"Probably not," said Immy. "But do *you* want to take her, and be there when she tells Amy JoBeth about the dead pig?"

Hortense considered for a moment. "If Louise is this distraught over the animal, her daughter will be influenced in geometrical proportion, I surmise."

"Yep. I think you're right."

"Until this most recent setback, I was contemplating how well Louise has been doing." They heard Louise start her car start and drive away.

"You mean…cuz her husband killed himself?"

"His suicide affected her severely. Her recent ebullient nature was, I understand, from what she's related to me in the short while I've been acquainted with her, the norm for Louise prior to that event. She's been morose to the point of morbidity until lately."

Immy picked up the last crumbs of brownie from her plate. "It's awful he got so all-fired upset about losing his ranch like that."

"That land had been in his family for generations," said Hortense.

"And Amy JoBeth is Louise's daughter? I should have figured that out. Now I think about it, they do kind of look alike." They both looked a teensy bit like sows. "They haven't been living here until recently, have they?"

"Louise has transferred her domicile here from Bootstrap, whence she retreated after the suicide. Louise's daughter was united in connubiality with Ernest Anderson, who was a member of the military establishment. I believe they were on various bases in this country and Europe until she returned to work in Wymee Falls a year ago. Amy JoBeth seems to have kept her matrimonial name of Anderson even after her divorce."

"How odd that I have her job."

"You're raising pigs now?"

"I am not raising pigs, Mother. She's the person I replaced when I went to work for Mike Mallett. Maybe you didn't hear me telling Louise. You were watching Drew with her new pig."

"My, my. Small world."

Immy retreated out the back door to the yard, where Ralph and Drew were leading Marshmallow around by his leash, acquainting him with his new quarters.

"I think the cement pond should go yonder." Ralph pointed to a spot near the corner of the pen. "I can rig up another pen for it, and a gate so Marshmallow can get there from his main pen. You'll be able to close it off to clean it up."

"And just how am I supposed to clean up a cement pig pond?" asked Immy.

"I will," said Drew. "I clean it up. All by myself. Like I clean my room. I take all the toys out and put them away."

Immy had to chuckle. "Cleaning up" meant straightening to Drew. She had never cleaned anything in her short life.

"Drew," said Immy. "I'm going to get a piñata shaped like a piggy for your party tomorrow. Would you like that?"

Drew's eyes sparkled and she jumped up and down. "Piñata pig! Piñata pig!"

"I think that means yes," said Ralph.

"We can pick it up after supper," said Immy.

"What are we having?" asked Ralph.

It looked like Ralph would be staying.

*****

After watching Ralph chow down on four pork chops and a mountain of mashed potatoes, Immy drove back to the pig breeder's spread for the piñata. She thought her mother's menu choice was unfortunate, but no one said anything.

She'd never had a pet, although she'd always wanted a donkey, or maybe a goat. While her father was alive he'd promised she could have a pet when she was old enough to take care of it by herself. But his death when she was twelve shut her mother down so completely and for so long, Immy hadn't brought it up again. She'd run into her own problems, letting that smooth-talking, exciting-looking, long-haul trucker talk her into fifteen minutes of passion in the bunk of his cab, and getting pregnant with Drew. He'd disappeared down the highway without Immy getting his name or license plate. Being pregnant had made her senior year of high school hard. But she wouldn't trade Drew for anything on the planet. And she never felt the need for a pet after she had the baby.

Maybe, just maybe, for Amy JoBeth, who had no children, losing Gretchen was a tiny bit akin to how it would be if Immy lost Drew. Hard to tell.

Now that she was on her way to Amy JoBeth's, Immy had to decide what to say to her when she saw her. She rehearsed some phrases. "I'm so sorry for your loss." "Sorry about the pig." "I heard about what happened to Gretchen." "I know what you must be going—" No, that wouldn't work. Immy had no idea why everyone was getting so upset about a dead pig. Pigs were slaughtered to be eaten every day. Of course, people probably didn't eat miniature potbellied pigs.

She braked in front of the white ranch house, glad this trip had been cooler than the earlier one. The sun was a couple hours from setting, now throwing long slanting rays across the roof of the house and outbuildings, casting the ground behind them in deep shadow. Snuffling, rooting sounds came from the pens behind the house.

Immy wandered around back first, thinking it might be feeding time, but Amy JoBeth wasn't there, and didn't come out of the house to see who was calling on her. Immy gave a tentative rap for her first attempt, and her second and third, expecting Amy JoBeth to come investigate. Her fourth and fifth were loud banging, accompanied by calling out Amy JoBeth's name.

Her white truck was there, beside the house. No lights were on in the house, but it was borderline whether she'd need them this hour of day.

Then Immy spotted the piñata. It lay next to the wrought iron porch railing and had a post-it note stuck to it. Immy pulled it off and read it.

'Immy, this is yours. Pay me later.'

So, Immy thought, she must be feeling bad about Gretchen, mourning her, and didn't want to be disturbed. Still, Immy thought she ought to make sure she was all right. Like, not suicidal or something. She might take after her father.

She'd seemed cheerful enough earlier in the day. Before she heard about Gretchen being shot. Maybe the potbellied pigs helped keep her out of depression. It would be terrible for her to slip back now.

So Immy opened the front door and poked her head in to see if Amy JoBeth needed anything.

*****

A fruitless fifteen minutes later, Immy emerged, puzzled. Amy JoBeth wasn't in her house. Maybe she was with her mother, Louise. She'd left the piñata on the porch. Her white truck was parked beside the house, so she hadn't driven herself anywhere. Immy carried the piñata to the van. Before she left, she gave one last sweeping glance around the grounds. Her eye was caught by a metallic glint near the tornado shelter.

Immy, who, whether justly or not, prided herself on her frugality, walked closer to see if the glint was money. When she bent to examine the small pile of metallic pink glittery stuff at the entrance to the tornado shelter, she saw it was confetti in the shape of pigs. She chuckled. She'd bet the piñata she'd stowed in the van was stuffed with this.

But she sat back on her heels and wondered why it was out here, next to the shelter. The tornado shelter was underground, except for the top foot and a half that stuck up and had grass-covered dirt mounded around it. The door, a rectangular affair on about a thirty degree slant, opened to the side and swung upward. A couple of fresh footprints had been left in the small dirt space outside the door. Could Amy JoBeth be in the tornado shelter? Should Immy be starting up the car and tuning the radio to the weather station? It didn't even look like rain when

Immy glanced at the sky, let alone a tornado.

There was no padlock, so she pulled the heavy door up and peered down the dark stairway.

"Yoo hoo," she called. "Anybody down there?"

"Go away," came the muffled answer.

Immy started to pant and her heart trip-hammered a few beats. The last thing in the world Immy wanted to do was enter that dark, underground place, exactly the kind of place that would trigger panic from her morbid fear of being closed in.

When five-year-old Immy had locked herself into a dark closet, she'd pounded on the door for what had seemed like hours, screaming for her mother to let her out. Hortense had been in the backyard hanging up clothes, so it probably hadn't been more than half an hour before she rescued her frantic child. Immy had never forgotten the terror she'd felt in the closet.

But Amy JoBeth, the poor woman, was in distress. Immy had to do something.

She slowed her breathing, but not her heart, and started down the steps, leaving the door open for light and quick escape. A loose spider web floated past her face and she batted it away. Amy JoBeth lay curled up on a mattress under a heap of blankets. It was a degree or two cooler under the ground, but the small enclosure was still sweltering.

"Oh my god, this is creepy. And dark. What are you doing here? Are you all right?"

No reply.

Immy squatted on the floor beside the mattress and put her hand on Amy JoBeth's forehead. She was drenched in sweat, but didn't seem feverish.

"I should have locked the door," muttered Amy JoBeth, turning her back to Immy.

"But what in the hell are you doing down here? The sky is clear. There's no tornado coming. The breeze isn't even very strong today." Immy's hands prickled from her fear of the closed in space.

"I don't care 'bout the weather." Amy JoBeth's words slurred slightly. Was she drunk? "Don't care 'bout nothin' anymore."

Was this the same bright, bustling woman who had, only a few hours ago, sold her a pig? Immy's scalp prickled to match her palms "C'mon, Amy JoBeth. Tell me what's the matter. Maybe I can help."

The air in the shelter was warm and still, with a slight smell of dampness. A portable toilet stood in the corner, beyond the mattress. The shelter was a prefab affair, unlike some of the homemade ones in Saltlick. It had built in shelves, a ceiling light and a ventilation turbine. The light wasn't on, though. The white walls would be black with the hatch closed. Amy JoBeth must have been huddling here in inky darkness.

"Can you resurrect Gretchen?" Amy JoBeth sat up and flung off the covers. "Some son of a bitch shot her. Some drunk bastard. Shot my pig! My Gretchen!" Her face crumpled and her tears streamed. "I knew I shouldn't've let those filthy Buckets take her. They let her get out, I know they did. It's their fault."

"Well, and the fault of the drunk hunter."

"Yes! It's everyone's fault. I wish they were all dead!" Amy JoBeth's fists clenched the blanket so tightly her knuckles whitened.

"Now how would that help anything?"

"It would even the score, I reckon. But it's mostly my own fault because I let someone buy her. How could I? How could I sell my baby? I let Tinnie talk me into it. I should be shot. Right after Rusty and Tinnie and the drunk asshole who shot her." She grabbed the top blanket and wiped her tears from her cheeks, then blew her nose.

Her grief filled the tiny space. Immy wanted to flee up the stairs so she could breathe more easily. "Can I get you to come out of here?"

"No, you can't. Go away." Shooting a sharp look at Immy, she said, "And you take care of that baby pig I just sold you."

"Oh, we will. He has a sturdy pen. And we'll probably keep him in the house most of the time."

"Yes, that would be good." Her crying had stopped.

"We've already taken him to Dr. Fox and gotten him all fixed up."

Amy JoBeth gazed at Immy for a moment. "You're a good person, Immy. You're kinda flighty, but Marshmallow will be okay with you and Drew. And Hortense. Mom said you're Hortense's daughter. She's been a good friend to Mom. He'll be all right."

"Oh yes! He will be." Now that Amy JoBeth had stopped crying maybe she could be reasoned with. "So, are you hungry?" That usually worked as a good distraction in dealing with her mother and with Drew. Worked well on Ralph, too.

Amy JoBeth set up a loud wail. "How can I eat? How can I go on?"

"Um, can I bring you some brownies?"

Silence. "Hortense's brownies? Mom's told me about them."

Immy nodded. "She made some this afternoon." If Ralph ate them all, maybe Mother can make some more, she thought.

"That might be good."

"All righty then." Good God, she sounded like Betsy, that dingy vet's assistant. "I'll go get some."

"I'll be right here," snuffled Amy JoBeth, swiping at her nose again. "You can leave the hatch open. It's dark in here."

Immy raced up the steps, glad to be leaving the dungeon.

The germ of an idea was forming in the part of Immy's mind devoted to detective matters. The fiery part, the part that held her burning desire to someday be a detective. Mother scoffed at her and belittled her dream. But her father had been a detective in the Wymee Falls Police Department, and, if he were still alive, would be proud she wanted to follow, somewhat, in his footsteps, Immy was sure. She didn't see how she could ever achieve the rank of Police Detective, but PI seemed possible. She had a book she had found almost new, in very good condition, called *The Moron's Compleat PI Guidebook*. With the help of that, and her new job working for a real PI, she was well on her way. True, all she'd done at work so far was typing and filing, but she felt she'd be able to investigate a case one of these days.

Maybe she could investigate the murder of Gretchen. It would be good practice, and maybe give Amy JoBeth a measure of closure. The Case of the Slaughtered Pig.

*****

There were a dozen brownies left, to Immy's relief. She told Hortense about Amy JoBeth shutting herself into the horrible tornado shelter and grieving.

"But I think we can lure her out with brownies," said Immy.

"That would be charitable and generous, dear," said Hortense. "It's felicitous that some of my bakery products remain." She bit off a piece of the jerky Immy had brought from Jerry's Jerky Shoppe. It was the last piece. "Maybe you can stop by and get me some more of this."

"They're closed this late, Mother. It's after seven. I'll get you some tomorrow after my hair appointment." The next day was Saturday, Drew's party, and Immy had an early appointment—at eight—to give her plenty of time to get ready for the celebration.

Hortense heaved a giant-sized sigh, the only kind she ever heaved. "I guess that will have to do. My, that Rusty Bucket makes good jerky."

"Why do they call the shop Jerry's, Mother? Why not Rusty's?"

"I believe it was already named when the Buckets bought it. The alliteration is pleasing, for one thing. For another, they probably decided it would be better for business to remain with a known name."

"Who was Jerry, anyway?"

"I do believe he was an old family friend of the Squire family."

The Squire family, of which Tinnie Bucket was a member, owned the biggest ranch in these parts. They were considered the local "rich" folks and everyone knew Tinnie's money had bought the jerky business. The Buckets never had two dimes to rub together. Rusty had played outstanding high school football, though, so he was considered a good catch for the local rich girl. And, since Jerry had been a family friend, Tinnie and Rusty may even have gotten a good deal on the property.

"Louise tells me," said Hortense, "that her daughter used to retreat to the tornado shelter on their ranch in times of distress. She has, in the past, suffered greatly from malaise."

"I thought she had depression," said Immy. "Mike Mallett told me my predecessor was put in the hospital a couple of times for depression when she worked there. I don't think he should have told me that. But, since I know about it, I'm thinking it might be depression again."

"Yes, but that's such an ugly word." Hortense finished chewing the last bit of jerky. "That batch of jerky tasted a bit different from the usual. I wonder if Mr. Bucket has a new ingredient, or a new process. I am unable to decide whether the taste is superior or inferior."

"I'll ask when I go by tomorrow. Right now, I want to get these brownies to Amy JoBeth and get her out of that hole in the ground."

*****

The poor woman was right where Immy had left her, but she was able to coax Amy JoBeth out from underground and into her own house. Immy was careful not to mention pigs while they sat at Amy JoBeth's kitchen table sharing the brownies with sweating glasses of iced tea. Amy JoBeth must have turned off the AC in the house. How long had she meant to stay in the shelter?

Immy was congratulating herself for rescuing the poor, distressed woman, when a rattling pickup pulled up in front.

"Sounds like Vern," said Amy JoBeth.

The vet assistant who had been stabbed with the syringe wandered in from the front of the house, evidently feeling at home enough to walk in. Amy JoBeth turned a fond smile on him and he stooped to peck her on the cheek. He on had the same ratty clothes he'd worn in the clinic earlier that day and carried a plastic bag.

So, Vern and Amy JoBeth. Small world, Immy thought.

"Evenin', Immy." His smile revealed those dimples.

He turned so Amy JoBeth saw his other arm and she sucked in her breath. "What happened to you?"

His short sleeved shirt revealed a length of gauze wound round his biceps where the needle had punctured him.

"Oh, an accident at work. That clumsy bitch, Betsy Wiggins. I oughta sue, get workman's comp or disability or something."

"I'm not sure you can get disability if you're not disabled, Vernie."

He frowned and the cute dimples disappeared. Immy didn't know if it was because he was being denied his rights, or because of the ridiculous nickname. "Anyway, I brung you something. Your ma said you was feelin' puny."

"I… I guess I was. Still am, but Immy was kind enough to bring me some of Hortense's brownies."

"These are Hortense's?" He scooped one up and mashed the entire thing into his mouth. "Tell her thanks, Immy," he said around the chocolate goo filling his mouth.

"Okay." Immy averted her head in case she wanted to eat another brownie.

"What did you bring me, Vernie Wernie?"

Immy stifled a groan. Vernie Wernie? What was with these two?

Amy JoBeth took the plastic bag from Vern, then shrieked. She jumped up so fast her chair crashed to the floor and she ran from the room.

"What in the hell did you bring her?" asked Immy.

He held up the package Amy JoBeth had flung to the floor. "I brung her some of Rusty's new pork jerky."

Immy's mouth dropped open. Pork jerky? To a woman who had just lost her pet pig? This was far worse than Rusty mentioning pork jerky to Tinnie.

"He says it'll be a real good seller. Tastes better than the beef to lotsa people. Wouldn't you think a pig person would like pork jerky?"

Immy ran after Amy JoBeth, but she had fled to the shelter. And this time she had locked the door from the inside. Immy was almost relieved she wouldn't be able to follow her.

Vern came up behind Immy and started pounding on the door. "Sweetcakes! Honey bun! I didn't mean nothin'. C'mon out. Please? Pretty please with a cherry on top?"

But no amount of cajoling, shouting, or pounding raised a sound from within.

"Aw jeez." Vern slumped onto the grass beside the tornado door. "What did I do now?"

"Vern, you're not serious. You honestly don't know what you did? You brought her a delicacy made from the body of a close relative of Gretchen."

He raised his head and gazed at the darkening sky. "I never thought of it that way. Aw shit." He got to his feet, dragged himself to his dusty black pickup and drove off.

Immy tried to coax her out for awhile longer. Telling Amy JoBeth that Vern was gone and there were more brownies failed to rouse her. Immy finally left, knowing Drew might be afraid if it started storming. She would tell Mother to call Louise. Maybe Amy JoBeth's own mom could get her to come out. Staying there all night wouldn't kill her, would it?

Four

There is nothing quite like the feeling of strong fingers massaging your scalp at the shampoo bowl, thought Immy. Cathy, of Cathy's Kut and Kurl, was the best. She was the *only* beautician in Saltlick, that was true, but still….

This was a good opportunity to gain some information since Cathy was usually a fount of gossip. The trouble was, Immy wasn't sure what questions to ask to track down a pig killer. Maybe an open-ended one?

"So," she said, her eyes closed in pleasure from the head rub, "did you hear we got a pig for Drew?"

"Drew wants a pig? For a pet or to eat?"

"It's a pet. A potbelly. She named it Marshmallow."

"Did you see the *Saltlick Weekly*? There's a funny article about a pig in it. It's one of them potbellies, too."

"The story is there already? What's it say?"

Cathy rubbed conditioner into Immy's hair and massaged some more. "It's a sorta local color humor, I guess. This here pig got killed somehow and some poor woman is god awful upset about it, like it was a kid or something."

Cathy dried her hands and left for a moment, then returned waving the paper.

"Here it is," she said, skimming the article. "It says the pig got killed by a drunk hunter after Tinnie Bucket, the owner, didn't shut the gate.

I didn't see it was Tinnie when I first read it."

A voice piped up from the next shampoo bowl where old Mrs. Wilson was waiting for her perm to set. "I heard the darn pig dug under the fence. Tinnie's pretty upset, you know."

"I saw her," said Immy, "and she was, but Amy JoBeth, who sold the pig, is more upset. She loved it." She groaned as Cathy resumed scrubbing her head.

"You can't trust a pig with a fence," said Mrs. Wilson, who considered herself an authority on most things.

Immy knew Mrs. Wilson didn't even trust their dog with a fence, since they kept their Rottweiler chained in the yard. She and Drew sometimes snuck stew bones to the poor creature.

"Well," said Immy, trying to dig deeper, "does anyone know who the hunter was?"

"Someone pretty close to the pig pen, wouldn't you say?" said Mrs. Wilson.

Cathy's massage stopped as she straightened and confronted Mrs. Wilson. "It happened there at Jerry's Jerky, on Rusty's property. Are you saying it was Rusty? Cuz I don't think you oughta be spreadin' stories if you don't know."

Cathy turned on the hose and started rinsing Immy. "I haven't knowed Rusty to be drunk all that often. So drunk he couldn't see what was a pig and what wasn't, anyways."

Rusty had neither looked nor smelled drunk yesterday. "What time was Gretchen killed?" Immy asked.

"Who's Gretchen?" asked Mrs. Wilson.

"That's the pig. Says so in the *Weekly*," said Cathy.

"Someone named a pig Gretchen? That's disgraceful. My sister is named Gretchen, Gretchen Newhouse. Well, I never." Mrs. Wilson rattled the pages of the magazine she'd been leafing through and went back to it, finished with this discussion.

"I don't reckon anyone knows what time," said Cathy. "But prob'ly late Thursday night. Maybe early Friday?"

It was Saturday morning now. Immy had been at the jerky shop Friday afternoon and Tinnie had been grieving then. But Amy JoBeth hadn't heard about it yet. So maybe Gretchen was killed during the day on Friday. Hunters usually went out early in the morning, but they weren't usually drunk until later. Immy had no idea when the crime had been committed. That was going to make it hard to investigate. She needed more details.

"One thing I heard 'bout that Jerry's Jerky," said Cathy. "There was a health inspector out there yesterday."

Immy hoped the Buckets wouldn't have a bad health inspection report to deal with, on top of everything else.

She tried to remember Dr. Fox telling them about Gretchen's death. Who had told Dr. Fox about it? That's who she needed to talk to. It might have been Tinnie. Dr. Fox said Tinnie wanted him to come autopsy the pig, which he hadn't done. Maybe he should have. What would it hurt? He could determine the angle of the lethal bullet. Immy knew that was important at a crime scene. Her second-hand copy of *The Moron's Compleat PI Guidebook* had an entire chapter on determining bullet angles.

But, right after her hair appointment, she had to drive into Wymee Falls to pick up Drew's pig-shaped cake at the Fancy Frosting Bake Shop. She would be pleased if they hadn't misspelled Drew's name D-E-R-W, as they'd done on her cake when she turned three. No one had noticed it until Drew did. A tearful time was had that year because neither Hortense nor Immy was able to transpose the letters of icing.

When her hair was clean and blow-dried, Immy turned her van out of the nose-in space in front of Cathy's Kut and Kurl, the vivid pink of the small wooden structure flashing so bright in the rearview mirror it made Immy's stomach hurt.

Directly across Second Street from Cathy's, where Huey's Hash used to be, stood the only franchise establishment in Saltlick, the newly opened Tomato Garden, a faux Italian chain owned by the Giovanni family in El Paso. Frankie Laramie, a Giovanni on his mother's side, was the manager, but most Saltlickians thought he didn't have enough gumption to run the place. Some gave it three months, some six.

Immy wanted to wish the place luck. It was good to have an eatery in Saltlick. The nearest Dairy Queen was in Cowtail. But she couldn't help the anger she felt when she passed by the door, never going in. She had owned the previous restaurant, a legacy from her Uncle Huey, and Frankie and his Uncle Guido had argued that the property was worth very little. They had argued so convincingly, she had sold it to them for very little. Afterwards, when she saw the booming business it did, she knew she'd been cheated. It was doing as well as the Wymee Falls franchise, which they also owned.

The restaurant was flanked by the glass windowed second-hand shop that used to be a video rental store and the town library, whose limited hours meant it was hardly ever open. The town had to save money somewhere, and replacing the yellow light bulbs in the blinking light on the main drag was expensive. The First Bank of Saltlick presented a staid façade next to Cathy's garish Kut and Kurl. Immy pulled into the All Sips "inconvenience store", as Hortense call it, across the street to fill the van's voracious gas tank, then began her drive into town.

Immy usually liked to drive past the placid cattle, chewing grass in the vast fields between Saltlick and Wymee Falls, but today she was in a hurry and had a lot on her mind. Turkey buzzards circled ominously above a slight dip beyond a far herd and Immy hoped a dead calf was not their target.

Wymee Falls, the county seat of Wymee County, was the nearest town big enough to have a bakery, a mall, and multiple strip shopping centers. The town wasn't exactly thriving, but it wasn't dying as actively as Saltlick and some of the other small surrounding towns. The oil boom had made the area, but the decline in oil drilling had brought about a decline here, too.

Saltlick has specialized in supplying oil drilling equipment to many local refineries. Now yards full of rusty remnants pocked the town. No one seemed to know what to do with the stuff that nobody wanted any more. The biggest employer in Saltlick was the school system. The biggest events were football games on Thursdays and Fridays in the fall. These were replaced by Go-Kart and riding mower races when football season ended.

Wymee Falls, on the other hand, survived on a few other things. There was the shopping mall, the only one for miles around, the sporting events—rodeos and ice hockey, and a nearby Air Force Base to supply shoppers for the mall and attendees at the events. Oil was still an industry, and pump jacks still dotted the landscape, but it was a much smaller part of the economy than in prior years.

After she saw the turkey buzzards, Immy passed one big pump jack and two smaller ones on the way into town.

The pig cake was beautiful, shaped like one of Disney's three little ones, with a cute snout and curly tail, frosted in pink, with Drew's name, spelled correctly, scrawled on its round belly. Immy was climbing into the van, balancing the cake to put it onto the front passenger seat, when her cell phone startled her. She nearly let the cake fall to the pavement, but managed to dig her phone out of her purse. It was Mother.

"Imogene, I am in extreme distress."

Now what?

"Would you be a dear daughter and swing by the apothecary for an anti-diarrheal drug? Maybe also an anti-emetic. If there is an all-inclusive medicine, that would be best."

Stomach trouble? Mother? She never had stomach trouble. Her vast abdomen was capable of taking in, Immy was sure, a small vehicle.

"I may have been poisoned."

Shit! Who would poison Hortense Duckworthy?

*****

Mother really was sick. Immy had never seen her so ill. She found her hunched over the toilet bowl, retching. Had her overeating finally caught up with her? Hortense grabbed for the bottle of Kaopectate the druggist had recommended to Immy. Instead of reading the directions, Hortense swirled the cap off and glugged from the bottle.

"Mother, there's only so much you should take," said Immy, but Hortense had set the bottle on the sink counter. With her weight she could probably absorb a lot.

"Do you suppose," Hortense groaned, "someone is out to get me?"

This was not a good sign. The largest word in that sentence was only seven letters. "Mother, maybe I'd better call the doctor."

"No, call the police. I want the perpetrator apprehended."

The Kaopectate must be working. "Perpetrator" was four syllables. Immy dutifully dialed the non-emergency number for the Saltlick police station. The front desk woman, Tabitha, answered.

"Tabitha, Mother wants me to—"

"State your name, please."

"It's me, Immy."

"First and last, and spell them please."

Immy ground her teeth. Tabitha could be such a bitch. They'd gone to high school together, but when she was getting all official, Tabitha acted like Immy was a complete stranger. Not that there were any real strangers in Saltlick, pop. 1234.

"Mother thinks she's been poisoned so I guess you should send someone over."

"That won't be possible at this time."

Tabitha was being impossible.

"And why not?"

"Both the chief and Ralph are sick. Throwing up all over the place."

Cathy's earlier words came to her. A health inspector had been at Jerry's Jerky.

"Tabitha, do you know anything about an inspector at the Buckets' jerky place?"

"Huh. I know they got inspected. Don't know if they passed. Hey, Chief was eatin' jerky yesterday. Do you suppose…?"

Ralph had chowed down on it, too. "Yeah, I do. I'll bet they all have food poisoning. I wonder what Rusty did to his jerky."

"Somethin' bad, looks like. Glad I never touch the stuff."

Immy did eat it occasionally, but hadn't had a chance to get any of the last batch she'd brought home for Mother.

"Tabitha, is there any word on Gretchen?"

"Gretchen Newhouse? Somethin' happened to her?"

"No, Gretchen, Tinnie's pig that was shot by someone. Can you tell me who's looking into it?"

There was a muffled sound on the phone, like someone strangling. "Hah! You think we'd investigate a dead pig? Only if someone got sick eatin' it." After a few peals of laughter, the connection cut off.

Immy called Louise Cotter after she hung up.

"Oh, Imogene, I'm so glad you called." Immy had to hold the phone away from her ear slightly so Louise's high-pitched screech didn't damage her hearing. "I can't get Amy JoBeth to come out of that damn shelter. She spent the night there. Could you go over there? Maybe bring her some more brownies?"

"I doubt that would work again, Louise. I don't think I can get there today. Drew's party is this afternoon and Mother is sick."

"Your mother is *sick*? Hortense? Sick?" Louise evidently found it as amazing as Immy did.

"I think it's something she ate. Some other people are ill, too."

"You know, you're right. Vern was here earlier. He looked awful. 'Course he's lost his job again."

"He got fired from the vet's clinic?"

"Yes, and he said he was sick to his stomach."

"Did he eat jerky from Jerry's yesterday?" Immy asked.

"He finished what I had here. I didn't eat much of it. Wasn't too hungry."

That wasn't surprising. Louise had filled up on brownies.

Immy hung up and pondered. She'd done a good job of detecting! These people were all sick from Jerry's Jerky. Well, Rusty's jerky. She would swing by there before the party and see what was going on. Drew's party was at two. It was now just after ten thirty. She had time to investigate.

Mother's extra heft gave her super recovery powers. No longer vomiting, she left the bathroom floor to help Drew make up party favor bags and Immy set off to detect.

Now she was working on two cases at once: The Case of the Slaughtered Pig and The Case of the Poisoned Jerky Eaters. How exciting!

First stop, Dr. Fox's vet office to question him in connection with Gretchen's murder. She'd find out who told him the pig was dead. That might hold a clue as to the identity of the killer.

Dr. Fox was busy and she had to wait twenty minutes to see him. A front desk woman she didn't know, much more subdued than Betsy, told her to sit and he'd be right with her, then rushed off to assist the doctor. It looked like both examining rooms were occupied and two more patients and their owners filled the wooden chairs in the waiting room.

It was probably practical to have all hard surfaces, tile floor, no curtains on the windows or artwork on the walls. But it made a loud room. The yaps of the Chihuahua beside her and the hoarse arf of the Akita beside him bounced around the room, pounding Immy's eardrums.

The two cats and their owners in the exam rooms finally departed and the dogs entered, their barks muffled by the closed doors.

Dr. Fox raised his eyebrows at Immy and she said she had a quick question.

"Is Marshmallow having a problem already?"

"Oh no, it's not Marshmallow. He's doing great. Used the litter box and everything. I'm trying to find some answers about Gretchen for Amy JoBeth."

Dr. Fox frowned, which made the slight furrows on his brow redden.

"Do you remember who called you to tell you Gretchen was dead?"

"No one called me. Someone, I don't know who, called Betsy and Betsy left me a note. I saw it while you were here and thought I ought to warn you. I called over to the Buckets' place before I talked to you, though, and got Tinnie. She was in a state."

So she would have to ask Betsy who called. "Is Betsy sick today?" Maybe she'd eaten jerky, too.

"She's taking a day off. Is that all? I have patients waiting."

"Oh yes, thanks. That's it for now. If I have more questions I'll be back."

Dr. Fox gave her an irritated look and opened the door to Room Number One. Immy glanced at her watch and decided she'd better move on to her second case, The Poisoned Jerky Eaters.

Jerry's was dead when she drove up. Except for a car leaving, whose driver had the same hairdo as Betsy. Was Rusty carrying on with her at his own place? What a prick. He was screwing Betsy *and* Poppy. And Tinnie knew it, too. She's mentioned Rusty's "other whore".

She had to get out of the van to read the note tacked to the door of the shop. It had been closed by the health department! As soon as she got home she'd call a doctor for Mother. She surely must have food poisoning.

On her way back to her car, Immy glanced at the smokehouse. The door stood open an inch or so. That was odd. She knew the door had to be closed when they smoked the jerky. Maybe the health department was airing it out. Maybe it had been left open by accident. Maybe she should close it.

She stole across the dirt parking lot and peeked inside. The tantalizing smell of smoked meat lingered, strong. It was dark, but the air didn't seem smoky. The door must have been open for awhile. She tried to push it open farther to see inside, but the door was heavy. Even with the door ajar, the smokehouse was hot. And dark.

She hesitated. Maybe she should try to raise someone at the house. The back door was closest to the shop so Immy rapped on it. Little Zack opened the door.

"Is your Mommy or Daddy home?"

He shook his head. "Mommy's sick. Daddy's not here." A tear squeezed out of his eye.

Oh dear. Maybe Tinnie was poisoned, too. "Can I see her? Maybe she needs some medicine."

"She said she needs Daddy to be dead."

Immy froze at the horror of those words. His mother must have spoken them to him. A four-year-old boy wouldn't come up with that on his own. What was the matter with Tinnie that she would do that? Was everyone going crazy this week?

"I'd like to see her," said Immy. She needed to make sure Tinnie wasn't having a breakdown, like Amy JoBeth. She shook her head, amazed that so many people could get so emotional over a pig!

Tinnie lay on her back on a rumpled bed in a floral bedroom, more suitable for a single woman than a married couple, Immy thought. One arm covered her eyes. The other hand fingered the fringed edge of the spread. The blinds were drawn and the room was murky, even in the middle of the sunny day. The room felt cold. The AC must have been turned down low.

"Tinnie?" Immy spoke as softly as she could.

"What?" Tinnie moved her arm and opened her eyes. "Who's there?"

"Can I do anything? Are you going to be all right?"

"No! You can't do a damn thing and I'll never be all right. Not until that bastard is dead."

Zack was standing in the doorway. "Zack," Immy said, "could you get a glass of water, pretty please?"

When he had gone she leaned close to Tinnie and whispered. "Do you see what you're doing to your son? You need to straighten up and quit talking that way about Rusty in front of him. You hear me?" Her hushed words came out harsh, but that was okay. Tinnie needed some sense knocked into her.

"I don't care. I can't do it." Tinnie sat up and started to wail. "And I don't know where Rusty is and that damn Poppy has disappeared. I never want her here except today and now she's, poof, gone in a damn puff of smoke."

Immy blew out her cheeks. She wasn't going to be able to make

Tinnie come to her senses. She could at least shield Zack. "I'll tell you what. I'll take Zack to our place for a few days until you feel better. Would that be good?"

Tinnie fell silent and reached for a tissue on the nightstand. "Maybe that would be a good idea." She nodded. "Yes, that would be good. I think I'll go to Mom's for awhile. A couple of days? We can probably get him then."

Probably? She'd keep Zack as long as needed. He was a sweet kid, wouldn't be a problem. "Drew's party is today anyway. He was planning on coming, wasn't he?"

"Oh god, yes. There's a present on his dresser. It's wrapped." Tinnie collapsed onto the dented pillow, took a deep breath, then sat up on the side of the bed. "I suppose I can help him pack a few things."

"Oh good." Maybe Tinnie *would* come around.

"Why did you come in here, anyway?" Tinnie asked.

"I almost forgot. The door to the smokehouse is open and I wondered if that was how it's supposed to be."

Tinnie frowned. "No, Rusty is smoking pork today. I know the health nuts closed us down, but he ought to be able to open up tomorrow. One of the cutting blades wasn't all the way clean, they said."

Immy was glad she hadn't looked inside to see a pig carcass smoking. "Some people are sick, you know. People that ate jerky yesterday."

"Shit. It's probably from that blade. That could do it." She gave Immy a look of alarm. "You think we'll get sued?"

Immy shrugged. "Not by us. Can't speak for anyone else."

"Shit." Tinnie rose to her unsteady feet. "I'll go get a duffel ready for Zack." She turned at the door. "I appreciate this, Immy. I really do."

"I'll go close the smokehouse door."

Tinnie nodded and left for Zack's room.

The smokehouse door, still ajar, creaked in a slight breeze. Immy started to pull the door shut, but changed her mind. First, she'd see what it looked like. She'd never seen inside one. Maybe it wouldn't be so bad. She put a tentative hand on the rough wooden door and pushed.

It was surprisingly heavy. The light crept into the dark room, fragrant with mesquite smoke. Immy followed it in and let her eyes adjust.

The carcass of a pig lay against the side wall, the back half in a plastic garbage bag. Immy gasped. It wasn't butchered, it was whole. She pushed it away from the wall to see it better. Something shiny and pink lay under the pig. Immy started to reach for it, then she realized that the animal was pure white, just like Marshmallow. Was this Gretchen? Was Rusty going to smoke Gretchen into jerky?

The door fell open wide enough that daylight illuminated the whole room. Sturdy hooks, screwed into the ceiling, held slabs of meat. All but one. That one held the owner of the establishment, Rusty Bucket. He looked smoky. He looked naked. And he looked dead.

Five

Drew's party was merry for the children, Immy hoped. Zack was subdued until the kids were brought outside to the backyard. When he saw the piñata he broke into a grin. After Drew's turn, since she was the birthday girl, Immy had Zack go next. Although she tied a bandana around his eyes, he could see perfectly fine when he tipped his head up. He gripped the broom handle and whacked the pig hard enough to split it in the exact spot of the dent Drew had made. The children squealed and dove for the candy, under a shower of metallic-pink pig confetti, miniature candy bars, and gum.

"Whew! It's fortuitous she only celebrates her birth annually," said Hortense later that evening, rocking in her rocker-recliner, sipping iced tea, and fanning herself. She turned the television on to a prime-time hospital drama. She liked those almost as much as daytime soaps. Hortense still looked ill and hadn't eaten any birthday cake, but wouldn't let Immy call the doctor. Being sick was a moral failure for Hortense.

The air conditioning was cranking out all the cool air it could, but it was hard to battle the triple-digit Texas heat of late June. After sunset, the temperature dipped into the nineties, but not that far into them, and not for long.

Immy surveyed the happy wreckage of ribbons, toys, and pig confetti tracked everywhere and decided to do cleanup later. Drew and Zack had been bathed, separately—Immy wasn't quite sure at what age it was appropriate or inappropriate to bathe together—and tucked into bed. Drew took her youth bed in Immy's room, as always, and Zack was bedded down in Immy's single bed. Immy planned to sleep on the couch until Zack returned home.

He had said a disturbing thing to Immy as she tucked him in. "That lady that works in the shop, that Poppy lady, told Mommy she gonna eat—" His soft chin quivered. "—eat Gwetchen. Soon as she's smoked, she said."

"Oh, darlin'." Immy sat on the edge of the bed and gathered him in her arms. The child shook with sobs for a good five minutes. Immy dried his tears with a tissue. "We might find Gretchen somewhere," she lied. "Or we might be able to get you another pig. Would you like that?"

"I want Gwetchen."

"But if we can't find Gretchen?"

He nodded. "'Nother pig would be awright. Mommy said Gwetchen is dead. Somebody shot her. But not Daddy."

The child fell asleep in her arms and she gently laid him on the bed and covered him.

After Immy'd seen the grotesque body of Zack's father, skewered through the shoulder onto a meat hook and swinging slightly from the breeze of the open smokehouse door, she'd shoved the heavy door shut and run back to the house. The thought had flitted through her head that she should take her time and investigate the scene of the crime, but she was afraid she might throw up all over the evidence if she lingered.

After a whispered consultation with Tinnie, they'd agreed Immy would take Zack to her house immediately while Tinnie phoned 911. Tinnie had relayed a message to Immy that she should be ready to give a statement later that day or the next.

It didn't occur to Immy until much later, after Drew's party that night, that Tinnie hadn't seemed grief-stricken about her husband being dead.

Mother was now watching a lawyer show in the living room.

"I think I'll call Tinnie and see what happened after I left."

"Why? Was something happening?"

"Oh!" Immy hadn't had a chance to tell her mother about Rusty. "Yes, something was happening. Or had already happened. Let me make sure the kids are sound asleep."

She peeked in and they were sleeping like a pair of rosy-cheeked cherubs. The room was sweet with bubble bath smell.

"You would think three recitations of *Goodnight, Moon* would induce somnolence, wouldn't you?" said Hortense when she returned.

"I don't know. Drew usually takes four."

"But tonight it was five. My word, I almost fell asleep myself."

"Mother, that Rusty Bucket is dead."

"Yes, I know. I noticed a hole in it the last time I watered the irises. Just throw it away."

"No, not *our* rusty bucket, Zack's father, Rusty Bucket."

"Zack's father is dead? Heart attack?"

"Not exactly. I found him...hanging in the smokehouse. On a meathook."

Hortense's eyes grew to their fullest, then spilled tears. "Oh, my poor baby. You had to find him?" She rose and pressed Immy to her bosom. "Life is not fair."

When Hortense returned to her television viewing chair, Immy said, "He was murdered, Mother. He had to have been."

"I don't suppose one could commit suicide that way," said Hortense.

"Well, he should have killed himself. You know who else was in there?"

"Two people were hanging from meat hooks?" Hortense muted the television and set her iced tea on the wobbly table next to the recliner. She must have been feeling a tad better because a thick layer of sugar lay on the bottom of her glass.

"No, the other body was on the floor. Not a person. Gretchen. The pig that got shot. She hasn't been skinned yet. I could see two bullet holes in her dear head. Poor thing. It looked to me like Rusty was thinking of making jerky out of her. Can you believe that?"

"I presume his spouse doesn't know of those intentions."

"Zack just told me that she does. I'm going to call Tinnie to see what's going on and how she's doing. Unless she's left for her mother's."

"Offer her a casserole, dear."

"Of course."

The phone at Tinnie's house rang and rang. Immy didn't have a cell phone number for her. "I guess I'll ask Ralph. Oh gosh! I'll bet the chief and Ralph had to go there to suss out the scene."

"One would hope so."

"But they both got food poisoning too."

Hortense had gotten up and dipped a finger in the icing of the left-over cake. If she was feeling better, maybe the other two were recovered. "Maybe you should offer to bring them the rest of my Kaopectate."

"Mother, you drank it from the bottle."

She nodded. "Yes, I'd forgotten about that. You should wipe the brim."

Hortense unmuted the drama and Immy went outside to call Ralph. She knew that he and the chief would be handling the call since they had jurisdiction for Cowtail, which was too small for its own police force.

The front yard was louder than inside the singlewide. Katydids were in the full bloom of their summer lust, jangling their mating calls from the live oaks and salt cedars overhead. A faint sliver of moon trickled its light through the small, hard live oak leaves and caught a few glints of metallic confetti in the grass, the tiny pigs turning to pinkish silver in the moonlight.

Ralph answered right away. "Immy? Are you all right?"

"Me? Yeah, I didn't have any jerky."

"Didn't you find Bucket's body? I thought Chief said—"

"Oh, yes, I did." She squeezed her eyes shut and the vivid sight of her discovery came back to her. Was this going to happen every time she closed her eyes? "I don't think I'll go to sleep tonight."

"Chief told me to get a statement from you. You want me to come over now? I'll be right there."

Before she could decide if she wanted to protest or not, the connection was dead. Ralph was, presumably, on his way.

*****

Immy ran inside to grab her book before Ralph arrived. The index of *The Moron's Compleat PI Guidebook* had an entry Immy had marked with a black Sharpie, "questioning of suspects". She quickly reviewed the tactics so she could pump Ralph. Being a cop, he should be wise to them. In fact, Immy thought, he should be using them, but Immy had never noticed him doing so. Maybe he was too polite to use cop tactics to grill her.

Immy returned to the front steps to meet Ralph. He leapt out of his truck and rushed over to stand at the foot of the stairs, looking up at Immy with genuine concern on his wide, ingenuous face. "Are you okay? How much did you see?"

She gulped and shut her eyes. She'd seen more than she ever wanted to. A blackened, naked, dry-looking body, speared through the shoulder, swinging, slowly swinging from a huge, thick, metal hook. Or had she imagined some of that, embellished the horrific sight with her mind's eye to the point it was even worse than what her real eyes had seen? Having a vivid imagination was a curse, Mother always said. Mother was, as usual, right.

This would never do. Immy opened her eyes and vowed to keep them open.

"I saw that it was Rusty."

Ralph wrote something in a notebook he'd taken from his pocket. Then he stowed it and put his warm hand on her shoulder. She turned to him, her tears spilling out in spite of her rapid blinking. Ralph pulled her up, lifted her off the step, and smothered her in a long, comforting bear hug. She wanted it to never end. Maybe the images would stay away if Ralph held her for a couple of days, or a week.

"I'm so sorry, Immy," Ralph crooned, over and over. "Next time you're going to discover a body, call me first."

Immy suppressed a half-hysterical giggle and pulled away. "Now, Ralph, how in the hell am I going to know before I discover it?"

She had him there. "Ralph, what do you know so far?"

"About?"

"About how he died. Did Rusty die in the smokehouse? Was he…smoked to death?" There hadn't been a puddle of blood under his body, so the skewering, which it seems was bloodless, hadn't killed him. Was he dead when someone stuck him there? He must have been.

"The autopsy isn't back. Won't be for a couple days, probably. Chief said it looked like he died of smoke inhalation, but that's not official."

If the cause and time of death weren't known yet, what info should she pump Ralph for? Then she remembered her original resolve to solve Gretchen's death.

"Did you see that Gretchen's body was there, too?" she asked. "With the confetti?"

"Confetti?"

Immy pointed to some pinkness glinting in the yard. "Like that."

Ralph got up and picked up a few pieces. "Yeah, this same stuff was found with that pig on the floor."

"Are you through getting my statement?"

"I can fill the rest in," he said, tucking his notebook back into his inside pocket.

That was kind of disappointing. She'd wanted to see what he wrote about her.

"Was it really Gretchen in the smokehouse? That pig was pure white, just like Marshmallow."

"Tinnie sure thought it was when she saw it." Ralph gave her a look of admiration. "You noticed a lot, didn't you?"

The body swung before her again, but this time her eyes were open. Was she always going to see it? The tears sprang again. "Yes, I did."

*****

On Sundays Immy usually took the opportunity to sleep in and have the trailer to herself, but she wanted a distraction from the recurring pictures that had interrupted her sleep half the night. So she decided to go to church the next morning with Mother and Drew, and Zack of course.

The sanctuary was dark and cool, welcome after the glare outside. Immy felt her body un-tense a bit, singing the old familiar hymns and listening to the rambling sermon from the elderly Reverend Klinger. He'd headed up the small Baptist congregation for most of Immy's life. Listening to him was easy, comfortable, and soothing.

Sonny Squire saw them enter and beckoned his grandson to come sit with them, but Zack stuck his lower lip out and shook his head. Immy recognized the expression. When Drew made it, her mind was made up and no one could change it.

This was awkward. Immy shooed Hortense and the children into a pew and went to speak with Sonny.

"He's not feeling well," Immy whispered. Whispering seemed called for after the recent events.

"Then he'd better be with his family." Sonny squinted and gave her a hard look.

Immy drew back from the whiskey fumes. "Speaking of family, where's Tinnie?" She and Zack usually sat with Sonny in church.

Sonny turned away from Immy without answering, so she made her way back to the pew, four rows behind and contemplated the back of Sonny Squire's head.

Immy probably only imagined she could smell Sonny from here. Came from being a wealthy rancher, Immy supposed. He was the only wealthy rancher who attended Holiness Baptist, but she knew he wasn't the only one who swilled whiskey when he drove his four-door, long-bed pickup across his land to survey the herds. She tried to keep her mind on Sonny Squire to prevent the other pictures that wanted to pop up in the dark places in her mind. Sonny also owned the First Bank of Saltlick but rarely put in an appearance there.

As they rose after the last Amen, Immy decided she was going to be able to go forward, to get past the crisis of finding Rusty's body. The service seemed to finalize his death. All she had to concern herself about in the coming week was her job, and she looked forward to that. She got a thrill seeing the words, "Private Detective," on the door every weekday morning.

Immy edged her way to the end of the pew behind Drew and Zack, Mother following at a slower pace, trailing them on their way to the door to file past Rev. Klinger to shake his soft, dry hand.

"Remember," Hortense said, "Chief is coming to dinner. He said he seemed sufficiently recovered to partake of my provisions. I assured him I would be serving poultry, one of his favorites."

"I'll shuck some sweet corn if you want," offered Immy.

"That would be—"

"Howdy, ladies," called Louise Cotter from the other side of the sanctuary. "Wait up, I'm acomin'."

Immy marveled that being a librarian hadn't affected Louise's speech the way it had Hortense's. Her vocabulary, in fact, seemed paltry for a woman who had probably read lots of books. And it was way too loud for a librarian.

Louise squeezed through a row of pews while Drew tugged on Immy's hand.

"Mommy, I wanna go see Marshmallow," Drew said.

"Wait a sec," said Immy, watching Louise's approach.

Sonny walked by and gave Zack a hug. He threw a glare at Immy, but didn't say anything to them. At close range, Immy again caught the brunt of Sonny's fragrance. It was strong today. She fanned her face after he walked away.

Louise emerged from her row and took a breath while they waited in the middle of the church, left behind by the departing crowd. Negotiating the small space between the pews was probably not easy for someone as rotund as she was. Mother barely fit.

"Tell you what, I've been trying to think of something to cheer up Amy JoBeth, and I've decided she needs a shower," said Louise.

"She didn't smell too bad when I was there Friday," said Immy.

Louise's sharp cackle made the departing parishioners stop and startle, alarmed. When they saw it was Louise, and not someone in the throes of death, they continued leaving the church.

"Aren't you a hoot! She doesn't need a bath shower, she needs a wedding shower."

"She's getting married?" said Immy.

"To Vern Linder. She's been so happy with him. She hasn't been in the tornado shelter for months and months until now. Not since she started on pigs. She said, after we lost the ranch and her daddy took his life, poor soul, and after her divorce, she wasn't inclined to even come back here. I had an idea we'd ranch together someday, but the family tragedy eventually turned Amy JoBeth clean away from cattle, straight into pigs. Fact is, the reason she divorced Ernie is because he wanted to take up ranching. She couldn't face that."

"She sure does love those pigs," said Immy. She thought it would be a nice thing to throw a party for Amy JoBeth.

"So you'll do it?"

Had she said that out loud? "Um, do what?"

"I'll help. I can do invites and cooking and all, if you'll just be the official shower thrower." She leaned close and Immy caught a whiff of her lilac eau de toilet. "It doesn't look good if her relatives throw the shindig, y'know?"

Louise winked and raised her elbow. Immy was pretty sure Louise was going to poke her in the ribs, so she took a step back.

"Imogene, that would be such a Christian act," said Hortense. "I'm proud of you for offering."

"Well…." said Immy.

"Either me or Vern'll bring over a list later. Y'all busy today?"

"Today would be fine, Louise," said Hortense.

"Well…." said Immy.

"See ya then." Louise strode up the aisle, slipped past the line for Rev. Klinger, and was gone.

"So," said Immy, "do we have it at our place?"

"I believe that is customary," said Hortense.

"Do we invite Vern, too?"

"We'll leave that to the discretion of Louise. I believe he'll be expected to make a brief appearance."

"I'll warn him not to bring any jerky."

"Any porcine products at all would be regrettable."

Six

T HE NEXT WEEK FLEW BY, although most of it was spent not working. When Immy first started the job, Mike Mallett had given her quite a free rein as to hours. He said he was mainly concerned with getting the filing and billing done, as well as typing up his occasional reports. Immy got behind in her filing during the week, what with planning Amy JoBeth's party and trying to track down Gretchen's killer, but knew she'd be able to catch up the next week. Her Poison Jerky Eaters Case seemed to be solved. Immy wasn't sure if she'd solved it or if it had just solved itself. The police were working on the case of Rusty's murder. But the pig killing wasn't going to be solved if she didn't do it. It was all hers. Besides, she thought it might be the key to solving Rusty's murder.

Monday morning, it seemed the same pile of filing greeted her that had been there last week. Mike got out the same files over and over, week after week. At least they all looked the same. Why couldn't she just leave them out? But she dutifully tried to put most of them back into the drawers. Sometimes she peeked inside, but they were mostly just boring notes about what people did every minute of the day. Lots of jealous spouses and suspicious employers in the world.

Immy took off early Monday because Louise was coming over to discuss party plans. Amy JoBeth was still spending most of her time in the storm shelter. Louise spent hours trying to persuade her out of it, but Louise had been to their trailer once when she wasn't busy guarding the tornado shelter door and helping with the pigs.

Driving past the pig breeding place a couple times, Immy noticed that Amy JoBeth's truck had been gone. The woman must have been making forays from her fortress. That was good, thought Immy. She was getting some fresh air anyway.

It was remarkable how much had to be decided for a simple wedding shower. Immy thought she could send out invitations, clean the trailer, make some cookies and punch, and that would be it.

But Louise thought they needed a theme.

"Without a theme," she said, "we won't know what kinda paper plates to buy and what color the food should be. They haven't set a date yet, so it's technically an Engagement Party. She never had one, so she won't think it's strange we're doing this."

Ha. Immy thought Amy JoBeth would know immediately what they were up to, trying to take her mind off Gretchen. If only Immy could track down the pig killer. That would cheer Amy JoBeth up.

"I found a list of themes in this magazine at Cathy's Kut and Kurl."

"Does Cathy know you took it?" asked Immy.

Louise frowned, but didn't answer.

The squeals of Drew, Zack, and Marshmallow came from the back yard. Louise gave a fond smile in the direction of the piggy noises. "Look here. There's your Alphabet Shower, but ya gotta have twenty-six guests for that one. Then there's your Makeover Shower. Maybe Cathy would like to do that."

If she's not mad at you for stealing her magazine, thought Immy. It was a new one, too, not one of the curled ones that had been there for years.

"And there's your Lingerie Shower. That sounds like fun. I guess it's too early for the Stock-the-Bar Shower. The stuff'd all be drunk by the time they get married, whenever that's gonna be."

Immy was beginning to think Stock-the-Bar would be the best idea. They could all finish off the presents at the party.

"Kitchen Shower. That sounds boring. Shower Shower? Oh, bathroom stuff. Kind of limited, I'd think. Recipe Shower?" Louise finally looked up from the magazine. "What do y'all think?"

Hortense cleared her throat to speak, but Immy jumped in first. "The Stock-Your-Bar sounds good."

Her mother ignored her. "I'm of the opinion that, Louise, in light of your offer yesterday, you should manage the celebration. What theme appeals to you?"

"I should take charge, huh? Lemme ask Cathy how she feels about doing a Makeover Shower. You think she'd do it for free?"

Immy and her mother answered together. "No."

"It would not be reasonable to expect that of her, Louise," said Hortense. "The woman makes her living as a beautician, applying makeup and coiffing hair."

"She usually just cuts and perms mine."

"Cathy would expect remuneration and she would be entitled to it."

"Should we pay her, though?" asked Louise.

Hortense rose and went into the kitchen.

"Yes," said Immy. "We should pay her."

"Oh good. You'll chip in?"

Hortense was back in a flash. "If you decide on this theme, *you* will pay her. We are opening our home for this and will put in our time planning, and don't mind minor expenditures, but you should bear the majority of the expense."

In case that was too complicated for Louise, Immy translated. "You really should pay for all the major stuff."

"Well, I'll see what Cathy says. We can always go with a Lingerie Party."

✳✳✳✳✳

It was obvious the police weren't going to treat Gretchen's slaying as a murder, so Immy returned to the scene of the crime late Monday night, after Louise left. At least to the scene where she had discovered the bodies. She equipped herself with what she thought she'd need and told her mother she was going for a drive to clear her head. Hortense wondered what was preventing its clarity, but Immy turned and walked out the door. The children were already in bed with the pig curled up on the floor beside Drew's cot.

Zack was still staying with them and Tinnie was still at her mother's in Fort Worth, so no one was at Jerry's Jerky or the Bucket house. Or the smokehouse. As Immy had suspected, Gretchen's poor body still lay in the smokehouse with the two bullet holes in her head. Things were happening to the pig that Immy did not want to think about. The dead body wasn't being preserved by being in the smokehouse. Probably because there wasn't any smoke left.

Immy stuck her head out the door and took a gulp of fresh air, then aimed her flashlight at Gretchen's head, took out the kitchen paring knife she'd brought, and dug the two bullets out. As the knife carved into the soft flesh, she swallowed down some bile, but didn't throw up. She was proud of that. She folded them into a paper napkin, having read in her Compleat book that plastic bags were not that good at preserving evidence, and stuck that into a paper lunch bag.

She would see if Ralph or the chief could at least get Gretchen buried.

After she got home, she wondered what she could compare the bullets to, but didn't come up with an answer. She would save them in her top dresser drawer and maybe they could be used in the future.

✶✶✶✶✶

Ralph came over Tuesday night to tell Immy the vet had taken Gretchen's corpse. That was a relief. Dr. Fox had a small burial plot for pets behind his office.

He also said the autopsy was done and Rusty had died of smoke inhalation and hyperthermia (which, if Immy had hyper and hypo straight, meant a high temperature, which made sense, him dying in a hot place). But, Ralph said, Rusty also had enough drugs in his system to knock him out.

"So, he was drugged before he died?" Immy asked.

They sat on the sagging green plaid couch in the singlewide's living room, sipping iced tea Hortense had brought them.

"The killer," said Hortense, "rendered him unconscious in order to transport his inert form into the smokehouse?"

"Looks that way," said Ralph.

"Should you be disclosing these autopsy conclusions, Ralph?" asked Hortense.

"This is all gonna be in the paper tomorrow, and probably on the news tonight, so I reckon it's all right."

"He could have ODed. What were the drugs? Did he use a lot of them?" asked Immy.

"He didn't take this drug," said Ralph. "It was animal tranquillizer. The stuff they use on horses."

"From a vet's clinic?"

Ralph shook his head. "You can't tell where it came from. But probably the vet clinic."

The vet clinic, Ralph said. There was only one in these parts.

"Are there any findings on Gretchen?" asked Immy.

"Uh, they don't do autopsies on pigs, Immy."

"But aren't the cops concerned about her? Are you going to make any effort at all to find her killer?"

"We'll be lucky if we can find Rusty's killer."

"No leads?"

"No one has confessed, if that's what you mean. Or blamed anyone else. Not even hardly any clues. The scene didn't give us much."

"So maybe someone who frequents the smokehouse?" said Hortense.

"Way to go, Mother. Good thought. If someone killed him, someone who goes there all the time, you wouldn't be able to get any useful clues."

"Smokehouses aren't good places to find clues, to begin with," said Ralph. "The Wymee Falls CSI did collect some prints, but I could tell there weren't many. They'd be pretty easy to see on those smoky walls. I bet people try to avoid touching those black walls when they're in there."

"How soon before you get the results from CSI?"

"No telling. They have to collect a bunch of prints from people, you know. The people that work there and stuff."

"For elimination, right? Do you know if there were any fingerprints on Gretchen's body?" said Immy.

Ralph puffed out his cheeks and blew. "Immy, for the last time, we didn't process the pig at all. We're not trying to track down Gretchen's killer."

"But what if the same person killed both of them? Have you thought about that?"

"No, we think Rusty probably killed the pig. Looked like he was gonna make it into pork jerky."

It all finally got to her. Immy ran to the bathroom to throw up.

*****

Wednesday Immy left work early again. As she was lifting her purse out of the file drawer, Mike walked into the front room. Immy thought of it as her office, but it was, she had to admit, the reception area.

"Leaving, kiddo?"

"I have some things to do. That shower this weekend, and we're running low on Cheerios. I swear that's all Zack eats."

"You get those bills sent out for the background checks?"

"I'll do them first thing tomorrow." She hiked the purse to her shoulder and shut the drawer. Standing, she stood eye to eye to the little man.

"And the filing for those child custody surveillance jobs?"

"I did most of them." She shifted to stand in front of the pile of folders awaiting a home in the gray metal file drawers behind her. She'd spruced the place up considerably since she started work in the spring. The bare walls now held travel posters from the agency next door. Her gray metal desk was adorned with a pretty, floral desk clock that matched the pen cup and blotter she'd found at WellMart. Several cinnamon candles scented the room while she worked. They helped to combat the walnut scented ones Mike always burned in his office, and of which Immy had gotten tired by her second week. Mike never seemed to notice her efforts, though. He seemed focused only on her filing and billing.

Mike peeked around her, at the pile of folders, and raised the eyebrows on his narrow, weaselly face. "Okay, kid, stay late tomorrow and you'll get caught up. See ya."

Immy let out a breath of relief. If she lost this job, she didn't know what she'd do. She might join Amy JoBeth in her depression, but not in that dark and dreary tornado shelter. She adored this job. She hadn't gotten into the good stuff yet, but she knew it was just a matter of time before Mike would trust her with some real jobs, not just typing and filing.

The van was parked two blocks away. Parking was a problem in Wymee Falls, at least right around here. If she got to work really early, within ten minutes of her start time, she could sometimes park right in front, but she was usually a block or two away. This seemed to be one of the few areas of town with full occupancy. Maybe the rent was cheap here.

As she passed the windows of the travel agency, Immy waved to the nice agent that had loaded her up with the posters for her office walls. The hamburger shop tempted her as she passed, as always, but she hurried to the van so she could pick up the groceries on the way home. Louise had given her a list for WellMart, too. The theme had finally been decided. They were doing a Makeover Party. Immy didn't want to be Madeover, but Louise was so excited that Cathy had said she'd do everyone for half price, that Immy didn't want to spoil her joy. Louise had an insidious way of getting people to go along with her. Well, maybe not insidious. Insistent. She kept after you and kept after you until you broke down and gave in.

Immy had forgotten why she was buying the paper products and not Louise. Something about hurting her foot. Or her hand. Or something.

She grocery shopped for Zack's Cheerios and some store-bought jerky for her mother. Hortense was missing Jerry's Jerky shop already. It was Wednesday and the shop had only been closed since Saturday. Immy hadn't had so many dreams of Rusty's swinging body last night. Maybe they would go away completely someday.

Next, at the WellMart at the edge of Wymee Falls, she steered her cart to the party goods section of the store, concentrating on the list Louise had given her. Louise had decided either tiger stripes or leopard spots would be good. What they had to do with the theme, Immy couldn't imagine. Maybe on Saturday night they would all be made over to look like cats.

Neither of them had thought how likely WellMart would be to carry tiger and leopard paper plates, napkins, and cups. Immy was also supposed to get matching plastic ware and placemats.

The only theme WellMart was stocking, a few days before the Fourth of July was firecrackers and fireworks. That had as much to do with makeovers as jungle cats, so Immy piled them into her cart. She was also supposed to order a cake so she made her way to the bakery counter, marking all the party paper products off the list.

A cart bumped into hers. Its driver was concentrating on a list, too. And its driver was Betsy Wiggins, the assistant at Dr. Fox's vet clinic.

"Well, well, WELL. Fancy meeting YOU here." She flashed a brilliant white smile at Immy, but it seemed cold, not warm.

It wasn't clear how she felt about meeting Immy here, but Immy knew how she felt about meeting Betsy, who had, Immy felt sure, not only slept with Tinnie's husband, but had dragged Gretchen's carcass to the smokehouse.

Immy didn't want to cross her, though. She remembered the ugly snarl Betsy had given Vern after she stuck him with the needle. It probably wouldn't take much for her to turn on Immy like that. Betsy wasn't from around here, so Immy didn't know her family or her background. She came from Dallas. You never could trust people when you didn't know their kin.

"Looks like YOU'RE going to have yourself a PAR-ty." Betsy glanced into Immy's shopping cart.

"Looks like you're having one, too," said Immy. Betsy's cart was full of wine bottles and cases of beer.

"Oh, I just like to have DRINKS on hand for when people drop OVER." She waved her red fingernails above the booze.

She didn't seem to be mourning Rusty's death. So, maybe she hadn't been sleeping with him. Wouldn't she be more broken up if she had?

Immy tried to find out. "Have you heard anything about Rusty's memorial service? The autopsy is done so they'll probably release the body." Who would take the body? Not Tinnie, Immy would bet. He was kin to the Yarborough twins in Saltlick. Maybe they'd take it.

"I'm sure I don't know. I probably wouldn't have time to go, we're so busy at the clinic with Vern gone."

"Where's he gone to?" This was a ploy. Immy had read in her *Compleat Guidebook* that an interrogator should play dumb to elicit information.

Betsy shrugged and shook her head. "No idea. Dr. Fox fired his ass. There's drugs missing."

Were these missing drugs what was used on Rusty?

"And *I* didn't take them." Betsy pushed past Immy and headed for the cheese case.

Immy wondered if Betsy *had* taken them, though. You just never knew about people who weren't from around here.

Seven

Emmet Emersen, the Saltlick Chief of Police, was expected for supper. The aroma of Hortense's homemade beef vegetable soup greeted Immy when she carried the party supplies into the trailer. She had to admit, having the chief over was good. The quality of the Duckworthy cuisine had picked up considerably since he'd started coming around. They used to have a lot of meals of SpaghettiOs and Dinty Moore beef stew, two of Hortense's favorites. But, when she began inviting the chief to supper, Hortense started pulling out the recipe file she'd collected over the years and never used until now. The relationship sometimes surprised Immy, but she was getting used to it. So far, it seemed platonic, or maybe gastronomic.

"Did you procure the Bisquick?" asked Hortense as Immy stacked the paper goods at the end of the kitchen counter. Immy waved the box she'd bought and got out a mixing bowl to put the biscuits together.

"Isn't it too warm for soup?" asked Immy.

Hortense simpered. "Emmett loves my soup so. He requested it for tonight, so, of course, I cannot refuse him."

He hadn't been "Emmett" all that long, but things were progressing quickly and Immy needed to decide what that meant for her and Drew. What if they decided they wanted to get married? What if they actually *got* married?

Chief Emersen lived in a nice doublewide on the other side of

Saltlick, which made it less than half a mile away. Immy thought it out. An engagement party in the backyard. A wedding in the church. A honeymoon, where? Maybe Fredericksburg? Then the happy couple would reside at the Emersen domicile. This could work out well. She might get the trailer to herself with Drew and Marshmallow.

*****

As they were finishing the blueberry cobbler, Ralph gave his special rap on the door and Drew raced to let him in.

"Unca Ralph!" She jumped into his arms and he hoisted her above his head with a huge grin.

"Hey, Drew. You missed me?" He set her down, then spied his boss sitting at the table. Marshmallow grunted at Ralph, who reached down to pat the pig's head.

Zack sat on the floor and watched without speaking, but smiled when the big policeman petted Marshmallow.

Immy could tell Ralph hadn't expected to see Emmett here, although the two of them had met here once before, when their social calls overlapped. Immy abandoned her last two bites and hurried Ralph out the front door.

"Was that blueberry cobbler?" he asked.

"Yes, but that was also your boss. I thought you might need to collect yourself."

"Maybe." Ralph's brow furrowed with thought.

"There will be some left when we get back. Let's walk." Immy needed to get Ralph alone, out of earshot of the chief, if she were going to learn anything.

They strolled through the warm evening, serenaded by crickets, locusts, and tree frogs. The constant wind was at a low point, barely stirring Immy's hair.

"What's happening with your case?" Immy tried to sound casual.

"Immy, don't try to pump me tonight. We're working hard to come up with something on Rusty's death. The autopsy came out yesterday, so we're not very far."

"No leads?"

"I didn't say that." He sounded defensive.

"You'll have to find her. She has to come back for Zack."

"We're looking."

"Well, who looks good for it?"

"We're questioning everybody. Everybody except Poppy Jenkins."

"Why on earth aren't you questioning her?"

"Because we can't find her. We can't find Tinnie Bucket either."

"She's at her mother's in Fort Worth."

"That's where she was. It's not where she is now."

"Who else is there to question?"

He gave her a playful look. "You want me to haul you in?"

"Um, no."

He grabbed her, tickled her, and they ended their match with a satisfying clinch.

Later, Immy wondered where on earth Poppy and Tinnie were. Was one of them a killer, a desperado, on the run from the long arm of the law? She hoped Tinnie wasn't a murderer, for Zack's sake.

*****

By the time Immy and Ralph returned for his piece of blueberry cobbler, the chief was gone.

"Drew's Mom?" Zack tugged Immy's sleeve as she washed Drew's face for bedtime. He couldn't quite say Ms. Duckworthy and she hadn't persuaded him to call her Immy, or even Miss Immy.

Smiling down on the child, she smoothed his fly-away blond hair. His shiny blue eyes looked sad. "Yes?"

"Do you know when Mommy will come and get me?"

Immy's smile faded. "No, I don't." And she didn't know how to reach her, or where she was. When Immy had called Tinnie's mother's house in Fort Worth after Ralph left, she'd learned Tinnie had left there on Tuesday. Tinnie's mother wasn't sure where her daughter was going, but probably not home, she said. She hadn't seemed overly concerned about her grandson.

"Well, can I get a new pig?" Zack said.

She stifled a laugh. From being forlorn about Mommy to wanting a new pig—kids jumped around a lot in their heads.

"We'll see." She didn't have money for another pig, that was for sure. Zack's Mommy had plenty, Immy was sure, but where was she?

"That means no, wight?"

"Noooo, that means we have to ask your Mommy. As soon as she comes to get you."

"Well, can we go wook at some?"

That might not be a bad idea. It would give her an excuse to check up on Amy JoBeth, and maybe it would get Amy JoBeth interested long enough in selling a pig to break the tornado shelter habit. Immy also wanted to see if this party on Saturday was going to come as surprise to her.

When Immy left work early Thursday to check out some pigs with Zack and Drew, Mike was out of the office. He'd been gone all afternoon and she had studied her text for her online PI course while the office was empty. The phone only rang three times, all with messages for Mike that didn't sound urgent enough for her to call him. She had his cell number in case someone needed him in a hurry. She had a test Friday and hadn't read half the material yet. The test was on The Crime Scene. The textbook emphasized that the subject could be a whole course by itself, a course they would sell you for an additional fee, so she thought she'd better delve deeply. It didn't seem, though, that a private investigator like Mike Mallett would ever be involved in investigating a crime scene. The cops probably wouldn't let him near it. She'd learned that much about allowing civilians at crime scenes in her course. She wanted to ask him about it, but he'd been busy lately and she hadn't spent too much time at the office this week.

After she picked Zack and Drew up from their preschool, she drove to the outskirts of Cowtail while the kids snacked on raisins and juice boxes in the back seat. She didn't have a car seat for Zack and worried about that.

She'd driven to the Buckets' house, which sat in front of the jerky shop, Tuesday after work, after dropping the kids at her home, hoping to somehow get a car seat, but no one had been there. The shop, of course, was closed and yellow police tape on the smokehouse fluttered in the wind. She didn't think Tinnie was there because the only vehicles on the property were the Jerry's Jerky van and Rusty's orange truck. Tinnie's Volvo, which held Zack's carseat, had been gone.

At least they didn't have to drive past Zack's home to get to Amy's Swine. She didn't want to do that to him.

She negotiated the dirt road and coasted to a stop at the pig farm. Snuffling, snorting sounds came from the pens behind the house. The pigs didn't sound distressed, so Immy assumed they were being taken care of.

The children ran to the animals as soon as Immy released Drew from her car seat. Amy JoBeth didn't appear, which wasn't surprising, since Immy assumed she was in the underground shelter. Immy knocked on its slanting door but didn't get an answer. She'd come prepared with a flashlight in case the light was off. When she pulled the door open, the interior gaped dark and silent. Immy switched on the flashlight and made her way down the steep steps, her hands sweating only slightly. It was not only dark, it was empty.

That was good! It must mean Amy JoBeth was feeling better. Immy hoped that's what it meant. She scurried up the stairs and ran to the front door of the house. No one answered her knock there, either. Immy tried the handle. Not locked. She pushed it open, stepped in and hollered, "Yoo hoo. Howdy. Amy JoBeth. It's me, Immy."

Her calls fell on the kind of quiet that signals an empty space, as empty as the tornado shelter. She took another look outside. Drew and Zack were the only humans in the yard. Amy JoBeth's white pickup stood beside the house, but Immy couldn't remember if she had another vehicle or not. Immy closed her eyes and tried to picture the last time she was here. Maybe there'd been a car? Maybe not, she couldn't remember, hadn't noticed. Maybe Ralph would remember, but he wasn't here.

Immy snapped her fingers with a thought. Someone could have picked up Amy JoBeth and gone somewhere with her. Probably her mother.

Well, she wasn't going to worry about it now. They'd come to see the pigs and they could do that without Amy JoBeth.

She pulled the door shut behind her and joined the kids, who were pointing at one piglet, then another, saying, "I want that one." "No, that one." "No, I want the other one, over there."

It turned out to be a good thing the pig seller was gone. That made it easy to tell the kids they couldn't get one today for Zack. The boy left, happy that he had made a selection.

Immy turned her attention toward the engagement shower when she got home. Louise was coming over after supper to see what Immy had bought the day before.

As Immy could have predicted, Louise wasn't happy with the firecracker plates and napkins.

"What do fireworks have to do with getting engaged? Or with makeup?" she said, shoving the packages away from her on the coffee table.

"Louise, be reasonable." Hortense came to her daughter's defense. "There isn't a wide array of availability in the local establishments. And there isn't time to drive to Dallas or Fort Worth."

Louise cocked her head at Hortense and considered. For a moment Immy thought she was going to counter that there *was* time before Saturday, since it was only Thursday. But she didn't. She gave in on the plates. She wasn't happy about the cake, though.

"Why didn't you get it at Fancy Frosting? Didn't you get Drew's cake there?"

How on earth did she know that? "I'm not made of money, Louise. I can't afford another cake from there so soon. You go get a Fancy Frosting cake if you want to and I'll cancel the grocery store cake."

"Unless, that is," said Hortense, "you're planning to reimburse Imogene for all the expense she's incurred so far."

Louise mumbled something about being short at the moment so Immy assumed she wasn't going to fork over any dough. Maybe Immy would send her a bill when this was done.

On Friday, Immy stayed an hour late at work and got all the billing caught up. While Mike was busy with phone calls, she stuffed the unfiled folders in the drawer of her desk where she kept her purse, called out her goodbye, and scooted out the door. Tonight she and Mother had to finish the baking for the party tomorrow.

She had taken her online test on The Crime Scene on her work computer while Mike was at lunch. It would take a week to get the results. The questions weren't too hard and she thought she'd known most of them. It wouldn't be too much longer before she finished her courses and could be a real PI.

On her way home, Immy swore she'd never get roped into anything by Louise again. She kept telling herself it was a good thing to do for Amy JoBeth. When the party was finished, she'd sit down with Amy JoBeth and see if she couldn't figure out a way to track down Gretchen's killer for her.

*****

The day of Amy JoBeth's party started fine. The weather had taken a slight cool turn and it looked like the icing on the cake would hold up.

Just before the guests were to arrive, Immy and Hortense bustled in and out, setting out sweating pitchers of iced tea, piles of festive red, white, and blue paper ware weighted with a couple of real plates, and platters of vegetables, dip, pickles, and cheeses. Drew and Zack were assigned the task of keeping Marshmallow away from the picnic table and there was only one minor mishap when the pig nosed a dish of ranch dressing dip onto the ground. Luckily, they had lots more.

Louise didn't show up until the first guests, some Cotter cousins from Fort Worth, had arrived. Soon, the yard was filled with Cotter relatives and a few locals that Amy JoBeth and Louise had met since they'd both moved to the area.

As the party was gearing up, Immy started to relax. She found an empty folding chair and sat to eat her cake and watch. Although she still felt she'd been railroaded into this, and wondered if Louise would ever repay her for the money she'd spent, she was doubly glad she'd done it now. Amy JoBeth, her wiry hair tamed into what might almost be a bob, and wearing a denim skirt and sandals instead of her usual overalls, looked relaxed. She sat on a lawn chair and chatted with some of her cousins about plans for the wedding—flowers and colors. Maybe Louise was right and this was just what she needed to bring her out of her doldrums and her bunker.

Cathy was due soon and they could get down to discussing makeovers. They'd decided she would just do makeup today, but would suggest new hair styles that would be optional, and would be accomplished by appointment in her shop, Cathy's Kut and Kurl.

At one point, Drew and Zack took the pig to the front yard to play, while the party continued in the back, under the spreading live oak tree next to Marshmallow's new quarters. Marshmallow hadn't spent much time there yet, though. He'd taken to the litter box inside and had slept with Drew every night after the first one, when he'd squealed for three hours outside until Immy let him in.

As Immy finished her cake and stood to toss her plate into the garbage bag tied to a lawn chair, the two children rushed around the corner of the house from the front yard. Immy's first reaction was alarm. Had Marshmallow run away and been shot? But he trotted behind them like a puppy dog.

Behind Marshmallow strode Chief Emmett Emersen. Immy wondered if he had been invited and, if so, why he was so late, but one look at his beefy red face told her this was a business call.

He stopped and surveyed the yard full of females, then made straight for Amy JoBeth. Now Immy pictured all of Amy JoBeth's pigs loose and lying dead, shot by drunken hunters. Immy started toward the chief.

Amy JoBeth's hand, holding a forkful of cake, stopped halfway to her mouth. Heads swiveled and silence fell at the sight of the beefy, ruddy-faced, fully uniformed cop.

"Amy JoBeth Cotter Anderson," Chief said in his most official tone, "I arrest you for the murder of Beryl Bucket, also known as Rusty." Amy JoBeth slumped to the ground, exactly as her mother had done in their kitchen a few days ago.

Eight

AT CHURCH THE NEXT MORNING, the sanctuary was abuzz with the news of Amy JoBeth's arrest as Immy and her family walked in. Louise hadn't shown up, so Immy thought most of the talk was speculation. She'd have to see if Ralph could give her some concrete information on the charges later.

The rumors were wild. Amy JoBeth was in a coma in the hospital. She was in a coma in the Saltlick jail. She was awake, but babbling incoherently. She was awake and coherent, but crouching beneath the cot. Immy knew this was possible because she'd spent a night there once herself and the cots were built as shelves, with one bunked atop the other.

Immy shuddered as she pictured Amy JoBeth hunkering on the floor of the cell, getting as close to being underground as she could, since she couldn't get into her tornado shelter. Once she got out of jail, she might never come out of her cave again, no matter how many brownies Immy offered her.

Mrs. Wilson, the woman who kept her Rottweiler chained in her yard, and one of the biggest gossips in Saltlick, gave two conflicting versions, the coma in the hospital and the incoherent in jail. She had another rumor, though, that Immy didn't hear from the other parishioners.

"I was talking to Ophelia Jenkins before the service," she whispered to Hortense during the offertory. Immy, on the other side of Hortense, could hear her perfectly. "She was praying at the altar, down on her knees, and bawling. She's just beside herself."

Hortense scanned the congregation. "Where is she coexisting next to her own person at the moment?" she asked. "She's not present in the sanctuary."

Mrs. Wilson shook her head to clear it of Hortense's extraneous words.

Immy leaned forward to whisper to Mrs. Wilson. "Mother means, where is Ophelia?"

"Oh. She decided she couldn't stay for the service. She's too upset about her daughter. Poppy didn't come home from her last shift at Jerry's Jerky. Ophelia doesn't know where she's at."

"That is peculiar," said Hortense.

"Has Ophelia investigated?" asked Immy.

"All rise," intoned Reverend Klinger, and they rose and sang the doxology.

Immy wondered if she should take on another case, The Case of the Missing Poppy. It sounded like a gardening mystery novel. Or a drug mystery?

After the service, Immy dropped Hortense and the children at home and swung by the jail to see if she could cheer up Amy JoBeth.

Tabitha, the bleached-out blonde guardian of the bullet-proof window in the small police station lobby, acted like she didn't know Immy, as usual.

"Please sign your name on the roster and write down who you want to see.'

"Tabitha, you know very well who I am and I want to see Ralph. Which you also know very well."

Tabitha looked up from inspecting her long nails. "You have to sign the roster."

"I didn't have to last time I came in here to see Ralph."

"Well, we have new procedures now."

"Since when?"

Tabitha went back to her nails, which badly needed cutting. But all she was doing was buffing the blood-red polish on them. Immy gave up and signed her name on a tablet on which Tabitha had printed headings: NAME, PARTY TO BE SEEN, TIME IN, TIME OUT.

She was able to put her NAME, Imogene Duckworthy, and her PARTY TO BE SEEN, Ralph Sandoval, but she didn't know what time it was. Probably about one. She wrote: daytime.

Tabitha examined the tablet, gave Immy a hard stare from under her pale eyebrows when she got to TIME IN, but left for the innards of the station. The innards were not vast, but were fiercely guarded by Tabitha during her working hours. Sometimes, when Immy came to the station after Tabitha had gone home, she could rap on the heavy door beside the empty glass cage and Ralph would usher her to his closet-sized office.

Tabitha returned after a leisurely ten-minutes and told Immy that Ralph wasn't in today.

"What the hell? You knew that when I walked in here. Why didn't you tell me?"

"I thought maybe Chief would want to talk to you."

"What are you doing working Sunday anyway?"

"Making up hours. I'm taking vacation next week."

"Good," said Immy, and left the station. Outside the door she reconsidered. She went back and asked Tabitha if she could see the chief instead.

Tabitha pointed to her damn roster and Immy filled it out, using Chief Emersen's name for her new entry, glaring the whole time.

Chief Emersen eventually ushered her through the door, down the hall and into his office. It couldn't be called spacious, unless you'd seen Ralph's office first. She'd never sat in his office before. She'd walked past it and peeked in the door, but it was even smaller from the inside. Bigger than Ralph's office, which had been converted from a storage closet, but not by a lot. A bank of tall file cabinets lined one wall and a computer with a bouncing screensaver logo took up a lot of the gray metal desk that, in turn, took up a good portion of the room. But the two side chairs were nice, with leather-looking cushions and arm rests. A window faced out on the side street to his right.

"Immy, how's your mother doing?"

Chief sure was becoming sweet on her mother. Could Immy use this? Turn it to her advantage? Probably not, Chief was an upstanding guy.

"She seems to like Drew's new pet," said Immy. "She decided to cook special treats for Marshmallow."

"The pig eats marshmallows?"

"No, no, Drew named the pig Marshmallow."

"That's right. I remember Drew telling me that."

"Mother thinks Marshmallow needs special pig treats. He seems to like Cheerios and popcorn just fine, but Mother found a recipe for peanut butter flavored pig treats in the 'Potbelly Insider Magazine'."

Chief drummed his pencil on his desk blotter and glanced at the clock on his wall. "Immy, what did you want to see me about?"

"Oh yes. I wanted to talk to Amy JoBeth. If I could."

"Why do you want to see her, Immy?"

"Well, I guess I want to cheer her up. She has a history of depression. It's not good for her being locked up."

"I don't believe being locked up is good for anyone. But we don't release prisoners because they're upset about being locked up."

"I don't want to get her released. I'm not going to try to spring her. Honest."

Chief pondered for a moment. "How about if I let you talk to her through the bars?"

"That's fine." Immy especially disliked the confinement of jail cells.

So she was escorted to Amy JoBeth's cell, relieved to find it wasn't the one she'd spent a night in once. She got a cold feeling inside when she glanced at that one as she passed it. Of course, there were only three jail cells, so it wasn't far away. The other cells were empty, and the chief left her alone to talk to Amy JoBeth. Immy was glad about that. It might give her a chance to suss out some good dope.

Amy JoBeth looked up at Immy with dull eyes. She wasn't on the floor under the cot, but she didn't look well. Immy stepped to the bars and grabbed them. They were as cold and unyielding as she remembered.

"Hi, Immy. What are you doing here?"

"I, uh, would you like some brownies?"

"No, Immy. I would not like some brownies. I would not like anything. Except to redo the past. I never should have left Ernest." Amy JoBeth returned her gaze to the concrete floor.

Did that mean she regretted killing Rusty?

"What are they charging you with? Do you have a good mouthpiece?" Immy had read every piece of detective fiction in the Saltlick library at a young age and slipped into the lingo with ease.

"What do you think? Murder. They think I killed Rusty."

"Why?"

"Because he killed Gretchen."

Oh. "That's not what I meant, but I didn't know Rusty killed her. How did you find that out?" How could she get her career going if all her cases were going to solve themselves?

"Vern told me Rusty did it. He said Rusty told him."

Immy pondered this for a minute. "When did that happen?"

"You know how Vern brought me that jerky when I came out of the storm shelter?"

That moment was vividly etched in Immy's mind. She hoped it had given Amy JoBeth an accurate assessment of Vern's intelligence level.

"Vernie said Rusty told him when he was there to buy jerky. He saw Rusty putting Gretchen into the smokehouse. Into the smokehouse! He told Vern to tell me he was so sorry he'd shot Gretchen."

Since she was still calling him Vernie, Immy guessed she still loved him. "Rusty told Vern that? Why would Rusty do that?" But then, why would Vern buy pork jerky for Amy JoBeth? And why in the hell would

Rusty think he should smoke Gretchen? Were those two men just that dumb?

"He said he'd take it all back if he could." Amy JoBeth squeezed her eyelids shut and tears streamed over her round cheeks.

"But the shop was closed so he couldn't, I guess."

"What?" Amy JoBeth looked straight at Immy for the first time, animation playing across her face.

"I said Vern couldn't return the jerky because the health department closed Jerry's Jerky Shoppe."

"I was talking about Rusty taking back what he did, not Vern taking back the jerky. Are you crazy, Immy?" She rose and approached the cell bars.

Ha. Coming from a person who locked herself in a tornado shelter, those were fine words.

Amy JoBeth dashed the tears from her face with her sleeve. "Why did you come here?"

Oh yes, she must remember her mission of mercy. "To cheer you up."

"You're doing a hell of a job." Amy JoBeth returned to the cot and slumped, hard, against the wall it was fastened to. "I feel *so* much better."

"Do you want me to figure out who killed Rusty?"

Hope glowed in Amy JoBeth's damp eyes. "You mean you don't think I did?"

Well, no, she hadn't thought that. Until now. But what if Amy JoBeth really did kill Rusty? She pondered that for a moment. She didn't think PIs were supposed to ask their clients if they were guilty. Maybe Immy had better figure out if Amy JoBeth did it or not. "Why do the cops think you're good for it?"

Amy JoBeth's shoulders rose and fell in a long sigh. "They have some pretty good evidence, my lawyer says." She held up her piggy fingers and ticked off her points. "First, because I knew he killed Gretchen. And I was mad enough to kill him, I admit. Second, because my signature confetti was found under his body. Third, I don't have an alibi."

Immy wondered if the cops would have connected the confetti to Amy JoBeth if she, Immy, hadn't pointed it out to Ralph. A spasm of guilt washed over her. "Isn't being in your cellar an alibi?"

"I wasn't *always* in my cellar. I have to go out sometimes."

"Often?"

"Not too often. But my slop bucket needs emptying when it starts to stink."

Ugh. How could she stay in that tiny space with a slop bucket? Double ugh.

"Why are you shivering? Are you cold, Immy?"

"So, the confetti was on the floor of the smokehouse. How do you suppose it got there?"

Amy JoBeth looked at Immy with admiration. "I don't know. I haven't thought about it."

An unwelcome idea ran through Immy's mind: *Is it because you had some on you and it got there when you killed him?* She used the interrogation technique from *The Moron's Compleat PI Guidebook* of maintaining silence so the suspects will spill their guts.

But Amy JoBeth cleverly turned it around on her. "Have *you* thought about where the confetti came from, Immy?"

"Well…it could get there from you, of course."

Amy JoBeth broke out in a shrieking wail. "Noooo! I didn't kill him!" She beat her fists on the cot and squeezed tears from her eyes.

"Don't cry, Amy JoBeth." Immy fished a tissue from her purse and pushed it into Amy JoBeth's hand. "I'm just saying that's one way. We need to think of other ways it could get there. Would Rusty have any confetti on himself? Did they use it in their business?"

"Why on earth would they do that?" She had recovered enough composure to speak at a normal volume, but her tears still streamed and her lip quivered.

It came to Immy in a flash of pink. After all, she had seen the pink stuff in the smokehouse.

"It was under Gretchen. Not Rusty."

"Huh?"

"I discovered his body, you know. And I saw the confetti underneath Gretchen."

Amy JoBeth's voice came out in a whisper. "You saw Gretchen? Dead?"

Immy nodded.

"How did she look? Do you think she suffered?"

"Um, no. She had, um, she had a peaceful look on her face." Immy wondered what that would actually look like. Pigs always looked peaceful to her.

Amy JoBeth crumpled against the wall again and drew her knees up to her chest. "Oh good. I'd hate to think she suffered."

Finally, she was making Amy JoBeth feel better. At least a little.

"What kind of person would kill a pig?" said Amy JoBeth.

"Well, slaughterhouses do. I think Rusty has to have dead ones to make jerky."

At that Amy JoBeth flung herself face down onto the hard cot and wailed again, a high, wordless sob, and beat her fists harder than ever on the flat pillow.

Immy quit trying to cheer her up.

Nine

Immy decided to shift her attention to The Case of The Missing Poppy. Since it was her newest one, maybe she'd make more progress on it. She should interview Poppy's mother, Ophelia. Marshmallow had one of her special potbelly pig leashes, but maybe he should have another one.

That made a good excuse for calling on her, anyway. She lived in a white-painted wooden house half way between Saltlick and Cowtail.

The woman looked horrible. Her prominent eyes were red rimmed and she was so folded in on herself that her long neck appeared almost normal.

"You want a leash at a time like this?" Her voice was thin and tremulous.

"Well…. Um. I work for Mike Mallett, the PI. Is there anything I can help you with?"

"You can find Poppy." She headed for a stiff, white couch and motioned Immy into an angular white chair. The whole room was white—walls, carpeting, furniture. The only touches of color were framed photographs of Poppy, some alone, some with her mother, some with her late father. Immy would have thought the woman's favorite color would be red, naming her only child Poppy like that.

"She went somewhere Saturday, you told Mother." Mrs. Wilson had told them today in church that Poppy had been missing since Saturday.

"Yesterday, right?"

"Oh no, not yesterday! Last Saturday."

"The day Rusty was killed?"

"That's just it. I thought she was going to spend the night with him." Ophelia dabbed at her eyes, then her nose, and straightened her spine. "Not that I approved of what she was doing. There's no talking to that girl. I'm thankful she confides in me."

Except she hadn't, had she? Immy had been right about Rusty and Poppy planning a getaway. Unfortunately, Rusty hadn't ever left his property.

"Is there anywhere else she might be?"

Mrs. Jenkins cocked her head so far over on her spindly neck, Immy thought it might fall off. "The deer lease. I hadn't thought of that. Sometimes she holes up there in the shack, or the blind, when she wants solitude."

"Have you been there?"

"No, but I should." She jerked her head up and drilled Immy with wide, buggy eyes. She looked frightened. "Will you go with me, Immy?"

Immy was afraid of what they might find there. Poppy had been missing for a week. What if she was dead? What if she'd been dead this whole time? Finding Rusty's relatively fresh body was one thing. Finding one that was a week old might be, well, repulsive. Sickening. It was warm out, after all.

But, was she a detective or not? She had to take the tough stuff with the rest of it. If being a detective were a breeze, everyone would do it.

Immy decided she wasn't going to get a leash for Marshmallow today.

"Point the way. Maybe we can find her."

The property Mrs. Jenkins owned was out of town a ways. Immy drove as Mrs. Jenkins directed her down one county road after another, until they were on one Immy had never seen before. Mesquite crowded the rutted dirt road, scraping against the sides of the van in places.

"Here," said Mrs. Jenkins, and Immy pulled onto a patch of dried grass beside a tiny wooden house. Its peeling paint had probably been white quite a few years ago. A porch, one step up from the ground, ran across the front. Two weathered rockers flanked the front door. Immy stifled a shudder at the slight gap in the door.

"Do you leave it unlocked?"

"Oh, lordie, yes. There's nothing to steal in there."

"Do you shut the front door, though?" Immy imagined possums and coons, maybe rattlers, nesting inside.

"The latch don't work right all the time. It swings open sometimes."

So maybe the door wasn't ajar just because someone had murdered Poppy and hurried away without closing it.

Immy let Ophelia lead the way. When they entered the house, it was empty, except for dried droppings from raccoons and possums that had probably nested there in the spring.

"We should try the blind," said Ophelia. "That's where she goes when she's upset."

Immy wondered if she should find a place to go when she was upset. Was she the only local gal who didn't have a hiding place?

The two women traipsed through the brush, following a rude, overgrown trail. Immy tried to discern signs of recent passage. She hadn't read up on tracking, but the trail seemed unused. No prior footprints disturbed the layer of soft dirt they were kicking up. Deer season was in the fall, so, if Poppy hadn't been here, it was possible no one else had for months.

The afternoon was wearing on and they were in the height of its heat. Immy reached behind her and pulled her wet shirt away from her sticky back.

"How much farther?" she asked.

Ophelia, in front, twisted her head on that stalk of a neck of hers to answer. "Just ahead a ways."

"A ways" turned out to be another fifteen minutes of walking, but they finally got to an open patch of ground where the hunters scattered corn to lure the deer. At the edge of the clearing stood the deer blind, a wooden box on stilts where the hunters hid and picked off deer from the rifle slits. Immy couldn't understand where the sport was in luring the poor things to a spot where you just shot them. But it seemed to hold great appeal for many Texas men.

Ophelia craned her neck to stare at the structure. "Maybe you could go up the ladder," she suggested. "You're younger."

But not braver, Immy wanted to add. She put a foot on the first wooden step, then another foot on the second, until she was at the top, holding her breath all the way. There was a crude door, shut tight. Immy tested the air with a cautious sniff, but didn't detect the odor of death, so maybe it would be okay.

When she pushed the door open, a furry demon sprang at her, chattering at her rude invasion of his quarters.

She lost her grip and tumbled down, hitting only a few of the steps on her way to the ground, eight feet below.

The triumphant squirrel stood on his hind legs and warned her to stay away.

"Oh dear, are you hurt?" Ophelia hovered over her, those buggy eyes full of concern.

Immy raised her head, then stood up. She patted her legs and stretched her arms. Everything worked and she wasn't dizzy. "I guess I'm okay."

"But where could Poppy be?" Ophelia broke into noisy sobs.

*****

"Mommy, we're out of Cheerios." Drew pouted as thoroughly as only a child can and plopped her chin into her hands at the kitchen table.

"You never eat Cheerios, honey," said Immy. "I thought you hated them."

"I eat them now."

Yes, that was true. Ever since Zack had, apparently, come to live with them, Drew had switched from Raisin Bran. Zack ate Honey Nut Cheerios for almost every meal. He could be coaxed into eating an occasional carrot, and once an apple, but his diet was mostly sugared oats. Immy was surprised he didn't whinny.

"Well, you and Zack have eaten them all and I have to go to work in a few minutes."

"That was Ophelia," said Hortense, hanging up the phone and joining the children at the table. Immy stood at the cupboard, searching for something the kids would eat. "Don't worry about it, dear," Hortense told her. "I'll take them out for something at All Sips."

"Dairy Queen!" insisted Drew.

"We will not have a vehicle after your maternal parent departs. Dairy Queen is in Cowtail. We will be able to transport ourselves by perambulation only. So it will be All Sips."

Drew understood the first and last parts anyway, and gave up her sulk.

Immy picked up her purse, ready to bolt out the door to be only, she hoped, ten minutes late for work. "What did Ophelia have to say?"

"She was remiss in not thanking you for taking her to the deer lease to ascertain that Poppy was not there. The poor, unfortunate woman is quite distraught. Her offspring hasn't been espied since a week ago Saturday. There has been no communication, even by cellular telephony. I cannot seem to forego obsessive thoughts about both Ophelia and Poppy."

She had been missing an awfully long time. Ophelia had turned down Immy's offer to call in the police, or even Mike Mallett.

Hadn't Rusty been telling Poppy something about the weekend when Immy overheard them in the packing room? She tried to picture little popeyed Poppy and big, strong Rusty together. That would have been Saturday before last.

Then she realized she was picturing them together at the sleazy motel at the far edge of Cowtail, misnamed Cowtail's Finest. Yes, that's where they probably would have gone. If they had made it there.

Rusty hadn't. By Saturday, he'd been dead.

*****

Mike was waiting beside Immy's desk when she rushed into the office. He'd taken the unfiled folders from where she'd hidden them in her desk drawer and strewn them on the surface. He raised his skinny eyebrows above his small, narrowed eyes. Immy had never thought Mike would be able to appear menacing, but his words chilled her.

"Keep showing up late, kiddo, and you'll blow this job. I gotta have someone here when we open, not a half hour later."

"I… I've had a lot going on. But I'll try very, very hard to be on time. And I'll stay late this week to get everything done."

"Good thinkin'." He swept his arm in an arc above her full desk. "You got a lot to get done here." He went to his own office to close the door and make phone calls.

Even after that unaccustomed lecture, it was hard for Immy to keep her mind on the mounds of filing on her desk. But it got easier after Mike gave her another stern look as he left for lunch.

"The rest of that filing has got to get done today, kiddo. I couldn't find a couple receipts this morning before you got here. No more excuses." He clapped his hat on his head and stumped out.

Was he getting angry that she was taking so much time off? The ill-fated shower was done with and most of Immy's cases were, too, so she ought to have time to do her real job. The one she got paid for. She gave a sigh of regret for not being a PI yet. She had to wait until Friday to get the results of her first exam in her online course.

Immy ran through her cases with part of her mind while another part recited the alphabet over and over, her hands automatically grabbing paper after paper and stuffing them into folder after folder, pausing to make new folders a few times. Her arms were a little stiff where she'd caught herself, tumbling down the ladder of the deer blind. She suspected she'd find a bruise on her hind end when she showered tonight, too.

She took a moment to set aside a few new file folders. She labeled two of them with her own cases: The Case of the Slaughtered Pig and The Case of the Poisoned Jerky Eaters. As she filed, she glanced at the folders.

The Case of the Slaughtered Pig. Rusty told Vern he killed Gretchen, but Rusty was dead, so no justice was to be had there. That case was finished for Immy. Did Rusty really kill the pig? Probably. Why would he have lied about it? And then why did he tell Vern? He should know Vern would tell Amy JoBeth, since they were engaged. Did Rusty want to hurt Amy JoBeth?

The Case of the Poisoned Jerky Eaters. Rusty again, as evidenced by the failed health inspection. And again, Rusty was dead. He wouldn't have poisoned his own customers on purpose. Bad for business. That was probably just an accident, sloppy cleaning, as Tinnie had indicated.

She hadn't ever labeled Amy JoBeth's problem. Maybe she should, The Case of the Depressed Pig Lady. But Amy JoBeth didn't need anything solved, she needed cheering up. Getting out of jail would do that. Solving Rusty's murder would do it.

Wait! Immy drew in her breath at the thought and dropped the folder in her hand. Rusty's murder was too much like a real detective case. She picked up the folder, one for invoices that were more than a year old. Immy wasn't sure she was up to something of the magnitude of an actual murder. That was real, hardcore crime. That case more properly belonged to the police.

There was one more, though. The Case of the Missing Poppy. She scribbled that on a third folder. That case was still open. It needed more investigation. And Immy knew just how to do it. She glanced at the clock. Forty-five minutes to go. Dare she leave early again?

She grabbed the next piece of paper and filed it. Her desk was empty. She'd finished the filing! Immy checked Mike's calendar on his desk. He had three consultations this afternoon so he wouldn't be back any time soon.

When she reached into her drawer for her purse, her glance caught a manila envelope full of clippings left behind, presumably, by Amy JoBeth when she'd quit the job. Something about them bothered Immy. She sat and pulled them out. They were birth and death notices, and a couple of marriage announcements. One headline said "Land Dispute" on a piece of newsprint that was extra brittle and yellowed. They were mostly about the Squire family, relatives of Sonny and Tinnie. Rusty and Tinnie's wedding notice wasn't among them, though. What tie did Amy JoBeth have to that family? Other than having sold her favorite pig to them? But that came after she left this job. She hadn't been raising pigs when she worked for Mike Mallett.

Immy stuffed the yellowing papers into the envelope and stuffed her speculations to the back of her brain. She was working on Poppy's case now.

The image of forlorn little Poppy waiting in a dilapidated room for Rusty to show up loomed before her on her way to Cowtail.

It hadn't been that long since Immy had been at the seedy motel called Cowtail's Finest. The town had another motel at the other end of town, all of five blocks away, that at least had water in the outdoor pool part of the year. It was a more likely candidate for the title of Finest. But this one did have a fly-spotted, buzzing neon sign that self-proclaimed "Cowtail's Finest." After dark it only proclaimed "Cowt l's F est" because some of the letters didn't light up at night. Since this was one of the last days of June, dark would come much later.

Immy pulled her green van next to the office and hit the desk bell when she got inside the air-conditioning. A Bassett hound on a doggie bed in the corner lifted his head at the sound. No one else responded, so Immy smacked the bell again.

She was surprised when a cute red-headed woman, maybe in her late twenties, rushed through the curtain behind the counter and breathlessly asked if she could help Immy. The hound dog lifted his head again and wagged his tail, but stayed on his bed.

"What happened to the manager?" Immy asked. An ancient, frail man used to run the place.

"Oh, that was my grandpa," the woman said with a cheerful smile. "I'm Wanda and I've taken over since he departed."

"Did he…?" Immy didn't want to say *die*, and learn that Wanda was happy about it. She looked so joyful.

"Yep." Her straight, shiny hair swung forward with her emphatic nod. "He retired."

"Oh. Retired." At least Wanda wasn't rejoicing at her grandfather's demise. "I'm looking for a…a friend of mine. I wonder if she's staying here."

Wanda pulled a computer keyboard toward her and poised her fingers over it. "What's her name?"

"Poppy. Poppy Jenkins. She might not still be here."

Wanda clicked the keys scrolling through a few screens. Immy leaned forward, but the angle of the monitor kept her from reading any names.

"What day did she check in, do you know?" asked Wanda. "I'm very new to all this, so bear with me."

Would she have checked in last weekend and waited for Rusty all this time? If she'd turned on a TV she would have seen the news of his murder. "Maybe last weekend sometime?"

"Mostly truckers stay here. Not many women. The only one was a couple days ago. And she sat in the car while the guy checked in."

Would she have come here with another guy? Maybe Wanda didn't really mean a couple of days. Maybe it was longer. But would Rusty check in with her, then go home and get killed? Should a detective be able to figure all this out? "She might have come here with a guy."

"Well, the guy's name is—" Wanda squinted at the screen "—Lernon Vinder." Wanda tapped the name on the screen. "He seemed kinda familiar, but I can't think where I've seen him."

"That's a strange name," said Immy. "Reminds me of something. Are they still here?"

Wanda shrugged. "He said not to disturb them and I haven't seen either one of them since they checked in. I didn't even go in to clean. His truck hasn't been here since that night."

"Was it an orange truck?"

"Orange? It was dark out, but the truck looked white."

Great, maybe ninety percent of the pickups in Texas were white. "Well, could I just knock on their door and see if she's here?"

"I don't know why not. It's room two-oh-five. One of our nicer rooms. It had a fire a few months ago and Grandpa had it and the ones next to it remodeled."

Immy walked around to the rear units and knocked on the door of 205. No one answered, but a buzzing sound drew Immy's gaze to the window.

The curtains were drawn. The glass was covered with huge, fat flies. Then she noticed the smell. She stood with her mouth half open for a long moment, frozen by the ice-cold blood running through her veins. Then ran to the office.

She had to ring the bell again. The hound had left, so she was alone in the office until Wanda again rushed through the curtain.

"Did you find her?" Wanda had such a cute, cheerful smile. "Is something wrong?"

"You should—" Should they inspect the room? Call the cops? Immy wanted to see for herself. "You should—" Immy was having trouble breathing. "You should open the door and see what's in there."

"They didn't want to be disturbed." Wanda frowned, keeping half the smile on her face. "He really insisted on it and even paid some extra. For later, he said."

"Have you been by there?" Immy's voice cracked.

"Not for a couple days. No one's using any back units right now. A few guys are in the front rooms."

"There's a...smell. You should go look. You really should."

Wanda kept her eye on Immy as she reached behind her for the key to Room 205.

Wanda didn't hurry on the way to the back units. The sun was heading for the distant horizon, heading for the cattle land surrounding Cowtail. As usual in this part of Texas, the wind blew, rattling the leaves in the grove of salt cedar and scrub oak that stood behind the motel. A mockingbird decreed the tallest tree his territory, trilling his stolen songs like the brazen thief he was. The scene was almost too peaceful.

Immy felt herself stiffen as they approached the door of room 205. The putrid odor seemed stronger.

Wanda saw the flies on the window. "Oh my God." Her voice was a whisper and her smile completely gone.

Wanda unlocked the door, averted her face, and flung it open for Immy to peek inside.

This was the end of The Case of the Missing Poppy.

Ten

THE ROOM HAD INDEED BEEN REMODELED. The headboard and nightstand were of light knotty pine and a colorful braided rug covered most of the floor. Large, rough-hewn logs criss-crossed the ceiling to form Xs, lending a rustic, Western feel to the room. The problem with the décor was that Poppy's slight body, now grotesquely puffy, hung from one of the sturdy beams. Her eyes, which Immy always thought bulged in life, almost popped out of her face in death. Maggots crawled over them. A scratchy-looking rope encircled her long, thin neck, and the flies that weren't trying to get out through the glass at the window swarmed in and out of her mouth and over her face. A strong gust from the wide-open door swung her, ever so slightly, and she twisted clockwise at the end of her noose.

Wanda was the first to throw up. Most of it hit the braided rug. Immy ran outside to do her vomiting. When both women were through retching, they walked wordlessly to the office, where Immy called the cops.

The computer screen still displayed the name Lernon Vinder. Immy stared at it through eyes brimming with unshed tears, blurring the words. She was going to try to hold herself together to speak to the police. It would be either Chief Emersen or Ralph Sandoval, or both, since the Saltlick cops served Cowtail, too. She didn't want to fall apart in front of either of them.

She blinked to clear her vision and took another look at the screen. Lernon Vinder. Lernon Vinder? Vernon Linder. The idiot. It was Vern who brought Poppy here.

*****

Chief Emersen walked into the motel office and nodded to Wanda, who was huddled miserably in front of her computer. She hadn't touched a single key, but had stared at the monitor through Immy's 911 call, the arrival of the cops, and the long wait after Chief had stuck his head in and told them to stay put until he had a chance to talk to them.

Now Immy and Chief Emersen sat on the hard chairs and Chief took out a notebook and pen. The Bassett hound padded into the lobby and lowered himself to his bed with a sigh.

Immy was glad the chief wanted to question her first. She wanted to leave this place. She told him about finding the body. But, when he wanted to know why she was here looking for Poppy, she stuttered.

"Poppy… Poppy's mother called my…my mother. Sh…she was l…looking for Poppy."

"And?" Chief's eyes were unreadable.

"And I found her."

Chief narrowed those unreadable eyes. "What made you look here?"

Immy considered. She couldn't make sense of what she knew. Maybe the police could. "I overheard her and Rusty make plans to spend the weekend together. Last weekend."

"Rusty was dead before last weekend was over."

"Yes, but this is where people go when they want to be together, and hide."

Chief's eyebrows rose. "You thought she would still be here, after spending a night with Rusty over a week ago?"

"I didn't know. I just thought I'd look. Maybe she was sad Rusty didn't show up and hanged herself. Except Vern's name is on the register."

It was obvious the chief hadn't believed all of her story, but he told her to go home, and didn't arrest her for murder. It did look to Immy like Poppy had hanged herself. But why had she come here with Vern? Lernon Vinder. That jerk.

When Immy got home, after a supper she barely touched, she brought her new case files into the singlewide and spread them on the kitchen table. She needed to relabel The Case of the Missing Poppy. She had solved that one. It was too bad the outcome wasn't better.

Technically, there was a new case, but she didn't want to waste a folder. She crossed through the penultimate word and wrote "Dead" above it. The Case of the Dead Poppy. Maybe, she thought, that word should be "Murdered." Unless Poppy hanged herself.

Should she make one for Rusty's murder too? Why not? She wrote The Case of Rusty Bucket on another file, aware that her labels were inconsistent, Rusty being The Case of Rusty Bucket and Poppy being The Case of The Dead Poppy. She would have to look up how to label case files in her *Moron's Compleat* book. But later. Now, she wanted to add notes to the files.

She couldn't locate any paper, as usual, but found an empty envelope in the junk drawer. The front had been used but the back was blank. Immy wrote a heading: The Case of the Dead Poppy. Was this even a case anymore? She didn't know if Poppy had killed herself or not. If someone else had hanged her, how would anyone be able to tell?

Poppy could have jumped off the bed. Or someone could have shoved her off. Or even lifted her to the noose if she weren't struggling too hard.

Immy closed her eyes and, after a shudder, willed herself to recall the sight of Poppy's dead body. Her eyes popped out. Her tongue stuck out. And it was swollen. The light outside had shown her clearly. Her face was the purple of a ripe plum. Immy squeezed her eyes harder. Poppy had swung in the breeze from the doorway and her left shoulder had rotated toward Immy. The left side of her face hadn't been purple. It had been a ghastly white. What did that mean? She'd have to see if she could find information on what happened to a person's blood after they were dead.

She got her copy of *The Moron's Compleat PI Guidebook*, which had been in good condition when she bought it, but was now looking like the used book it was, with dog-eared pages and wrinkled spine. She leafed through it to the section called Body Trauma. It didn't list Hanging, but she found it indented under Causes of Death. Immy thought she might offer to help re-index the book for the next edition.

It said the face could take on a slight bluish tinge, but it could also be red. Nowhere did it mention the peculiar white spot she'd seen on Poppy's cheek, or only having purple skin on one side of the face.

Ralph knocked on the door, his special dum, da dum dum. He'd missed supper, Immy realized. Poppy's case must have kept him busy tonight.

Drew threw down her Barbie and ran to the door. "Unca Ralph!" She jumped up as Ralph scooped her into his arms. Zack stayed on the floor where he rested his blond head on Marshmallow's pillowy tummy.

"Drew, honey, let Ralph sit down before you attack him," Immy said. He looked bone weary, in spite of his smile for Drew. "Have you been at the motel all this time?"

"Most of it." He took the beer Hortense handed him and sank into the green plaid couch. Immy waited while he glugged half the can before starting in.

"I have a question about Poppy," she said.

"I might not be able to answer it, you know." Sometimes Ralph couldn't answer questions because he wasn't allowed, but sometimes it was because he didn't know the answer.

"How did Poppy's skin get that way? All purple except the left side of her face. My book doesn't say you get that from hanging."

Drew, who had gone back to Barbie on the floor, looked up. "Poppy has purple skin?"

Ralph and Immy exchanged looks.

"Mother," said Immy. "Ralph and I are going for walk. Little pitchers."

"Why do you always says 'little pitchers' when you go for a walk, Mommy?"

*****

"She was moved?" asked Immy as they were nearing the intersection. She was limping a bit from her fall.

"Seems like it," said Ralph. He'd brought his beer can and he took a sip now and then as they strolled the dark road. The sound of small firecrackers popped from a few blocks away. Ralph turned in the other direction. "I don't want to see who's lighting Black Cats inside Saltlick. I'd have to at least say something to 'em."

Ralph could be so sweet sometimes.

"I guess that means she didn't off herself. Or she did and then someone moved her? Did she die at the motel?"

"Probably not. And not recently, either."

Immy thought for a moment that some of the maggots from Poppy's eyes were crawling up her spine. She tasted the bitterness of bile, but didn't throw up again. "Can I have a swig of that?"

Ralph handed her his can. "I thought you didn't like beer."

"Just a swallow. Thanks." She handed the can back. "I guess the forensics people from Wymee Falls can tell where she died?"

"How would they do that?"

"Can't they find fibers and hairs and DNA on her?"

"I'm sure they can. But what would they match them to?"

"Did Vern kill her?"

"Why would you think that?" Even in the dark, Immy could see his puzzled look. "Oh, because of the drugs?"

"Drugs?"

"Vet drugs were found in her body, the stuff you give horses to calm them down."

"Just like Rusty." And drugs had been reported stolen from the vet. "So she was killed by drugs?"

"No, the doc said he didn't want to make a report yet, but he thinks, yeah, it's like Rusty. She was drugged to begin with. She took a blow to her cheek."

"That's that white spot. Dr. Fox is missing some drugs, so do you think they came from there?"

"They probably did, but we don't know that yet. We questioned Dr. Fox today, and—"

"You questioned the vet?" Immy raised her gaze to the stars, thinking. "So you don't believe the drugs were really stolen?"

"We don't believe or disbelieve anything, Immy. You know that. We have to nail down facts and give them to the DA. There might be some sort of problem with accounting for drugs at the vet's clinic. Dr. Fox, Betsy Wiggins, and Vern Linder all had easy access to those drugs. We're going to question all three of them. At least."

"But Vern has to be the most likely."

"Why? Because Dr. Fox fired him?"

"No, because he and Poppy signed in together. Don't tell me you don't think Lernon Vinder isn't Vernon Linder."

"Lernon Who? What are you talking about?"

"It's on the computer. Wanda looked it up for me when I went there to find Poppy. She said Poppy was the only woman who checked in lately and she checked in with that Vinder character."

"I wonder why she didn't say anything to us. She wouldn't say when Poppy got there or who with. To tell you the truth, I think she was shocky. She might remember more tomorrow." Ralph studied the top of the massive live oak in the Yarborough twin's yard. A light night breeze rustled the small, tough leaves. "So Wanda saw Poppy check in?"

"Didn't exactly see her. Poppy was in the car. They checked in a couple days ago, Wanda said."

Ralph almost lost a mouthful of beer. "That body's been dead a lot more than a couple days. Chief noticed some bruises on her neck. Said he thinks she was strangled by hand, maybe a week ago, then hung up there more recent."

"Vernon checked in with her two days ago, though."

"If it was Vernon. Someone else might be trying to implicate him. Whoever it was, Lernon Vinder or Bucky Rustet, must have checked in with another woman. Or a dead one."

*****

Hortense led the way down the aisle of Holiness Baptist Church at precisely two-thirty Tuesday afternoon. Immy, Drew, and Zack followed, like ducks in a row. They were early enough to get a seat within three rows of the front, but not so early they were the only ones there. Mother, Immy thought, knew just how to time a funeral entrance.

The Widow Untermeyer coaxed a series of wheezy hymns out of the elderly organ as the citizens of Saltlick, Cowtail, and neighboring ranches gathered to give Rusty Bucket a sendoff.

Before they'd left home, Hortense had explained to Zack that his paternal parent was deceased (Immy told him his dad was dead) and that they would be in attendance for his memorial service, taking place at the habitual house of worship (Immy said they would go to the funeral at the church). Zack had nodded solemnly. Immy wondered if he'd already suspected his daddy was dead. She had wanted his mother to be the person to tell him, but they still hadn't been able to contact Tinnie.

Tinnie must have claimed Rusty's body after all, though, since she was sitting on the front row, flanked by her mother and father, Sally and Sonny Squire. They had been divorced long enough that they could sit a few feet from each other. Zack and Drew were busy scribbling pictures of pigs on the offering envelopes, so Zack hadn't spotted his mother yet. He was too short to see her without sitting on his legs in the pew. When he tucked them under him and lifted his head from his task, though, he caught sight of her.

"Mommy!" the boy screeched, and shot out of the pew, up the aisle, and onto her lap.

Drew stared after him, looking sad, as well as startled.

Immy leaned over to her daughter. "Zack's been missing his mommy, sugar. He needs to sit with her for awhile."

Drew nodded. "And his daddy is dead," she said. She returned to her scribbles.

Tinnie's head shook emphatically with her whispers to Zack. She wrapped her arms around him, but he squirmed out of them and ran up the chancel steps to the side of the coffin, which was balanced on sawhorses draped with white cloth.

"Zack!" Tinnie shouted and started after him, but she was too late.

"I wanna see Daddy." Zack grabbed the edge of the casket to pull himself up. Tinnie was in time to snatch Zack away so the casket didn't land on him as it seemed to dismount from its perch in slow motion. It wobbled, wobbled again, then rolled.

Zack and Tinnie tumbled down the carpeted steps. The casket landed on its side at the top of the stairs. The exposed top half of Rusty's body flopped forward in a grotesque bow to his family.

At least the cold, dead body hadn't touched the boy. That, Immy thought, was a blessing.

Until Zack again evaded his mother's grasp, scrambled up the steps, and started pulling Rusty out.

Most of the congregants were on their feet by now. The hush that had accompanied the scene of horror erupted into babbling and movement. Zack's shrieks of "Daddy! Daddy!" rose above the tumult.

Sonny, being in the front row, got there first. He squatted next to his grandson and spoke to him quietly. He was able to calm Zack and convince him to lightly touch his father's face. Zack's hand drew back as if stung from the feel of the cold, embalmed flesh and a sober little boy returned to the pew and sat with his family.

Several burly ushers stuffed Rusty into his resting place and hoisted the whole thing onto the sawhorses. In the process, the cloth was dislodged and one paint-spattered sawhorse leg showed for the rest of the service. Immy couldn't keep from staring at it.

Somewhat after three, the scheduled time for the funeral, the Reverend Klinger entered the sanctuary, robed and miked. He was, apparently, oblivious to the recent drama.

"Dearly beloved, brothers and sisters in Christ," intoned Rev. Klinger, "we are gathered together today to witness to the life of Beryl Isaiah Bucket, known to us all as Rusty."

Beryl *Isaiah*? You sure found out things at funerals, Immy thought.

The Yarborough twins, Rusty's third cousins twice removed, sat in the second row, nodding at the preacher's words. They were cleaner than usual, but Immy wondered what occasion would be solemn enough for them to forego their Carhartt coveralls. Rusty didn't have any other relatives that Immy knew of. No brothers or sisters in these parts. His daddy had been a bad one and was generally thought to be in prison, and his mama was long gone to her maker.

The minister made it sound like Rusty had died a peaceful death at home in his bed. He reviewed the decedent's life just like he always did at a funeral, saying what a good provider, good husband, good father he'd been.

Immy wondered if Rev. Klinger knew anything about Rusty. The biddies behind her, led by Mrs. Wilson, the lead gossip of Saltlick, murmured their rebuttals.

"If he was such a good provider, why was old Sonny Squire about to take the shop away from him?"

"That's not what I heard. I heard the bank would get it."

"You know Tinnie left him."

"That was because of all those women."

"I'll bet she was heartbroken, the poor thing."

"She left him, and she left the little boy, too. Does that sound heartbroken?"

Hortense finally turned and skewered them with the librarian glare that made the bravest people shut up.

After everyone rose and recited the Twenty-Third Psalm, the casket was lifted onto a gurney and wheeled out, followed by Tinnie and Zack, then Sally and Sonny Squire, walking stiffly beside each other.

"I wonder who's helping with the sandwiches," Hortense said.

Mrs. Wilson said she and the Ladies' Circle were making them.

It was such a lovely day, Immy wanted to go to the graveside service, but Hortense decided to wait at the church for the mourners to return to eat. She would be nice and close to the food.

"Do you want to go to the cemetery, Drew?" Immy asked.

"Is Zack going?" That decided it. Immy left Hortense to help in the kitchen and she took Drew and lined her van up behind the short row of pickups following the hearse out of the church parking lot.

The Saltlick Cemetery was at the edge of town, next to the Emersen Memorial Park, named for Chief Emersen's great-grandfather. Carolina jasmine on the fence washed the gathering in sweetness. The wind blew from the north, which was lucky. If it shifted and came from the south, the stench from the dump, on the other side of the cemetery, would have overpowered the flowery smell. As it was, a hint of rotted garbage underlay the delicate scent.

Ralph Sandoval, in uniform, had been in the back of the church for the funeral, but wasn't at the graveyard. Immy wondered if he had been there to spot the villain. Would the villain be more likely to give himself away at the cemetery than in the church? Immy had better sharply observe everyone here.

She tried to stand close to Tinnie, but Betsy Wiggins elbowed her way to the front. From what Immy could tell, she just wanted to be there to smirk at Tinnie. And to put on a boo-hoo display when the short service ended. Betsy seemed oblivious to the oh-please looks she was getting.

Was it strange for the widow of the deceased to put on a stone face and for the mistress to display so much grief that it looked fake? Sonny Squire was too liquored up to express much emotion at all and his ex-wife tried to stay at least two or three people away from him. The Yarborough twins hadn't made it to the cemetery.

Tinnie and her family left quickly after the short service. Immy wondered if they left so soon to get away from Betsy. The others started to follow. Drew stood rooted beside Betsy, fascinated by her continuing display. Zack watched his mother leave with a solemn expression on his young face.

By the time Immy, lost in musings on relationships, realized they were the only three there, besides the funeral workers who were waiting for them to leave so they could lower the casket, Betsy was beginning to wind down.

"Oh, Immy," she said, hugging Immy as if they were friends. "I'm going to miss Rusty SO much." Betsy released Immy and caught her hands. Immy felt that one of Betsy's hands held a damp tissue. "WHY did he have to DIE? Why? Why?"

Immy wanted to slap her and say, "That's enough, Betsy. Your audience is all gone." Instead she pulled her hands out of Betsy's and dug in her purse for her Purell.

"C'mon, Drew, let's get back to the church."

"Aren't you working for a PI, Immy?"

She turned to Betsy. "Yes. Mike Mallett."

"He any good?"

"I… I think so. Why?"

"Could he find Rusty's killer? Could I hire him?"

"He doesn't really do that kind of thing. He's more of a PI for people getting divorced and hired and stuff like that. The police will find out who killed him."

"What makes you think that? They think I killed him, for godsake."

"At this point, they're questioning everyone, not just you." At least that's what Ralph had said. She had reached her van and boosted Drew into the car seat in the back.

"The cops asked ME if I stole drugs from Dr. Fox. I'M the one who told Dr. Fox that VERN stole them. So, what the hell?"

"They questioned Dr. Fox, too, you know."

"So they think we're all lying?"

Immy smiled. "The cops always think everyone is lying." Ralph often told her that.

As Immy drove back to the church she wondered who the hell *was* lying. Someone used drugs on Rusty *and* Poppy. Someone stole those drugs. If she could believe Betsy, it was Vern. Unless Betsy stole them and led people to believe Vern did it. Unless the vet used his own drugs and reported them stolen. Rusty had been banging Betsy and Poppy. Poppy and Rusty were dead. Should Betsy be worried?

Eleven

DREW AND ZACK, WHO HAD COME HOME WITH THEM from the funeral, were playing Barbies on the living room floor. Drew had been ecstatic to find out he loved them as much as she did. The other Barbies were having a funeral, complete with a dead Barbie laid out on a napkin. Immy worried about the future of this whole generation of four year olds.

After supper, her thoughts were still a tangled mess and she decided to tackle her case folders again. After all, she had new information. She pulled them out of the carryall she had used to bring them home from the office and spread them on the coffee table.

The sight of the folders gave her a slight twinge of guilt. After all, she had stolen them. She had also left very early to attend Rusty's funeral, but Mike Mallett couldn't blame her for that, could he? She didn't choose when to schedule the funeral.

She opened the folder labeled The Case of Rusty Bucket. There was nothing inside. The Case of the Dead Poppy contained the used envelope with "Cause of Death" written across the end, under the case name. Finding another envelope in the kitchen wastebasket, she printed "The Case of Rusty Bucket" and "Cause of Death" across that one, too.

Placing them side by side, she wrote "Drugged" on both lists. She put "Inhaling Smoke" next, for Rusty, and "Being Strangled" for Poppy. Rusty was found in the smokehouse, hanging, and Poppy was found hanging, too. But the hangings weren't the causes of their deaths, from what Ralph said.

She wrote "Suspects" on Rusty's list, and wrote the names of Tinnie, Vern, and Amy JoBeth. Also Poppy, because she could have killed Rusty before she died. Then she added Betsy, just because Immy didn't like her. For "Motive" she put "Affairs" beside Tinnie's name and "Other Affair" beside both Poppy and Betsy, in case one mistress was jealous of the other. Beside Amy JoBeth, she wrote "Rusty killed her pig, Gretchen" and, after pondering, put the same thing beside Vern's name. Since Vern supposedly loved Amy JoBeth, it would upset him, too, that Rusty shot the pig. She added Sonny Squire on the strength of the gossip she'd heard at the funeral about him not liking Rusty as a son-in-law. Maybe he threatened to take the jerky shop away from Rusty and they fought. Sonny wasn't young, but he was strong. And usually drunk.

She pushed the paper aside and started on Poppy's.

"This one is, *too*, my mommy," said Zack, raising his voice at Drew.

"Well your mommy doesn't have brown hair," said Drew. "You need a blonde one. And here's a Ken to be your daddy."

Immy looked over at the children.

Zack bowed his blonde head. "My daddy is gone."

"But you can pretend," insisted Drew, shoving a Ken doll at him.

"Mommy says, now that Daddy is gone, our troubles are over. That's what Mommy said at his fune-rull. So I shouldn't have a doll for him."

Immy's mouth dropped open. She snapped it shut before the children saw her watching them. She grabbed her pen and added a note beside Tinnie's name on Rusty's list: "End of troubles."

She jumped up to give them each a cookie and pat their darling, innocent heads.

When a knock sounded on the front door, Immy waited for Drew to jump up to let Ralph in. Drew stayed put, chewing her cookie.

"Mommy?" Drew said, looking up at her.

Immy realized she hadn't heard Ralph's knock. Hortense was deep into a prime-time drama, so Immy opened the door.

Tinnie Bucket stood on the front porch.

"I didn't get a chance to talk to you at the funeral today," said Immy. "I'm so sorry about Rusty's death."

"Thanks," she said and brushed past Immy.

Hortense looked up. "Oh, my dear Christina." She grunted as she rose from her recliner and caught Tinnie's slim hands in her meaty ones. "Allow me to express my heartfelt condolences at this sorrowful time, upon the demise of your conjugal mate. This must be a devastating—"

"Thanks, Hortense. I've come to take Zack home. I appreciate y'all keeping him for me." She turned to include Immy. "Really, I do. I knew he'd be fine here."

Zack had jumped up at the sight of his mother and wrapped his arms around her legs, Drew, Barbie, and Ken all forgotten.

Immy inched her way to the coffee table to slide a magazine on top of her folders and envelopes.

Hortense, irritated at being snubbed by Tinnie in the midst of her heartfelt condolences, clomped to the bedroom to collect Zack's things. Hortense couldn't really manage a haughty looking-down-your-nose glare, since she was considerably shorter than Tinnie, but Immy knew that chin in the air was an attempt as Hortense handed Zack's suitcase to Tinnie.

The children said good-bye to each other matter-of-factly, in the universal manner of children.

Immy trailed them outside to Tinnie's Volvo, leaving Hortense to her drama and Drew to her Barbies. "Are you going to be all right?" she asked Tinnie.

"Why?"

"Well, you know. Rusty's dead. Murdered."

"That's nothing to do with me." Tinnie straightened from buckling Zack's car seat and slammed the rear door. "I mean, I had nothing to do with his death. He did tell me he shot Gretchen, but, the more I think about it, I don't see how he could have. He wasn't out of my sight that night for more than a minute or two. Anyway, thanks again for keeping

Zack." The Volvo dug a rut backing up through the grass, and left rubber on the road speeding away.

Immy had never seen Tinnie in what you'd call a good mood, but her disposition tonight seemed worse than usual.

Ralph's pickup came from the opposite direction.

He jumped out and stared as Tinnie's taillights disappeared around the corner. "Was that Tinnie Bucket? We've been looking for her this evening."

"She's going home, I think. She just came to pick up Zack."

"Where's she been?"

"No idea. Is she a suspect?"

Ralph looked at her for the first time. "That's a good question. A suspect for what?"

"Well, for the murders."

Ralph was trying the silence thing on her, obviously. It worked. She broke.

"You know, Rusty and Poppy."

"No suspects yet. In fact, only one murder at the moment. That'll change tomorrow morning, though. Chief has the autopsy results for Poppy on his desk. I just saw 'em. He'll probably announce tomorrow morning that she was murdered."

Immy tried to think how she could get Ralph to tell her exactly what he would announce.

"You want to come in?" she said. "There's some leftover chicken."

"Tell you what. I'll try to come back later. I think I'll see if I can question Tinnie tonight. See you." He snatched his radio mike as he climbed in and drove off in the direction of Cowtail.

Immy went inside and pulled out her lists again. Then it struck her.

Rusty and Poppy, both drugged. Both hung after their deaths. They were both murdered by the same person. Immy would put money on it. If she had any to spare.

Twelve

The next knock at the door was Louise Cotter. Immy was at the kitchen table with her folders. Hortense had gotten up to get herself another glass of iced sweet tea during a commercial, so she let Louise in.

"I've never properly thanked y'all for Amy JoBeth's shower," Louise gushed. "That was a bright spot in my poor girl's life."

Immy watched from the kitchen as Louise dabbed at her eyes with a crumbled tissue. She perched on the edge of the couch.

Hortense lowered herself to sit next to her. The couch groaned and threatened to give way.

"Immy," she called. "Could you bring Louise some sweet tea?"

"Please," said Drew from the floor. The Barbie funeral was over and it looked like she was playing "school" now. The napkin Marshmallow was chewing on might have been the one the children had used for the coffin.

Hortense blinked. "Yes. Please, Immy."

It was still an order, no matter how she phrased it, thought Immy. She got up to get the tea from the fridge. Drew, trailed by Marshmallow, ran through the kitchen and out the back door.

Louise stifled a couple sobs with her fist. She was acting like her daughter was dead. She was only in jail.

"We missed you at the service today, Louise," said Hortense.

"Yes, well, I'm not fit company for man nor beast lately. I can't sleep for thinking of Amy JoBeth in jail like that."

"It's not too bad a place," said Immy, handing Louise a tall glass of sweet tea. "I stayed there once."

Louise gave her a hard stare and sipped her tea. "Is there more sugar?"

Immy returned to the kitchen to get sugar.

"Have you thought about engaging the services of a private detection agency?" said Hortense. "To investigate the unlawful death of Beryl Bucket?"

"Who's that?"

"She means Rusty," said Immy. "To clear your daughter." She plunked the sugar bowl onto the coffee table, then resumed her seat in the kitchen before her folders. She couldn't help eavesdropping, though. Especially when Mother had just mentioned a private detective.

"I don't know. They cost money," said Louise. "Who was at the funeral?"

"Well, Rusty's family, of course," said Hortense. "His widowed spouse, Christina—"

"Tinnie," called Immy.

"—and their child, Zachary. And Christina's father, James Archibald."

"Sonny Squire," called Immy.

"Imogene," said Hortense. "If you would like to partake in this discussion, please place yourself in our proximity."

Immy shoved the envelopes into the folders and came to sit in the recliner usually occupied by Hortense, since the couch was full of Louise and Hortense.

Louise stared at Immy even harder than she had when Immy had said she spent the night in jail.

"What?" said Immy.

"Did I just hear you say that Sonny Squire is Tinnie Bucket's father?" Louise looked angry.

"Yes, he is," said Hortense. "Having all that wealth handed to him has not been beneficial to him."

"Oh, I wouldn't say that," said Louise, her voice quieter than usual. "It got him a bank."

"His daddy owned the Saltlick bank before he did, I think," said Immy.

Louise nodded, then gulped some of her tea. "It wasn't much though, until Sonny Squire pumped all that oil money of his into it. That was back when we lived here."

"So, technically," said Immy, "his money didn't get him the bank. His family gave him the bank."

"I have to go." Louise slammed her glass onto the coffee table, sloshing out some tea, and left.

She hadn't thanked them for the tea.

Hortense tapped her fingers on the armrest of the couch. "Learning that Sonny Squire is Tinnie Bucket's father has upset her."

"Looks that way," said Immy.

"People are strange."

Small words for Mother, thought Immy.

*****

Ralph stopped over to the house after questioning Tinnie. Immy tried pumping him for insider dope, but he wasn't giving anything away.

"Well, who you going to pin these killings on?" she asked.

"Immy, we aren't going to pin anything on anybody. We're going to investigate the murders and track down the killers."

They sat on the front steps of the trailer to talk, partly for privacy, and partly not to disturb Hortense's television viewing.

"But don't you think there's only one killer?" asked Immy.

"We don't draw conclusions until all the evidence is collected."

"What else do you have to collect?"

"We have other suspects to question."

"And re-question, right? To see if their stories match up? So you can trip them up?"

"Well, yeah, sometimes."

Immy had learned some things from her online course and her books.

Ralph looked tired and Immy suggested he get some rest.

"Yeah, we're announcing the autopsy results on Poppy Jenkins tomorrow morning, so I'd better be there bright and early."

That would be another tough funeral. Poor Ophelia, thought Immy. She'd lost her only child. How must that feel? She couldn't imagine losing Drew.

Immy tried to get some autopsy details, but Ralph held firm. She walked him to his car, the second-best Saltlick cop car. The night air was soft and sweet. Fireflies sparked in the jasmine-scented darkness.

"Your eyes look tired," Immy said.

"Yours look…they look…." He pulled her to him before he opened the door and gave her a kiss that woke up everything inside her, right down to her toes. Reeling a bit, she watched him drive away, then returned to the trailer that held her family.

She stood just inside the door. Hortense, watching her show from her recliner, sipped tea and munched on a handful of mixed, salted nuts. Drew tried to do a cheerleading pyramid with her Barbies, and almost succeeded.

"Bath time, sweetheart," Immy said to her daughter. Drew picked out two lucky Barbies to share the bubble bath with her. Half an hour later, Immy leaned down to inhale the aromas of clean hair and her child's sweet skin, then kissed her daughter and tucked her into her cot in the room they shared.

She worked the rest of the evening on her lists without adding anything useful.

Thoughts of Ralph's kiss strayed through her mind from time to time and put the hint of a smile on her still-tingling lips.

But she did think she was on the right track. Rusty and Poppy were probably killed by the same person. And the person was probably not Amy JoBeth, who had no access to horse tranquilizers. That she knew of.

*****

Immy raced out of the house, not quite late, but almost. At least it was summertime and she didn't have to drop Drew at nursery school this morning. That had often made her late for work the first few months she worked for Mallett. She glanced at the dashboard clock as she cranked the engine and backed onto the hardtop road. Maybe there was enough time.

She nosed into a parking space in front of the Saltlick police station and ran inside. It was so nice that Tabitha was on vacation. She was such an obstructionist when Immy wanted to get inside the station. Ralph came to the heavy door that led to the hallway.

"Hi, Ralph—"

"Aren't you supposed to be at work?"

"In a few minutes. Let's go back to your office. I want to get a copy of Poppy's autopsy." She tried to shoo him through the door so she could follow.

"I can't give you that." He didn't budge and he filled the doorway. She also wanted to check in on Amy JoBeth, but couldn't if Ralph wouldn't let her inside.

"Why not?"

"For one thing, we haven't released it yet. The press conference is in Wymee Falls at ten this morning, Chief decided."

"In Wymee Falls? Maybe I can take an early lunch and hear it."

"You're not invited. It's just for press."

What good did it do a person if a police officer kissed her, if he wouldn't give her any privileges? Of course, being kissed was better than not being kissed, but still….

"Well, can I talk to Amy JoBeth?"

"Immy, you're late for work. Come back after you're through."

She tried a cute little pout, eyelashes batting and head at an adorable angle, but Ralph stood in the doorway until she had to leave.

Sure enough, she was late for work.

*****

Immy didn't understand why Mike had been so upset she was late. Her filing was all caught up, and she might catch up with the billing notices today. She wasn't that far behind. What a stickler. Maybe that went with being a private eye. She would know soon enough. She had her online course book in her top drawer and she studied the next lesson when Mike closed his door to work on the phone. The next chapter was on Using the Internet. It would be handy to try some of the techniques on her office computer, but too risky with Mike in the building. If he left for lunch, maybe she could visit some of the sites mentioned for researching felons.

With dismay, she watched ten o'clock come and go. She was missing the press conference. If Mike had left for a morning appointment, she would have tried to sneak in to the interview. Except, she realized, she had no idea where it was being held. Ralph hadn't even told her that. She was getting more and more upset with Ralph. And with Mike.

She pulled out the envelope of clippings left behind by Amy JoBeth one more time, trying to decipher their importance. Most of them were about the Squire family. Some of them were about things going on at the Saltlick bank. Sonny was mentioned in most of these. The divorce of Sonny and Sally was included, and the engagement announcement of Tinnie and Rusty. Zack's birth announcement wasn't there.

Where on earth had Amy JoBeth gotten all these old articles? She hadn't been back in this area that long. A year, her mother had said. Some of them were from the top of the newspaper page, some were cut from the middle of the page. But she thought most of them must have come from the *Saltlick Weekly*.

The bigger question was, why was the Squire family so intriguing to the Cotter family?

Immy vowed to stop by the office of the Saltlick paper and see if Amy JoBeth had been doing research there. Maybe someone there knew why she collected these clippings.

She hadn't noticed Mike open his door, but there he was, at her elbow.

"How is this helping you get invoices typed, kiddo?" He reached for the brittle pieces of paper, but Immy quickly shoved them into the envelope and opened her drawer to put it away.

"Hey, what's this?" He grabbed her course book where it lay open in her drawer. "You studying to take my job?"

Immy hoped her expression was indignant and self-righteous. "I'm studying to become a better employee. The more I know about how private detecting works, the more—"

"The less use you are to me. That's the way I see it. I'm the detective here, sweetheart. You're the file clerk and typist. So type. And file."

He left the office and walked up the street, no doubt to have a leisurely, delicious, expensive lunch.

She pressed her lips together and blinked back the tears that threatened to fall. Those were the meanest words he had ever said to her. She'd show him. She got out the list of bills to be typed and started pounding the computer keys. But tears continued to blur the words in front of her and she mistyped every third word, having to hit backspace almost as often as she hit the space bar.

to let you go."

"Go?" Immy picked up the broken keyboard. "I can fix this." She tried to push the key caps back onto the keys.

"Yeah, let you go."

"I don't need to go anywhere." No, that wasn't right. The W didn't belong on the bottom row.

"Yeah, you do, kid. You need to go wherever it is you been goin' when you're supposed to workin' here, for me."

"You…you're firing me?" She dropped the keyboard again. Two more key caps popped off.

"You're a nice girl, Immy, but this hasn't worked out."

He was firing her? The words didn't seem to make sense. She had lost her job? Her PI job? Her face felt numb.

"Go ahead. Get your purse and leave."

"What about two weeks? Don't I get two weeks?"

"No, I don't think you do. Go on." He waved his hand toward the file drawer that held her purse. She pulled it open, dropped her purse on her first try, then picked it up. Her body was having trouble responding to the commands she, and Mike, were giving it. She stood up. Mike backed to give her room to leave and she walked out the door.

*****

Immy had forgotten Ralph was coming for supper that night. Hortense had spent the afternoon brewing her special spaghetti sauce, fragrant with oregano and thyme, using tomatoes from Ralph's vegetable plot behind his house. Immy heard him arrive, but stayed in her bedroom until Hortense called her to eat.

Ralph was helping set the table, but putting the flatware on all wrong. He put the fork on the same side of the plate as the knife. Immy's waitressing experience at her uncle's diner had taught her how to lay a table, if nothing else. But she was too weary to correct him. What did it matter anyway?

She sat in her usual chair to watch Hortense dish up the sauce and spaghetti noodles.

"Imogene, would you be so kind as to grate the cheese, please?" said Hortense.

Were there not bigger words for grate, or cheese? Immy tried to think of some, but she couldn't. With lead in her limbs, she rubbed the wedge of Parmesan against the raspy metal barbs. She felt like her heart was being grated with the cheese. She hadn't realized she'd left her course textbook in her desk drawer until she was home, in her room. She'd been studying the section on Using the Internet. She wouldn't be able to study the internet without her book, or without Mike's computer.

When she nicked a knuckle she dropped the cheese and the grater and stared at her finger.

"Immy, you've cut yourself." Ralph wet a paper towel to sop up the dot of blood.

"Yes, I see that," she said, making a point of not holding out her hand to him.

"What's the matter?" He lowered his face and tried to peer into hers. She held her chin firmly against her chest, refusing to meet his eyes. She was afraid she would start crying if she told someone she'd lost her job.

Since walking in the door and shutting herself into her room, she hadn't spoken to anyone. She had sat on the edge of her bed, letting silent tears flow and imagining what Mother would say when she found out. The last time she left a job, Mother hadn't taken it well. Not at all.

"I can't persuade her to communicate with me, Ralph," said Hortense, ignoring the fact that Immy was standing right there in the kitchen. "I've been trying ever since she got home from work, but it has been akin to extracting incisors. Maybe prandial nourishment will make her feel better."

Food. Mother's cure for everything, thought Immy. She sat and pushed the spaghetti around on her plate and swirled the sauce, but took very few bites. When she did, they were difficult to swallow. Her pain lay like a lump in her throat.

Drew chattered about Marshmallow's amazing accomplishments of the day. They mostly consisted of eating enormous amounts of food and using the litter pan.

When the dishes were cleared, Hortense pulled a plate from the cupboard. "There are cinnamon cookies for dessert," she said, her voice brittle with forced gaiety, an obvious effort to counteract Immy's gloom.

"None for me, thanks," said Ralph. "Immy, let's go for a walk."

Immy started to shake her head, but Ralph pulled her up by her elbows and propelled her toward the door.

"No dessert, Ralph?" called Hortense. "Are you sure? I'll save you some."

"I want dessert, please," Drew was saying as the front door closed behind them.

"Okay," he said, once they reached the road. "Tell me what's going on."

Immy opened her mouth, but nothing came out.

"Something happen at work?"

"Work!" she wailed and buried her head in his chest. Ralph patted her back and stroked her hair and the tension she'd been holding all afternoon and all evening drained out of her. She lifted her face, damp now with tears. "I got fired."

"Wow." His jaw dropped. "Fired."

"He fired me. He let me go. He said I wasn't..." she paused to blubber, "...wasn't doing the work."

"Were you?"

"Well, nooooo." She felt like sitting down on the road and bawling like a newborn calf. She stuffed a fist into her mouth to stifle the loud wails that wanted to escape.

"Why would anyone fire you, Immy? I would never fire you."

"You don't hire anybody. Nobody works for you."

"True. But if I did hire people, I'd hire you, and I'd never fire you."

"That's because...."

"Because, Immy, I love you."

Ralph had never said that before. But Immy realized she had known if for awhile. A warm feeling trickled inside her, then spread, starting with her curling toes and ending up prickling her scalp. A smile slowly spread across her face and her tears stopped. The pain of being fired shriveled up into a corner inside her.

"You're so sweet, Ralph."

They kissed.

*****

Immy and Ralph returned to the singlewide, strolling through the dry grass and holding hands. They spotted Louise Cotter's car, a perpetually dusty, old brown Buick, parked in front.

"Wonder what she wants now?" muttered Immy.

"Be nice. Her daughter's in jail."

Ralph's phone beeped and he looked at the screen. "Call out. Looks like one of the Yarborough twins peed in the neighbor's yard again. Gotta go pick him up and dry him out."

He gave her a brief peck that was nothing like their last kiss, but was still nice, and off he drove.

Louise sat at the kitchen table, having cookies and coffee with Hortense. Drew must have gone to the bedroom.

"You look improved, Imogene," Hortense said.

Immy realized she wore a goofy grin. She tried to tamp it down, but it sprung up again.

"Is Ralph not coming in for dessert?"

"He got beeped. I don't know if he's coming back or not." Immy sat at the table.

"Oh, Immy, just the person I want to see," chirped Louise, at her normal full volume.

Immy squeezed her eyes shut, but that didn't stop Louise's voice. Although Immy could feel Ralph's lips again with her eyes closed.

"I'm been so beside myself, what with Amy JoBeth being in prison and all."

"She's not, technically, in prison," said Hortense. "She is merely in the Saltlick jail. She is, however, awaiting an arraignment that will determine whether or not she stands trial for a capital offense."

"Exactly," said Louise. "And we don't have a lawyer for that arrangement thing. We can't pay for one."

"You have to be given a public defender if you can't afford to pay a lawyer," said Immy. "Have they assigned you one?"

"They keep trying to, but I've advised my daughter not to accept one of those free ones. They're probably no good."

Immy and Hortense passed a look between them.

"How do you propose to proceed?" said Hortense. "You seem to be tying your own hands behind your back. It is imperative that you either accept the legal representative chosen for you by the state of Texas, or that you engage an attorney on your daughter's behalf. One or the other."

"That's what I wanted to talk to y'all about." Louise flashed a hopeful smile. "The Hail County Rodeo is coming up. Next weekend, in fact. Now here's what I've decided we should do. Sell Hortense's brownies at a booth to raise money for Amy JoBeth's defense."

Visions of Immy doing all the shopping for ingredients, decorating the booth, and shelling out her own cash flitted through her head. Not that there was much left of Immy's cash.

Hortense didn't give her opinion away on her face, but Immy must have. Louise turned to her.

"It's for poor Amy JoBeth. It would cheer her up so much to know that people are on her side."

Immy tried to hide her grin of disbelief in the woman's brass.

Hortense opened her mouth, closed it, then decided to go ahead and speak. "It is doubtful, no improbable, that enough currency would be obtained in the vending of my bakery products to employ a member of the bar."

"Oh no, we wouldn't have a bar. They'll have the usual booth for beer and—"

"You wouldn't," said Immy, stifling a guffaw, "raise enough money for a lawyer that way." She put two fingers to her left temple, where a headache was threatening to erupt.

"But you'll bake brownies for it, won't you?" Louise's voice still sounded hopeful, eager. "Maybe we don't need a fancy lawyer. Maybe a PI. Do you think you can ask the detective you work for to look into

Amy JoBeth's case?"

That stopped Immy's grin. A couple tears sprang from her left eye.

"Amy JoBeth says he might be able to do some good," Louise continued. "She thought so much of him when she worked there. Great guy, she always said. The only reason she quit was that her depression got so bad, you know."

Three teardrops escaped Immy's right eye.

"Are you all right, dear?" said Louise.

"No, she is not," said Hortense.

"I don't work for him," Immy managed to say, her voice croaking like the tree toads outside.

She opened her eyes. Both women were staring at her, both mouths agape and, miraculously, both of them silent.

"He fired me today."

"Oh, darling." Hortense rushed to her daughter, hoisted her up, and smashed Immy's face to her pillowy bosom. "I'm so sorry." Hortense rubbed Immy's back and Immy shook with silent sobs for a moment.

This was not at all the reaction Immy had expected. She raised her face to talk. "He told me to take all my stuff. But I forgot my book."

"What book, Imogene?" asked Hortense.

"It's for my course. I have to study for my next test. And I guess I left that envelope there, too." She twisted her head from Hortense's breast and looked at Louise. "The one your daughter had in the desk."

Louise said she had no idea what Immy was talking about.

"The envelope with all the stuff about the Squire family. Amy JoBeth was saving clippings about them and I was trying to figure out why. And now I don't even have it."

Louise took a sip of coffee. "I can't imagine why Amy JoBeth would be interested in *that* family. We have no connection with them." She picked her purse up from the chair next to her. "I'd better be going. Think about my booth, ladies. I'll be back in touch. Thanks for the cookies, Hortense."

After she'd gone, Immy asked her mother what they were going to do about Louise's booth.

"I'm not sure. I do not propose to bake vast quantities of brownies and give them to her for a lost cause. I wonder why she wanted to ask you about hiring Mr. Mallett. She wouldn't need your permission for that, even if you still worked there."

"She wants him for free."

*****

The next morning, Immy felt like crawling into Amy JoBeth's tornado shelter. After all, she wasn't using it as long as she was still in jail. Immy thought she had been depressed before in her twenty-two years, several times in fact, but she now realized those times had been mere sadness.

The worst had been when the trucker left her pregnant. However, her mother's disapproval, the difficulty dealing with her high-school classmates, the physicality of pregnancy, and the thought of what she might have done to her future, were all balanced by the joy and wonder of the seed growing inside her. And, when that seed became Nancy Drew Duckworthy, nothing was left inside her but elation.

She had wanted a job exactly like the one with Mike Mallett for years. When she landed it she thought she was on her way to fulfilling her career goal. But the job hadn't been what she'd thought it would be.

This morning, Hortense and Drew had walked to the park so Drew could play on the swings. The trailer was quiet now. She could hear Marshmallow grunting as he rooted in the backyard. The morning sun streamed in through her bedroom window. Her mother and her daughter had tip-toed around her while they got dressed, letting her sleep. She hadn't been asleep, though, just too drained to move.

She pushed herself out of bed and walked to her dresser, opened her top drawer, and pulled out a scarf. She unwound it to reveal her father's detective badge. He'd achieved the rank of detective in the Wymee Falls police force before his death by gunshot wound from a robber.

Hortense's reaction to his death, when Immy was only twelve, had been to ban anyone from speaking his name, and to eat. In a few years she started referring to him again, but always as "Your dear, dead, sainted father" when talking to Immy; "My dear, dead sainted husband" when talking to others.

Her other reaction had been to forbid Immy from even thinking about becoming a detective. She hadn't banned Immy from taking the PI job, maybe because it was actually a secretarial job, not, as Immy had deluded herself into thinking, an entry level position at Mike's PI firm.

Immy ran her finger over the smooth metal of Detective Louis Duckworthy's badge. She had been kidding herself. She was not on her way to being a detective of any sort. She'd been a lowly file clerk and typist. She had no qualifications. Wasn't even qualified for the typist job, if she were honest with herself. She would never be a detective.

She carefully rewrapped the badge and placed it back into her drawer. The room seemed too small. She pulled on a pair of shorts and a t-shirt and went to the kitchen to get something to drink, but the whole trailer felt too small. After she ran a brush through her hair, she got into the van and drove.

A hot wind blew into the open windows as she headed out of Saltlick. The highway felt only slightly less confining. Because the stricture was inside her.

She ended up at Amy JoBeth's pig farm. How had that happened? Maybe because they had something in common. So much was wrong in her life, and nothing was right for Amy JoBeth. Both their lives were in chaos.

The van door sounded loud when she slammed it. Several pigs answered the noise with grunts from in back of the house, but Immy ignored them and walked slowly toward the tornado shelter. She pulled the door up and let it drop fully open, then descended the steep steps.

Under normal circumstances, Immy's heart would be hammering at entering the dark, underground cavern, but her senses were so dulled that her fear didn't register more than a light frisson up the back of her neck. She wondered if her heart were broken and just couldn't hold any more. She plopped onto the mattress Amy JoBeth had spent so much time on lately.

It sat directly on the concrete floor and wasn't any more comfortable than the one in the cell poor Amy JoBeth was presently using. The portable toilet was clean, Immy noted. She wondered if Amy JoBeth had cleaned it before she left. Or maybe Louise or Vern had come over and tidied up.

No, no one had tidied. The floor became more visible as Immy got used to the light coming through the small rectangle of the door opening. Three Styrofoam coffee cups, some fast food hamburger wrappers, and a small container half full of French fries littered the cement.

At least Immy could clean up the debris. She picked up a couple of cups and looked around for something to put the trash in. The edge of a white plastic WellMart bag poked up from between the mattress and the wall. She reached for it and gave it a yank. It must be stuck, she thought, so she put the cups back on the floor and pulled out the mattress. There were three bags, not one, stuffed behind the mattress and they each contained something. She pulled one bag out. It held a few bottles of pills. She reached in and pulled out another. The second bag held a box addressed to Dr. Fox.

Immy's numbness vanished. The bag tingled in her fingers. She had found the stolen drugs.

The rattle of a vehicle pulling up outside alerted Immy. The engine cut off and Vern's voice called out.

"Immy? Immy, you down there?"

Oh shit.

By the time his shadow blocked the light from above, the bags were back behind the mattress, the mattress pushed to the wall, and Immy was sitting on the edge of it, trying to act calm and remember what she'd felt like, being depressed, so she could pretend she still was.

"Oh hi, Vern." She made her voice flat, but her heart whooshed in her ears.

"I saw your van. What the hell you doin' here?" he snarled. He clattered to the bottom of the steps in an instant. His first glance was toward the wall, then he riveted her with his blazing, angry eyes.

"I was so depressed." She kept her voice quiet and her hands still in her lap.

"What the hell you depressed about?"

"I lost my job, Vern." She didn't have to act to put a quaver in her words.

The edge came off his anger, just a tad. "Yeah, I know, I heard about that at the bank. I lost mine, too." The moment of semi-softness vanished. "But so what?"

"I wondered if it would make me feel better to curl up here. Since this is where Amy JoBeth goes when she's sad about things. I guess it makes her feel better, huh?"

"It don't make her feel better. Makes her feel worse. How long you been here?"

"I… I just got here. Just right before you pulled up. Just reached the bottom of the stairs when I heard your car. I think you're right about this place. I think I'll go now." She stood up but he blocked her exit. "Excuse me."

"You sure that's all you're doing here? You're not doing nothing else?"

Immy looked around at the bare space, avoiding focusing on the place where the mattress met the wall. "What else would I be doing? There's no TV or anything."

Vern stepped aside. "Don't come back here." His tone was hard with anger.

Immy, thoroughly chilled, fled up the steps.

Fourteen

IMMY WAS NO LONGER DEPRESSED. But she sure was frightened. Did Vern know those drugs were there? If he did, he wouldn't want Immy to find them, would he? That might be why he got so angry and wanted her to leave, and not come back.

It also seemed that what Betsy Wiggins had told her must be true. Vern must have stolen horse tranquilizers from Dr. Fox, and been fired when they came up missing.

Did that mean Vern had used the drugs on Rusty? And Poppy? He had plenty of access to syringes, too. But why on earth would Vern want to kill either of them?

Wait a minute, Immy thought. It might make sense.

Amy JoBeth was in jail for killing Rusty, and that was because she thought Rusty killed Gretchen. Maybe the cops were almost right. Maybe Rusty did die for killing Gretchen, but maybe, instead of Amy JoBeth, it was Vern who killed him in a twisted attempt to set things right for Amy JoBeth. He'd made clumsy messes before. If Vern thought a powerful lot of Amy JoBeth, he had odd ways of showing it.

No matter what, Immy had to tell someone about the drugs. She drove toward the Saltlick police station.

Vern's black pickup came up behind her on the highway and she slowed to let him pass, but he rode her tail, following much too closely. A glance in her rearview mirror showed a scowl on his angry face. No sign of dimples. Immy couldn't believe she'd ever thought he was cute.

She slowed further. His front bumper disappeared from her rear view mirror as he crowded her vehicle. He crept closer. His grill disappeared. Then his windshield was all she could see, with Vern's enraged face behind it. His car had to be inches from her rear bumper. She held the steering wheel tight and braced for an impact.

Her mind raced. He must have figured out that she'd seen the drugs.

What if he ran her off the road and she rolled over and died? She looked around frantically. The ditch beside the road was deep. She might not be found for days.

What if he rammed her from behind and pushed her into oncoming traffic, causing a fatal head-on collision? That wasn't usually much traffic on this highway, but, just her luck, a steady row of eighteen-wheelers headed toward her.

His car nudged hers with a jolt. She skidded sideways, toward the oncoming behemoths.

Her van shuddered in their slipstreams as two of them roared by, inches from her door.

She jerked the wheel to the right. What if a long haul driver fell asleep for a moment, right when she was meeting his truck? She stayed as close to the far edge of the road as she could.

Vern dropped back and Immy assumed he would hit her again, maybe push her into the next bunch of eighteen-wheelers.

She waited for impact. It didn't come.

What the hell was he trying to do? Follow her until she stopped, then drug her and kill her? She considered that the most likely scenario.

She wouldn't stop, that was for sure. Vern drove closer and gave her car another jolt, this one harder than before.

She sped up and kept her course for Saltlick. Her mind furiously ran through the index of her PI Guidebook. She'd glanced at a chapter on losing a tail.

Approaching the outskirts of Saltlick, she swerved onto the first street, just before the stop light, but Vern followed her.

She made a hard left, then a hard right. The left wheels of the van left the pavement, squealing for a sickening moment, then crashed down.

There weren't too many more streets in Saltlick, so Immy was relieved when she lost Vern a block from the police station.

Should she wait in the van to make sure he didn't double back, or should she make a run for it? Maybe both. Immy waited a long ten minutes in the van to make sure Vern wasn't around before she got out. Then she fled the van as quickly as she could and ran inside the glass double doors, catching a glance of a dirty passing truck, hoping it wasn't Vern.

It was—and it wasn't—convenient having Tabitha on vacation. When she was on the job, at least someone was present to ignore Immy. She stood at the window in the lobby calling Ralph's name, pacing and glancing out the front window, expecting Vern to storm in any minute and haul her off in his truck. Finally, the chief poked his head through the door.

"Can I help you, Immy? Ralph is out talking to Mrs. Jefferson about her barking Basset hound again."

"She's too deaf to hear it," said Immy.

"I know. It's kind of a problem. What can I do for you?"

"I found something." Immy looked around to see if Vern had showed up yet. No sign of him. But she didn't want him to see her talking to the chief. "Can we go to your office?"

Chief positioned a guest chair beside his desk and sat, waiting for Immy to begin. Some framed photos of a much younger chief with his late wife perched on the edge of the desk. A picture of the chief shaking hands with the mayor of Saltlick hung prominently over his desk. It was the mayor before this one, Immy thought, or maybe the one before that. The chief had held this job for many years.

Where to begin? Was Ralph supposed to have told her about the autopsy results? Did the cops know Vern had been fired for stealing drugs?

"I have some other things to do, you know," said Chief. He lowered his blonde-white eyebrows.

"I know. But, well, I found some drugs."

The chief waited for her to elaborate. She waited for him to interrogate her. The chief won.

"I found them in Amy JoBeth's tornado shelter."

"Am I supposed to know what you're talking about, Immy?" Those bushy eyebrows raised up a discreet notch.

"The drugs that were used on Rusty and Poppy. I found them."

"Do you mean you found some of the same type? The ones used on them have been, well, used."

"Where did they come from, though? Dr. Fox, right?"

The chief maintained his silence.

"I was in Amy JoBeth's tornado shelter because I thought it might be a good place to be depressed."

"I imagine you're right about that. It seems to work well at making Amy JoBeth depressed."

"No, I mean…well, anyway, I was depressed. And I went there. And I found some drugs. And I think they were stolen from Dr. Fox. One box had his name and his clinic address on it."

"I admit that's interesting. But what do you propose I do with this information?"

"Well, I guess, go get the drugs and arrest Vern Linder."

The chief shook his head and his face reddened slightly. "I'm not sure I'm following you. You say the drugs are on Ms. Anderson's property, in Ms. Anderson's shelter. She is being held on suspicion of murder. So far, so good. We could search for and retrieve the drugs, if we find them there. But what does Vernon Linder have to do with anything?"

Immy frowned.

"I wonder," Chief said, studying the ceiling, "when they were put there. We searched her place Saturday, right after we arrested her, and didn't find any animal drugs other than what she uses on her pigs."

"Well, they're tucked behind the mattress. Maybe you missed them."

His beefy face purpled. "We saw everything, Immy. We did not miss them. They were not there." His voice had that steely edge that Ralph's sometimes got. "Again, what does Vern Linder have to do with this?"

"Well, Betsy Wiggins told me Vern stole them from Dr. Fox."

"She told us that, too, but Dr. Fox says he can't seem to tell if he has any drugs missing."

"That's sort of a problem."

"Yes, but not our problem. Not right now."

"Well, why did Dr. Fox fire Vern then?" Immy asked.

"We asked him that, but he doesn't have to tell us, and he didn't."

Chief agreed to have another look in the shelter and Immy drove home. She was too discouraged by his attitude toward Vern to mention that he tried to run her off the road. She'd also let him figure out for himself that Vern had been at the hotel with Poppy.

She walked around the van when she got home. The van's rear bumper had a new dent, but it didn't show up all that much because of the other ones from Immy backing into things.

Inside, she glanced at the clock on the stove. 11:45. Her mother and daughter would be home for lunch soon. Meanwhile, Immy had a new case to work on. Since she didn't know who was involved, she'd call it The Case of the Purloined Drugs.

Of the folders she'd taken—borrowed—from Mike's office, she had two left. When she got a new job and got paid, she'd replace them. She printed "The Case of the Purloined Drugs" on the tab.

But was that right? According to Dr. Fox they weren't missing. Did Dr. Fox drug Rusty and Poppy? Did he tell Betsy that Vern took the drugs—when he didn't? Because he himself, Dr. Fox, used the drugs for his evil deeds? Or did Dr. Fox not keep very good track of his drugs?

Immy bowed her head to think. After rummaging through the drawers where she usually found paper, she found a grocery list with no writing on the other side of it and put "Dr. Fox" and "Betsy" at the tops of two columns. Then she started the rows, recalling the chapter on MMO, Motive, Means, Opportunity, in her *Compleat Guidebook*.

Motive: the same one Amy JoBeth or Vern would have—Rusty killed

Gretchen. It occurred to Immy that a lot of people had liked that pig.

Means: the drugs, which Dr. Fox had, and a rope, which everyone had.

Opportunity: maybe not. Dr. Fox had been in his clinic when Rusty was killed, sometime Saturday morning. The clinic was usually packed then with people who couldn't make it in during the work week.

Immy moved on to Betsy, who'd told Immy and the police that Vern stole the drugs. Did she make that up? Betsy and Vern didn't like each other, that had been obvious to Immy during her visit to get Marshmallow's shots. Betsy might like working there without Vern much better than with him. She might even have stolen the drugs herself to get him fired.

Motive: a better working environment. That seemed weak. They hated each other? But why murder Rusty now and not awhile ago?

Means: the drugs and a rope. Easy for Betsy to find and use.

Opportunity: Think back, Immy, think back. She'd seen Betsy at the clinic Friday, and then the next day leaving the smokehouse. Immy had gone to the clinic Saturday morning and someone else was working that day. Dr. Fox had said Betsy was taking the day off. To murder people?

Immy looked at her paper. Who else would be a suspect besides Amy JoBeth, Vern, Dr. Fox, and Betsy?

The phone rang.

"Hi, it's Louise," Immy heard from the high decibel shriek. "Is your mother there?"

"She will be in a few minutes. She's at the park with Drew."

"I just wondered if she's given any more thought to that charity booth for poor Amy JoBeth. Even if we don't raise enough for a lawyer, it would help to pay that PI."

Immy would let Hortense tell Louise herself whether or not she was going to spend hours baking for a few dollars' profit for poor Amy JoBeth. "I'll have her call you when she gets back."

"Oh."

Louise sounded so disappointed, Immy added, "How about seeing if Tinnie's family will donate some jerky to your booth? There's always jerky for sale at the rodeo."

"Tinnie *Squire*? Definitely not."

After she clicked the phone off, Immy picked up her pencil, drummed it on the table, then put "Louise" at the top of a third column. Same motive as Vern. Doing it for Amy JoBeth. But how could Louise get vet drugs? From Vern?

Whether the drugs were missing or not, two other cases did center around them, Rusty's and Poppy's murder cases. Someone had to get to the drugs from somewhere, to use on both of them.

Immy heard her mother and daughter returning and stuck the paper inside the folder. The more she thought about these deaths, the more confused she became.

*****

After Drew's nap, Ralph showed up. Immy was surprised, since it wasn't near a mealtime. He refused to come in, so they spoke on the front porch.

"I wanted to let you know both Chief and I searched Ms. Anderson's storm cellar and there's no drugs there."

"They're stuck behind the mattress. If you pull it out—"

"Immy, we moved everything, looked under and behind everything. The only stuff there is the mattress, a wastebasket, and a small potty. I'm glad it was emptied recently because the chief had me dump it and look inside."

Either Vern had snatched them before he took off to run her off the road, or he'd gone back and taken them. "Vern has them."

"If you say so."

"You'll have to search him quick, before he gets rid of them."

Ralph avoided her eyes. "We can't do that."

"Why? Do you think I'm lying?"

"No, but Chief is ticked at you right now. He says we were on a wild goose chase at the shelter. Says we wasted half a day."

"Ralph, he tried to run me off the road."

"Vern did? What happened?"

"He was tailgating me something awful."

"And?"

"And he bumped me."

"Let me see." Ralph got up and strolled to the back of the van.

Neither of them could detect any new scratches or dents. The van was kind of dirty, but nothing stood out.

She puffed out her cheeks in frustration and stalked back to plop on the steps. Ralph joined here.

"I'm not saying he didn't hit you, just that you don't have any proof."

Immy listened to the prosaic afternoon sounds of the neighborhood. The barking dogs two streets over, the drone of the katydids, which would get deafening after dark. She could even faintly hear the clank of the oil pump jack on the edge of town.

She might think the drugs were the most important part of the cases, but the police did not. What other avenues were there for helping Amy JoBeth? There was no way that little gal could have killed and hung up two people. Immy would never believe that.

"Why on earth does Chief think Amy JoBeth is guilty of murder?"

"The only evidence we have points to her, Immy. That's all we can go on. When we turn our findings in to the DA, it's his job to decide who to prosecute. We follow the evidence and see where it leads. We have her motive and we have physical evidence, that pink pig confetti."

"There's got to be something that points to someone else. Besides the drugs."

Immy tried to think what else could be evidence in this baffling case.

Well, there was one thing that baffled her besides the case, something she couldn't connect to the murders. It connected to Amy JoBeth, though: that envelope of clippings. Couple that with Louise's hateful comments about the Squires, and something simmered under the surface that Immy couldn't see.

She had to get those clippings back.

"I keep thinking about that packet I left at Mallett's office."

"What packet?"

"Something Amy JoBeth left behind, from when she worked there. I need to see it again."

"Just don't send us to get it."

After Ralph went inside and gave Hortense and Drew quick hugs, he left to return to work.

Immy called Mike Mallett's office, but there was no answer.

"What's a matter, Mommy?" asked Drew, who was stuffing rice cakes into Marshmallow's eager mouth.

"I'm not sure, sugar. I'm overlooking something. I might have to do a B and E tonight. As soon as it's dark."

"What's a B and E?"

"It's an expression, honey."

After supper, which was just the three of them for once, Immy got her purse and the keys to the clunker van. She could ask Mike, in the morning, to let her look at those papers in her desk, but he might not let her. And besides, she didn't want to see his mean face anytime soon.

"Gotta drive into Wymee Falls, Mother," she called, and ran out the door before she could be given an errand in town.

Mother said something about Ralph. Maybe he was coming for dessert? She would ignore that. Detective Duckworthy had a mission.

*****

Immy decided to run surveillance for awhile, to get the lay of the land, before she rushed into anything. She regretted not equipping herself for a stakeout. She knew, from her *Compleat Guidebook*, that she should have provisioned herself with food and drink, and probably should have procured a disguise. It was bad enough she had to do surveillance in such a conspicuous vehicle as a huge green van. If only she had her own car, she wished for the millionteenth time.

Hortense had left a plastic rain hat, festooned with orange and yellow flowers, on the floor of the van and Immy tied it on. Hoping Mike Mallett wouldn't recognize her in the rain hat and shorts and a t-shirt, she parked two blocks from her office and strolled down the street, trying for the casual shopper look.

She got some odd looks from a couple hurrying past. She heard the woman ask the man if it was supposed to rain soon.

"Maybe in three months," he said.

Immy huffed her indignation. That was not true! It was very likely to rain in June. Just not July and August. Then she realized that today was the first of July. So the man was right, it probably wouldn't rain any time soon. She left the rain hat on, though, as it was the only item of disguise she was wearing.

When she got to the travel agency next door to Mike's office, she stopped and spent a few moments looking at the toy cruise ship and the airplane in the window display. She sighed. Wouldn't that be nice? To take a ship or a plane, or maybe a bus, and escape? She couldn't even afford a second-hand car, so a vacation trip wasn't in her foreseeable future.

Finally she summoned the courage to gaze directly at Mike's office. It was dark. She walked to the front. All the lights were out. If she were Mike, and if she were between receptionists, she would probably leave the lights on to deter thieves. He was just advertising that the place was empty. It was time for the office to be closed, but still….

Immy looked to the west. The sun was almost at the horizon. She got into the van and waited for full darkness. She rummaged through the accumulated layers of stuff in the van, looking for something she could use to break into the place. When she came upon the tire iron, she hefted it to feel its sturdy weight. That should do.

Finally, at about 8:30, when she couldn't wait any longer, the sun set and she again made her way to Mike's office.

She carried the tire iron pressed to the side of her leg. She couldn't conceal it since she was wearing shorts, but held next to her leg she didn't think it was too conspicuous. It took her some seconds before she could make herself attack the glass door panel that said 'Mike Mallett, Private Investigations'. How many times had she pictured her name below his: Imogene Duckworthy, Assistant? Or maybe Partner?

Since her name was never going to be painted onto the door, with or without a title, she closed her eyes and swung the tire iron, one-handed, overhand. It bounced back and whacked her on the side of the face.

"Damn!"

She looked around. No one was in sight. Even the cars usually parked at the curb during the day were mostly gone. She touched her cheek. It was numb from the blow of the wrench, but no blood anyway.

This time she gripped the metal tool with both hands and chopped the window with all her might. It shattered with an explosive noise. Most of the glass fell away, but the first two letters, MI, remained on a hanging shard. Jagged pieces stuck up from the bottom of the frame, too. She wasn't sure if she could reach in without cutting herself. Maybe she should take the time to knock the rest of the glass out.

Headlights appeared a few blocks away. She had to get out of sight. What if Vern was still tailing her? Laying low until he saw his chance to ambush her?

She reached through the opening and struggled to open the door, narrowly avoiding getting cut by the jagged glass. Damn. It wasn't locked. She hadn't had to break the damn window after all.

She opened the door and slipped into the building, just as the car reached the corner. It seemed to be slowing.

She hurried to her desk in the dark and opened the drawer that held the envelope of clippings. Except it wasn't there. She rummaged through the papers by feel, searching for the envelope. It was large enough that she should have run across it right away. It simply wasn't there.

That was puzzling. Where would Mike have put it? Had he thrown it away? Unlikely, since he didn't even clean the desk out before Immy started to work for him. Her course textbook was in the middle drawer and she stuck that into her purse.

The room suddenly lit up. Something terribly bright shone through the window

"Come out with your hands up," called a voice of authority through a speaker.

She was busted.

Fifteen

Iₘₘy walked out the ruined office door with her hands raised, her purse over her shoulder. She slipped a little on the pebbled glass fragments underfoot. The searchlight, bright as daylight after the dark interior, blinded her.

"Do you have to shine that thing in my face?" said Immy. "I'm going to fall and cut myself."

"And whose fault would that be?" said Ralph.

Ralph! What in holy hell was he doing here?

A police officer who wasn't Ralph stepped into the circle of light and roughly stuck her upraised hands behind her back. Her purse slid to the glass-strewn sidewalk. He started to wind plastic bands around her wrists.

"Wait," said Immy, trying to snatch her hands away. "It's okay. I belong here. I used to work here."

He pulled the bands tight. "So why did you break the window?"

"I… I was just going to call that in…that broken window. Someone busted it. It's terrible what people do. Destructive."

"We saw you do it." The guy whipped out a notepad. "Name please."

"Where's Ralph? Officer Sandoval?" Immy squinted against the searchlight, but couldn't see Ralph. Had she imagined his voice?

"State your name."

This guy was beginning to bother Immy.

"My name is Imogene Duckworthy. What's yours?"

His eyebrows shot up. "Officer Hadlock." The eyebrows went way down and he pressed the tip of his pen into the page of his notepad. "What were you doing here?"

"I left some personal effects behind, in the office. In my desk. I was retrieving them."

"Immy, he saw you break in." Ralph again. So he really was here.

She tried to peer past the searchlight to see where he was. She flinched with the pain of the light and her eyes started tearing.

"How did you know I was coming here, Ralph?" she said in the general direction of the light.

"Drew asked me what 'B and E' meant. She said you had to do one tonight."

"How did you know I was doing it here?"

Ralph groaned.

Oops. Had she just admitted something?

*****

After a long discussion between Ralph and Hadlock, outside the car, which Immy couldn't hear because she was inside enjoying the eau de vomit and pee in the back seat of the Wymee Falls cruiser, Ralph opened the door and pulled her out. Rather roughly, Immy thought.

"Hey!" she said.

"Be quiet. Don't say anything." He sounded serious.

He pushed her toward his Saltlick cop car and opened the back door. "Get in."

She had never sat in the back seat of Ralph's car before, and it was humiliating. But his back seat smelled much better than Hadlock's back seat. Her face was sore where the tire wrench had whacked it but she couldn't rub it because she was still cuffed. They drove out of Wymee Falls toward Saltlick. Ralph must have been awfully mad at her because he didn't say a word—and she didn't dare to—until they reached the Saltlick police station.

Ralph helped her out of the car, gripped her elbow, and walked her inside. She was happy to see her purse in his other hand. "You can thank me now, Immy," he said.

She stopped in the lobby, tried to wrench her elbow from his grip and faced him, her mouth dropping open. "For getting me arrested?"

"For bringing you to spend the night here instead of in the Wymee Falls jail."

That was a good thing, she supposed, but she'd be damned if she was going to thank him for anything tonight.

Chief was inside, to Immy's surprise. He stuck the fingerprint gizmo at her and, after Ralph snipped off the plastic cuffs, wordlessly rolled her fingers through the goo.

"So, what did you do?" she asked Ralph over her shoulder. "Send a BOLO to Wymee Falls?"

"What *could* I do? Drew told me you were going out to break the law. Your mother said you'd been fretting about leaving something in Mallett's office."

Any other time, Immy would be reassured by Ralph's strong hand on her upper arm. But his intention was probably to make sure she didn't run out the door as he steered her to a cell.

After Ralph locked her into the cell and left, Immy sat on the hard cot and wondered if it would be physically possible to kick herself. On her rear, where she needed it. Probably not. She had heard tell of an automatic ass-kicking machine once, probably from one of the Yarborough twins, but you never could tell how much of what they said was true.

How could she have forgotten to try the office door? But, on the other hand, why was it unlocked? With a loud sigh, she settled her head in her hands.

"Who's there?" came a voice from the next cell.

"Amy JoBeth," Immy said slowly. She rose and went to the bars at the front of her cell, but couldn't see into the one next to hers, since the cells were side by side.

"No, that's me. Is that you, Immy?"

"Yep."

"Who do they say you killed?"

"I didn't kill anybody."

"Well, neither did I," said Amy JoBeth.

"I committed a minor crime. I think it's technically a misdemeanor. I broke into a place." Immy stopped to think for a moment. "Hey, I broke in to Mallett's office to get that stuff you left there. You know, those clippings?"

Silence came from the next cell.

"You know, all that stuff about the Squire family?"

"I don't want it, Immy." Her voice shook. Was that fear Immy heard in her words? Or anger? "I'm surprised Mike didn't pitch it."

"Ha. He doesn't ever clean anything out. You ought to know that."

They both let out a shriek as the heavy metal door to the cell block clanged open.

"Visitor," said Ralph. "For Amy JoBeth."

Vern Linder followed Ralph through the doorway. He stopped in front of Immy's cell.

"What's she in for?" Vern asked.

"I'm not at liberty to say," said Ralph.

Immy could have kissed him for that. It was mortifying enough being seen here by him. It was none of his business what she'd done to get thrown into the clink.

"So, what'd you do?" Vern asked Immy.

She turned her back on him and he proceeded to Amy JoBeth's cell. Ralph locked Vern in with Amy JoBeth for a visit, then left, without a glance at Immy.

Somehow, Immy avoided regurgitating at the billing and cooing that ensued between Vernie Wernie and Amy JoBethy Wethy. She had to resort to sticking her fingers into her ears to keep her dinner down.

How could Amy JoBeth stand the guy? Did she know he might be a murderer? Was Immy, in fact, sitting one cell from a murderer? Had Vern murdered Rusty because Rusty killed Gretchen?

Then she backtracked. Had it really been established that Rusty killed the pig? She tried to remember where that intel had sprung from. Amy JoBeth had said Vern told her Rusty killed Gretchen. How did Vern know that? Was it even true?

Mercifully, Ralph returned after about ten interminable minutes and Vern gave Amy JoBeth a noisy kiss.

"Vern," Immy said when he was in front of her cell. "What makes you think Rusty killed Gretchen?" She stepped to the bars.

"He told me he did it. Right there in his shop."

Immy narrowed her eyes at him. "Why in the hell would he tell you that?"

Vern lunged toward her and she backed away from the bars. "Are you calling me a liar?"

Ralph grabbed Vern and, after a brief tussle, hustled him out.

Immy hadn't been calling him a liar so much as she was calling him a killer. She no longer believed anything Vern had said. Tinnie didn't think Rusty had killed the pig, even after Rusty had told her he did. Maybe he'd told Vern, too, but why would he?

She leaned her forehead against the cool bars. Her cheek throbbed and burned where the tire iron had hit her. She wondered if she would have a bruise tomorrow. Maybe she could claim police brutality. Should she accuse Officer Hadlock? No, Ralph would only back up the Wymee Falls cop. She'd have to accuse Ralph. She'd been alone with him.

Oh shoot, she couldn't do that. She blinked to keep tears from starting. The floor glittered through her tears. A bright pink sort of glitter. Then she noticed what she was seeing. After Ralph wrestled Vern away from her cell, she'd seen that one of Vern's pant cuffs was drooping. Ralph must have turned it down during their scuffle.

And, on the cement floor in front of her cell, were a half dozen tiny pink, metallic pigs. Confetti that had dropped from Vern's cuff.

"Ralph!" Immy screamed. "Come here!"

He raced through the door and she stuck her hand out of her bars to stop him before he stepped on the evidence. She pointed to the pile of incriminating pigs. "From Vern's pant cuff."

Ralph's eyes grew as big as she'd ever seen them. "Holy shit," he whispered.

*****

Ralph apologized that he couldn't release her that night. He needed to contact a judge or someone who was unavailable until morning. So she got to see Vern brought in and thrown into the third jail cell. Since the Saltlick jail only had three cells, Immy hoped that, for the rest of the night, no one was out driving drunk or peeing on neighbor's trees. Amy JoBeth's cell was a buffer between her and Vern, for which Immy was thankful. Vern ranted and screamed at Immy half the night after Amy JoBeth told him Immy had spotted the confetti, calling her horrible, obscene names that she totally did not deserve. All she'd done was point out the incriminating evidence he'd left on the floor. In the police station, of all places. The guy was an idiot.

Had he not changed his pants since the day he murdered Rusty? It was a wonder he didn't smell worse than he did. Maybe Amy JoBeth couldn't smell very well from being around pigs so much. They smelled a whole lot worse than cattle. Immy was glad Ralph usually changed Marshmallow's litter box. She did hate the smell of it.

But maybe Vern took his pants off so carefully the confetti never dropped out? Nah. They hadn't been washed, though. They couldn't have been. Immy was thankful her mother taught her better than that.

When Vern finally quieted down, Immy grabbed a few hours sleep before the chief banged open the metal door, rattling his keys.

"I'm releasing both of you," he said. "Immy, we got hold of the judge, who contacted Mike Mallett, who said he doesn't want to press any charges. Amy JoBeth, it looks like we got a slightly better suspect for the murder, so you're free for now. But don't leave town."

Immy noticed that Amy JoBeth didn't walk over to Vern's cell to tell him goodbye. Maybe she was finally done with him? He sure had called Immy some nasty names last night. Maybe she could see his true colors now.

*****

In the morning, Immy came through the front door of the trailer and Drew leaped on her, clasping her hands around her mother's neck when Immy picked her up.

"Mommy, Mommy, Mommy!" the child shouted, then broke down in heartrending sobs.

After wiping the corners of her eyes with the hem of her muumuu, Hortense gave her daughter a fierce hug. "I didn't know what to think when Ralph called to tell us you were incarcerated. He said you had entered the premises of Michael Mallett without authorization and caused egregious property damage. Is that true?"

"Um, sorta."

"Are there charges we're responsible for? Remuneration for repairs?"

"I don't know. Maybe. I'll talk to Mike. He's not pressing charges, Ralph said."

"What is that smudge on your face, Imogene?"

She fingered the bruise on her cheek. "It's from the tire wrench."

"I don't believe you're making sense, dear. You'd better have some provender to keep up your strength."

Immy followed Hortense and Drew to the kitchen, where she was overjoyed to see the waffle iron warming on the counter, a bowl of batter and a fat bottle of maple syrup sitting next to it. All three of them put away as many waffles as they possibly could.

After a short nap in her own, wonderful, soft bed, Immy walked to the library to see if she could log online to get her test score for her PI course. The library wasn't open very many hours of the week, but Friday morning at ten was one of them.

Cornelia Puffin, the Saltlick librarian, reigning behind her high counter, peered over her wire-rim glasses and kept her sharp eyes on Immy as she climbed the stone steps and entered the sanctum sanctorum, as Hortense sometimes called it. Immy headed toward the two public computers and Cornelia nodded, satisfied that Immy had not come to wreak havoc or steal books. She had very little reason to think Immy would, but Immy knew she always suspected everyone. Immy had very seldom stolen books from the Saltlick library.

Immy had used the library computer before and went straight to the entry screen for Stangford Institute of Higher Learning, where she entered her ID and password. The S in Stangford was so fancy Immy knew it was a reputable establishment the first time she saw it. And the Crime Scene course had taught her a ton of things she hadn't known, like how to take notes and measure things. Above all, to observe every detail and note it down. To always carry a flashlight, notebook, and pen. She had been surprised to learn that one should turn on all the lights when investigating a crime scene so they could see everything well. On television they always stumbled around in the dark with their flashlights when there were perfectly good light switches on the walls. Her course book had said to use the flashlight if the lights didn't work, or to find small objects on the floor, underneath things or in tight places.

She fiddled with the mouse, making circles on the screen while she waited for the screen with the test scores to load. The library used a dialup connection which was much slower than Mike's nice cable connection. She sure wished she still had that job.

Finally, the list appeared and she clicked on her name. The number 97 appeared beside her name. For a moment, she wondered what that meant. Was that her student number? Then it dawned on her. She'd gotten an A on her first test! Imogene Duckworthy was Detective Material. Here was the proof. She printed the sheet, wondering if it would prompt Mike to give her back her job.

"Silence, please."

Immy must have squealed. "Sorry. I just found out I got an A."

"Very nice for you, I'm sure. I didn't realize you hadn't graduated from high school yet," said Ms. Puffin.

Immy stood and walked, holding her paper, to Ms. Puffin's counter. "I finished high school some time ago. This is a graduate class."

Ms. Puffin straightened her back even further than her usual ramrod posture and patted her graying bun. "How nice for you. My, that's a nasty bruise on your face."

Immy left before the librarian could question her. She wasn't sure this was actually a graduate class, not being sure what that meant. But she knew she'd finished high school. What an old biddy Cornelia Puffin was. Hortense didn't like her much either, but that might be because Cornelia now had the job that Hortense had loved for so many years before her retirement.

After carefully folding the paper that had her stellar grade emblazoned on it and tucking it into her purse, she pondered, what would a detective do next, upon her release from stir? What cases should she work on? Maybe The Case of The Mysterious Papers, the missing clippings. She thought she knew where she might be able to find copies.

Sixteen

Around the corner and down a block from the library stood the *Saltlick Weekly*. In its former life, the building had been the home of the Bunyun family. Technically, it still was, even though the Bunyun family today consisted only of Paul. He lived in the back of the house and conducted his newspaper business in what used to be the living and dining rooms.

Immy stepped onto the small porch, shady under the overhang of a sagging square roof, and fanned herself from the exertion of the short walk. The day was becoming very warm. She squinted at the tiny hand-lettered sign tacked to the wooden door.

"Hours of Operation Th-F 11-3"

It was three minutes past 11:00, so she was in luck. She pushed the door open and entered the cool flagstone house. Editor Bunyan had erected a plywood counter across part of the living room and, propped beside a stack of newsprint and a box of print cartridges, stood a sign proclaiming him Editor. The man himself sat at his computer, tapping out a story and, probably, she thought, putting the latest issue to bed. Bunyan was not only the Editor, he was the Reporter, the Photographer, the Newspaper Boy, and everything else.

"Mr. Bunyun," Immy said softly. He didn't seem to have heard her come in and she didn't want to startle him into making a typo. There were enough of those in the paper already. Hortense complained about them in every issue.

He jumped up and dashed to the counter. He was so short he had to raise his arms above his shoulders to rest them on its linoleum surface. Immy wondered why he had made it so tall.

"Can I help you, Immy?" he asked, pushing heavy glasses up his small, sweaty nose with a stubby forefinger. "Do you have a story for this week's edition? I have room."

"No, I wanted to see if you kept old editions around. I'm looking for some information you published awhile ago." She wondered if his eyeglass prescription was up to date. He hadn't commented on her bruise.

"I keep all my issues in the morgue." He waved an arm toward an archway that led to the dining room. Immy had been inside a few times to drop off notices of Hortense's librarian meetings, but had never noticed that all four walls of the former dining room were lined with boxes, to the extent of blocking the windows. "Can I help you find something specific? Do you have a date?"

He darted into the makeshift morgue and flipped on the chandelier that hung from the ceiling, the only remnant of the room's former use. The boxes had date ranges on the ends, printed with a thick black marker.

"Um, no." One announcement not among the missing clippings had been Rusty and Tinnie's wedding. She wondered why it hadn't been there. "Do you have wedding announcements in a separate place?"

"No, but I remember most of the dates. Whose wedding?"

"Rusty and Tinnie Bucket."

"Oh yes, I remember that one well. The Squire family knows some prit-tee important people in Wymee Falls. It was a big affair. Shame about Rusty." He shook his head, then turned to a stack of boxes and pulled one out. Immy saw that they were on shelves, not just stacks of boxes as she'd first thought. He set the box on the floor and squatted in front of it. She watched him rummage through the papers, then sit back on his heels and frown, scratching his balding head.

"That's odd," he muttered, and pawed through the papers again. He finally pulled an issue out of the back of the box. "Misfiled," he snarled as he snatched it. But when he unfolded it to the page of wedding announcements, Immy saw a rectangular hole neatly cut from the middle of the page.

"Someone mutilated the archival copy," Mr. Bunyun said softly. He shook the page as if he could make the missing paper materialize, then quietly, sadly folded it and filed it in its proper place, in date order.

"Do you have Zack Bucket's birth announcement?" That was another clipping that might tie some things together.

He pulled down a second box with the same result, a cutout instead of an announcement, and more muttering and head scratching. "How could anyone do this?"

Someone who wanted to hide articles about the Squire family, Immy thought. Amy JoBeth had told Immy to throw away the ones from her desk, too. Was it her, and what was she trying to hide?

Immy left the little man pulling boxes out and trying to find more mutilated issues to fret over. This was damage Immy couldn't be blamed for, anyway.

She walked toward home, kicking the chunks of graveled tar that had come loose in the road and pondering The Case of the Missing Clippings, which is what The Case of the Mysterious Papers had morphed into.

What could be so valuable about newspaper clippings that someone would steal them, first from Bunyun's dining room archives, then from her desk at Mike Mallett's office? Amy JoBeth? Immy would go see her after lunch to try to shake some information out of her somehow. She'd review the Interrogation chapter of her *Compleat Guidebook* first.

*****

Immy leafed through the *The Moron's Compleat PI Guidebook*, propped on the kitchen table, until she got to the section labeled Interrogation. She munched her PBJ sandwich while she studied it. She had used some of these tactics in the past: she had answered questions with questions, let silence impel the perp to talk, acted friendly and casual at first to put them off guard. There was one effective way, though—put the perp in an uncomfortable chair in a stark, empty room. She would probably never be able to do that last one. At least uncomfortable chairs were still allowed. It was a pity rubber hoses and hot lights were out of favor these days.

"Mommy," said Drew. "Can I play with Marshmallow now?"

"You were with him all morning," said Hortense. "He might be getting weary of being pursued."

"You're chasing him?" asked Immy.

"It's Pig Scramble tomorrow," said Drew. "At the rodeo. I hafta practice."

"Tomorrow? The rodeo's tomorrow?"

On cue, Louise Cotter yoo-hooed at the front door and walked in. "Rodeo's tomorrow," she shrieked. "I got the permit for the booth." She waved a piece of paper at Hortense as she plopped into a kitchen chair.

Hortense rose with a grunt and carried her plate to the sink. "How nice for you."

"So, are you doing brownies?"

Hortense turned to face the brazen woman. "I do not intend to swelter in my kitchen all day for the sake of raising a paltry sum for your daughter's no doubt astronomical defensive costs."

Louise looked blank.

"No," said Immy. "She's not."

The woman's face caved in on itself and she lowered her head. Immy had never seen Louise so deflated.

Hortense's voice was softer when she continued. "I regret that I'm unable to assist you, Louise, but it's just not possible at this moment in time. I'm so sorry."

Of course it was possible for Hortense to bake all day, even in July. She'd done it before. She wasn't saying that she didn't *want* to do it, but Immy knew that's what she meant. Louise must have known it, too. When she raised her head, her face had hardened and her expression was black.

"You're not going to help us. I got lawyer's fees, you know. How are we going to pay them, Hortense? I had to put down a retainer when she was first arrested."

"You could probably get the retainer back," Immy said.

Louise pushed herself up, took an apple from the bowl in the middle of the table, and took herself off with a strut in her step that Immy thought was to mask her defeat. She slammed the door loudly on her way through it.

After they heard her car drive away, Hortense's shoulders slumped. "That woman."

"You can't, Mother. You can't give her an inch. We know that."

"Yes, we do. But I regret the whole situation."

"I hope she's not there when I go see Amy JoBeth."

"Why are you seeing her?"

"I have to find out about those stupid articles. I'm missing something. I can't see why they're so important."

"Do be careful, Imogene. If Louise is present, bide your time. Come back later to talk to Amy JoBeth."

"I think I'll do that."

"I'm gonna practice some more." Drew dashed out to the backyard.

"I think I'll bake one small batch of brownies," said Hortense.

Seventeen

Immy knocked on the front door for the third time. She'd been around to the back of Amy's Swine and the pigs were the only live beings there. Amy JoBeth's white pickup was parked beside the house in its usual place. It was not as clean as usual, though.

Immy turned and watched dust that her van had raised on the dirt road, still floating in the hot afternoon wind. She knew, of course, where Amy JoBeth was. And she didn't want to go there right now. But she had to find out about those clippings.

When Immy raised the hatch on the tornado shelter she was surprised to find the inside lit. The ceiling light must work, after all, she thought. Amy JoBeth sat on the mattress wiping moist, red-rimmed eyes. Immy picked her way down the steps.

The shelter was hotter than it had ever been and reeked of the unemptied toilet in the corner. Immy concentrated on the heat and the bad smell to keep her fear of closed in spaces at bay.

"Hi Immy." Amy JoBeth's voice was dull and flat, like the first time Immy had found her here.

"Aw, Amy JoBeth. Why are you here again?"

"Wouldn't you be if you were engaged to marry a murderer?"

"I'd probably just stay in bed at home. It's a lot more comfortable. And cooler." Immy fanned herself and she felt a stream of sweat trickle down between her breasts. Amy JoBeth shivered as if the place were cold.

"Are you sure Vern killed Rusty?"

"Heee," she wailed, "he told me he did. He whispered to me in the jail."

Immy lowered herself to sit beside her on the mattress and stroked Amy JoBeth's corkscrew hair. It didn't appear that she'd brushed it lately. There weren't any tissues handy.

"Are you sure you heard him right? The acoustics aren't that good in jail."

"I heard him," she blubbered. "He said he killed Rusty. For me. For *me*. How *could* he? How could I think I loved that, that, that horrible Vern?"

Immy didn't have one single answer to any of those questions. She dug for tissue in her purse and handed one to Amy JoBeth. It looked like it might have been used to wipe Drew's face, but Amy JoBeth didn't seem to notice. She stuffed it against her streaming nose, then smashed her face into her hands.

"Vern told you he killed Rusty? He actually confessed? Do Ralph and the chief know he said that?"

Amy JoBeth shrugged without lifting her face. The tissue had disappeared somewhere. Immy would make sure the cops knew about Vern's confession.

If Vern had suddenly started telling the truth, he had killed Rusty. But she'd bet Rusty hadn't killed the pig. So who killed Gretchen? This was all so confusing!

Immy couldn't talk Amy JoBeth up the steps, so she left with a mission. She was back to trying to solve The Case of the Slaughtered Pig. And she had clean forgot to ask Amy JoBeth about those damn clippings.

*****

Immy worked on the case until late into the night, jumping at the frequent firecrackers the younger citizens of Saltlick were tossing in the streets on the night before the Fourth of July. Drew had fallen into bed exhausted and confident of winning the Pig Scramble, a contest for youngsters in which they attempted to catch a young pig and stuff it into a sack. The rules forbade harming the piglets, but Immy was sure none of the piglets enjoyed being chased, caught by a hind foot, and deposited in a dark place. The rules also gave the winner—that is, the child who caught the first pig—the chance to keep the pig if they wished. Immy devoutly hoped Marshmallow would not be joined by another pig. This one would not be a cute miniature potbelly, it would be one of the regular kind that grow into huge porkers.

Immy still thought, as she had right at the first part of this case, that Amy JoBeth could be helped by finding out for sure who killed Gretchen. She would make sure Vern didn't find out, though, until he was convicted and in prison, so he wouldn't go off half-cocked and kill that person.

Immy had been around and around the scarce facts she knew. Gretchen had been shot, so the person who killed her had a gun. In her top dresser drawer, Immy still had the two bullets she'd dug out of Gretchen's head. But they were useless if didn't have other bullets or a gun to compare them to. Narrowing down Gretchen's killer to someone with a gun, in Saltlick, was like narrowing down a Texan to one with a pickup. It was easier to cross off people who didn't have them. Guns as well as pickups.

What else did she know about Gretchen's death? She'd seen what was surely Betsy Wiggins dragging the pig, in a big plastic bag, behind the smokehouse. Tinnie had taken Gretchen's body to the vet's, then Betsy had taken her back to Tinnie and Rusty's place. Gretchen had been killed, but where? She'd gotten out of the fence, but how far out? Who the heck could Immy ask? Surely it was important to find out where the pig was killed. Tinnie would know. Would Tinnie talk to Immy?

It was too late to drive over and call on her. Zack would be asleep, but it was around ten, Immy's calling cut-off time. So she phoned Tinnie.

"Tinnie? I have a question."

"Do you know what time it is, Immy?"

"I think it's just after ten. Could you tell me where Gretchen was when she was killed?"

"It was *not* my fault. I didn't know she could get out of that fence. It's not like she came with instructions."

"I'm sure it wasn't your fault at all, Tinnie."

"I didn't leave the gate open either. I should sue for slander. That damn Bunyun said I did in black and white."

"I was just wondering if I could figure out who shot her."

"Why?"

Immy took a breath. "Because, well, because I think it would help Amy JoBeth recover from her grief. It might help you, too."

"Everyone thinks Rusty did it."

"That's only because Vern says Rusty admitted it to him. I'm not sure. Can you believe what he says?"

"I don't know Vern all that well, but it doesn't seem like Rusty was out of my sight for long."

"Well," said Immy, "can you tell me who all was at your place the night Gretchen was shot?"

"We were all here. Me and Rusty and Zack. And Daddy was here, too. He ate dinner with us that night."

"Do you remember what happened?" Immy wished she weren't conducting her interrogation on the phone. It was so important to see if the suspect was fidgeting, or looking to the left, which meant they were lying. Or was it to the right that meant lying? She ought to look that up. Except Tinnie wasn't really a suspect for Gretchen's shooting. "Where was everyone?"

"Daddy was out target shooting after we finished eating."

"So it was dark out?"

"Yes, it was nighttime. Zack was in the bathtub and I was bathing him. Rusty was inside with me then. Zack had fed Gretchen some of the dinner scraps before his bath. He loved that pig so much, even in the short time we'd had her. She was a—" Immy heard sniffling. "—a really cute thing. So sweet."

"So, if someone was target shooting, how did you hear the shot that killed her?"

"I don't remember. Maybe Rusty or Daddy told me they heard the shot. Rusty and I went outside after Zack went to bed. Rusty started shooting with Daddy. Then I saw Gretchen was gone and the gate was open. She'd been in her pen before Zack's bath, when he fed her."

Something else Bunyun got wrong? Or did Immy hear that from Dr. Fox? Or was Tinnie lying? "Gretchen must not have gone very far if she'd been in her pen so soon before."

"No, she didn't. Rusty went looking and found her right across the road, partly in the lane. He saw her when a truck swerved to miss her. It's a wonder she didn't get hit. In the morning, Rusty took her into Dr. Fox for me, to see if he could tell anything, but he just said she was…dead." Another sniffle followed by a loud nose-blowing honk. "Dr. Fox was no help at all."

Immy wondered what help Tinnie had expected. Resurrection?

After she hung up, Immy revised some of her information. Dr. Fox had told her Tinnie heard the shot. Now, if she was telling the truth, Tinnie wasn't sure. Besides, two other men were shooting guns right there.

No drunken hunters had been mentioned in this conversation. But one of the shooters, if not both of them, was probably drunk. Rusty could have been drinking, should have been. It couldn't be pleasant for him to have dinner with the father-in-law who thought he was ruining the business he'd bought for his daughter. That would drive a man to drink. And Sonny? Immy hadn't seen Sonny Squire very often when he was sober.

Dr. Fox had said he'd warned them that the chicken wire they were using was inadequate. Tinnie probably wouldn't admit that.

Rusty had driven the pig to the vet's, then Betsy—as a favor to Rusty?—had hauled the carcass back to the smokehouse. Had Rusty told her to put it there?

Immy had seen Betsy drive away from Tinnie's the next day, just before Immy found Rusty's body.

How long had Rusty been hanging in the smokehouse when Immy found him, dead?

Eighteen

RODEO DAY DAWNED HOT AND DRY. Sunshine flooded across Immy's bed and spilled, more gently, onto Drew's cot against the other wall. Immy never tired of watching her daughter's sleeping angel face. If the world were a perfect place, Drew would stay four years old forever.

But, if the world *were* a perfect place, Immy would be a PI by now. She'd have a badge similar to her father's. She'd be driving herself to stakeouts in her new car, gray for anonymity. She would at least have a job at a PI office and would not have been fired. And people wouldn't kill each other. Or pet pigs. Of course, there might not be a need for PIs then, either.

Immy rose quietly so she wouldn't disturb Drew, slid her top dresser drawer open, and unwrapped her precious memento. Immy wasn't sure if her mother knew she'd kept the badge or not. Probably not. Hortense wouldn't want it in the house, a reminder of how her husband died.

She'd never really gotten over his murder.

A uniformed man had pounded on their door late at night and Immy, twelve years old at the time, had crept out of bed to see what would cause such a rare happening.

"Ma'am, Mrs. Duckworthy," Immy heard the man say from her spot in the hallway. "I have bad news."

"I didn't think it would be good news, coming this time of night. Where's my husband?"

"Would you like to sit down?"

"Where's Louis? What's happened?"

Immy heard the man cross the room to stand beside her mother before he spoke again.

"There was a robbery, and a shooting at Huey's restaurant."

"Is Louis all right?"

Immy had never heard her mother's voice screech and tremble like that.

The man must have shaken his head or something, because the next thing Immy knew, her mother was sitting on the floor, sobbing. Immy knew her daddy was not all right. And she knew her mother was not all right either, from that night on.

No one had witnessed what happened, no one who would talk, but Immy always imagined him dying as a hero, trying to stop the perps. Sometimes she dwelt on that event more than was good for her. But both brothers were now gone, Louis and Huey, both murdered. Immy shook off the memories. The past was over and done with.

She wrapped the badge in the soft scarf and returned it to its nest in the back of the drawer. The drawer squeaked slightly when she shut it.

Drew opened her green eyes wide, going in an instant from sound asleep to let's-go-what-are-we-waiting-for that four year olds are so good at.

"It's the rodeo today!" She threw off her covers and jumped on her bed, then climbed onto Immy's and started bouncing.

"Drew, don't jump on the bed."

"Five little monkeys, jumpin' on the bed," Drew chanted.

"No more monkeys jumpin' on the bed." Immy cut to the last line of the rhyme, grabbed Drew, and started tickling her. "C'mon, you need a good breakfast on rodeo day."

"For the Pig Scramble!"

Hortense was as excited as her granddaughter and dropped two eggs on the floor making an omelet. Her culinary efforts had expanded beyond dinners with the chief, to other meals for just the three of them. Marshmallow continued to benefit, too. The pig treats Hortense had made last night were on the counter, cooled and ready for consumption. She was experimenting with pig shaped rice cakes. Immy would be amazed if Marshmallow liked rice cakes. Did anyone? But, she admitted to herself, Marshmallow had yet to turn anything down, even if it did seem like cannibalism, eating things shaped like pigs.

They piled into the green van, the sun beaming warm rays, not yet the sweltering hot ones that would come in an hour or two, and drove to the Hail County Rodeo grounds on the west side of Wymee Falls.

The road approached the rodeo grounds from a hilltop, the vista laid out before them like a Google satellite map.

Trucks pulling vans full of bawling, bleating, nervous animals navigated the passageways between the rows of pens set up to house horses, calves, bulls, and other kinds of animals, too. The pens for the bulls were set out a ways from the ones for the other animals. The bull pens weren't too close together, either. Cranky animals, bulls. Their pens gave them room to move around so they wouldn't get any more agitated than they already were. They hated being confined too tight.

Cowboys and cowgirls pitched tents so they would be able to bed down next to their animals that night. Some were pitching tarp roofs above the pens to shade the livestock, too.

A new arena with covered seating had been built at the edge of the grounds a few years ago for this annual event. Smaller rodeos were held on private ranches throughout the summer, but this was the Big Daddy rodeo of the season. The one that attracted champions from out of state.

Since the Fourth fell on a Saturday this year, the two-day event was being held over July fourth and fifth, with the concluding fireworks Sunday night. Immy wondered about the wisdom of fireworks around skittish animals trained to buck, but the decision, obviously, wasn't hers to make.

Immy descended the hill and drove onto the grounds through the iron, grille-work gates, paying the spectator fee, as well as Drew's entry fee for the Pig Scramble.

"Where's the Pig Scramble gonna be?" asked Drew, stretching her neck to see the excitement. She managed to bounce slightly, even in her car seat.

"Probably in the main ring," said Immy. "I think everything is there."

"That would be an intelligent deduction," said Mother with a smile to lessen the sting of her sarcasm. "Since there is only the singular ring."

"But," said Drew, undeterred by sarcasm, since she didn't understand it, "where *are* the pigs? I don't see any pigs."

"They'll be in one of the pens," said Immy. "Maybe they're not here yet. The scramble is later on, after the parade."

The first event, the parade, wasn't scheduled until noon, but folks usually showed up early to look around, socialize, speculate on the outcome of the contests, and start eating.

Immy nosed the van into a slot near the arena and they got out to walk around and see people and, for Drew, pigs.

Drew ran ahead, peeking into the pens until she found the piglets for the scramble. They had arrived, after all. Hortense hurried after her, but Immy spotted someone she wanted to talk to next to a penned bull. Wanted to interrogate, actually, but this wasn't a good place for a formal interrogation. No small rooms with bright lights and wobbly chairs.

"Well, HELL-o, Immy," said Betsy Wiggins. "What on EARTH did you do to your face?"

Immy ignored her comment about her bruise. She'd thought it was fading in the bathroom mirror this morning, but maybe it looked worse outdoors. Betsy, every hair soldered into place as usual, was outfitted in red leather and fringe. She was going to be hot later, Immy guessed. The lanky cowboy next to her wore a white shirt and jeans pressed with a crease down the front of each leg. When Immy saw cowboys in jeans like this, their dress-up jeans, she wondered who put the crease in the jeans. The cowboy? His girlfriend? His mama?

"This here's Kyle Joe. He's a BULL rider." Betsy batted her lashes in his direction on the word *bull*. Immy wanted to add something about bull, but didn't. His goofy look testified that he had noticed Betsy's lash batting. The woman sure recovered from her grief fast. "And this here's Immy Duckworth, Kyle Joe. She lives over to Cowtail."

"Duckworthy. And I live in Saltlick."

"Oopsy. MY mistake."

Did the woman really put the tip of her index finger on her teeth? The three-year-old look seemed to appeal to Kyle Joe. How on earth was Immy going to pry him from Betsy's side? Immy needed to grill Betsy about what she saw when she dragged Gretchen around the smokehouse?

A clank and the sounds of snorting and pawing solved Immy's dilemma. Two boys had thrown a rock at a bull in a nearby pen. The huge, muscular beast pawed the ground and pushed its horns against the metal pen, itching to get at the miscreants, gore them, and trample their bodies. In Immy's experience, that's what bulls always wanted to do. One of the boys cocked his arm back to throw another rock.

Kyle Joe yelled at the boys and took off after them. They, naturally, ran away, darting among the animals' pens and trying to stay ahead of the bull rider. The cowboy caught them, though, one tee-shirt sleeve in each hand. They were too far away for Immy to hear the words, but the boys looked like they were getting the point. Don't throw rocks at the bulls.

Their timing couldn't have been better if Immy had paid them. She would have to work fast, though, before the besotted wrangler finished with the juvenile delinquents.

"So, Betsy, I want to make sure. That *was* you I saw putting Gretchen's body behind the smokehouse that Friday afternoon, wasn't it?"

Betsy frowned and opened her mouth. Then she shut it. Her fringed shoulders slumped. "Oh, hell. You saw me?"

"Yep."

"Rusty called my cell that morning and told me to fetch it. That was my day off, but I wanted to help Rusty out, so I went in to the clinic. Dr. Fox said he wasn't going to do what Tinnie wanted, cut it open and examine it. Dr. Fox was wondering what to do, cuz he didn't want it there, so he was happy to have me take it. I brought it back to Rusty's place, like he'd asked me to. He thought Tinnie might want to bury it."

What kind of a person works with animals and calls them "it", Immy wondered. What with Vern and this bimbo, Dr. Fox didn't get very good employees. "Dr. Fox said someone called you to tell him Gretchen was dead."

"Tinnie. She was about hysterical."

"What about Rusty? Where was he?" Immy asked.

"After he dropped it off at the vet's? He went back to work."

"And that was you leaving Jerry's Jerky the next day, the day I found Rusty."

"I went to see Rusty about...something."

Something like, your affair? "Did you find him?"

"Rusty was, just, just hanging there." Betsy's eyes widened in what seemed like genuine horror to Immy.

"You saw his body in the smokehouse?"

She nodded, the terror spreading to the rest of her face, to her trembling body. "I looked around for him and...."

"And you left and you didn't tell anyone?"

"You can't blame me, Immy. I've been so afraid someone would say they saw me. They might think I killed him. I could tell somebody had killed him. You don't put yourself on a meat hook. But I didn't. I wouldn't kill Rusty."

Immy believed her. She didn't think Betsy had the strength to get Rusty's body onto the meat hook.

"I'm not guilty. I swear I'm not." Betsy was shaking so hard her fringe danced at the edge of her jacket.

The only thing Betsy was guilty of, besides sleeping with a married man, Immy decided, was stupidity. "You need to tell Ralph or the chief what you saw."

"I can't do that. Oh HI, Kyle Joe. Aren't those boys NASTY?"

"What can't you do?" he asked.

"I could NEVER hit an ANIMAL with a rock. Or mistreat them in ANY way."

"Remember what I just said," said Immy. "I will if you don't."

She heard Kyle Joe ask Betsy what in the hell that woman was talking about as she walked away.

When she found Drew and Hortense, they were pointing to one piglet after another and squealing about how adorable they all were.

"Have you picked one out?" said Immy.

"Not yet," said Drew. "They're all too cute. Oh!" She looked across the pen. "There's Zack!"

Immy was surprised to see Tinnie looking over the piglets with her son. Drew scampered around the pig pen to greet Zack and Immy trailed after her, wondering what to say to Tinnie.

"This must be a difficult time for you, surveying piglets so soon after the most unfortunate demise of your own dearly beloved pet."

Immy hadn't realized Mother had followed her.

Tinnie gave Hortense a wan smile. "These aren't really anything like potbellies," she said. "They're okay, but potbellies are so much cuter."

"We getting new one, wight, Mommy?" Zack turned his eager, shiny, irresistible eyes to his mother.

She gave a doting-mother smile to her son. "We'll see."

Sonny Squire appeared behind Hortense, bearing corn dogs for his daughter and grandson from the food wagons near the arena. "Time for chow, kids."

He handed a dog to Zack and one to Tinnie, then almost dropped his. "We gotta go back for drinks," he said. "Or we can get a table and I'll get 'em."

Sonny, swaying slightly, had already had a few drinks, Immy thought. His group headed for the picnic tables set up under the dappled shade of a half dozen spreading live oaks at the edge of the grounds, just beyond the vendors. Immy and her crew headed in the direction of those vendors to seek lunch.

Rodeo goers were already lining up in front of the food trailers beside the arena. Immy's family took a place in line and contemplated the goodies. Hortense and Drew both wanted corn dogs, but Immy chose corn on the cob and some cole slaw. She didn't feel like eating something that might have pork in it right now. With corn dogs, you just never knew what might be in there.

Drew wanted to sit by Zack, but all the spaces in that row of tables were taken, so they found a place to sit two rows from Zack's family. Immy went to get cokes and soon returned with sweating waxed cups brimming with crushed ice and sugary, caffeinated goodness. They never drank cokes at home, so this was a treat for all three of them.

Hortense and Drew swizzled their dogs in paper cups of mustard and Immy went back to the vendor trailers for napkins, and a fork for her slaw. On an impulse, she got in line for a funnel cake for the three of them to share. With a pang at the sight of how little cash she had left, Immy paid for the cake. Mother's pension check from the library would not arrive until the fifteenth of the month and there was precious little left to tide them over. Immy would have to job hunt in earnest next week.

She turned from the funnel cake trailer, bearing her precious treasure before her, balancing to keep it level on the paper plate so none of the powdered sugar would slide off.

Her only warning was a whiff of whiskey breath. Then Sonny Squire's hefty form lurched into her side. The paper plate flipped and the cake fell to the ground.

Neither of them moved for a moment. Then Immy squatted to retrieve her cake, but it had landed in trampled dirt. A tear splashed to the ground beside the confection. She couldn't buy another one. Money was too tight. She looked up into Sonny's hangdog expression.

"Oh my god. I'm so sorry, Immy."

"Oh, you're sorry, are you?" That loud voice was familiar. "So what are you gonna do about it?" Louise Cotter stood a few feet away. She probably thought she was muttering, but that squawk of hers cut through the noise of the crowd.

"Mother," said Amy JoBeth, hurrying onto the scene, carrying lemonade cups. "Calm down. It's only a funnel cake." She thrust a cup at her mother.

Immy was glad to see Amy JoBeth out of the storm cellar. This wasn't the place to ask, but Immy wondered what had drawn her out.

Louise lowered her voice somewhat, but she couldn't speak as quietly as most people could. "Well, the lousy bastard should buy her another one."

"Mother, come on." Amy JoBeth pulled her mother's arm.

But Louise sidled up to Immy and whispered to her in the softest tones she'd ever heard the woman use, "You ask that uncle of yours about that Squire family." She did a double-take at Immy's face. "That's a nasty bruise, Immy."

"Mother, come have some lemonade." This time Amy JoBeth succeeded in pulling her mother away.

Immy watched them go, fingering her sore cheek. She turned at a nudge from Sonny.

He stuck a five dollar bill at her. "Here. Get another one."

She took it and he hauled a flask from his pocket, took a deep swing, recapped it, and staggered toward his family who were waiting in the shade.

This time, when Immy carried the funnel cake to Hortense and Drew, she kept track of her surroundings. A PI should never walk with her head down. She could, obviously, get side-swiped that way.

Nineteen

Louise's words didn't hit Immy until she was sitting at the picnic table, half done with the funnel cake she was sharing with Hortense and Drew. Louise had said to ask her uncle something. Oh yes, to ask him about the Squire family. That sure sounded crazy.

"Do you have a brother?" she asked Hortense.

"What an odd question. You know I don't. I am an only child, born of only children. I've reiterated that numerous times."

"Yes, you have," said Immy. And her Uncle Huey was dead, murdered in the spring of this year. So what uncle was Louise talking about? Immy shrugged. The woman was nuts. She finished her meal so they could go to the arena and watch the parade that kicked off the rodeo.

Hortense and Drew went on ahead while Immy scooped up their paper waste and found the trash barrel at the far edge of the picnic area. The Squire family had left a few minutes before. While they'd been eating, Amy JoBeth and her mother had arrived. They took places at this end of the area, sitting off to themselves at the end of the row of redwood tables and benches. Now they sat across from each other, apparently finished drinking their lemonade, but staring down at their empty paper cups in silence.

Immy wondered what it must be like to be a member of a family that wasn't constantly talking. Between Hortense and Drew, there wasn't much mealtime silence in the Duckworthy household, either when they ate at home or, like today, dined out.

How was Immy going to get Amy JoBeth by herself to ask her if she knew what her mother was talking about? Louise still looked angry and Immy didn't feel like talking to her while she was in such a snit. Besides, Immy usually ended up doing something she didn't want to when she talked to that woman. But Louise's words hung in her mind. Did Immy have an uncle she didn't know about?

Louise Cotter shoved her cup and napkin at her daughter, got up, and left. Amy JoBeth, still almost as dejected as she had been in the tornado shelter, picked up the trash and headed toward the barrel where Immy still stood. They were playing right into Immy's hand.

"Oh hi, Immy." Amy JoBeth pitched her trash and dusted her hands off.

"Hi. Enjoying the rodeo?"

"It hasn't started yet."

"Well, lunch is part of it, I think."

Amy JoBeth looked so sad.

"Are you missing Vern?" Immy had to ask.

That sparked some emotion. Anger flared in her eyes. "That louse! How could I have been so stupid? No, I'm not missing him. He's a horrible person. He killed Rusty."

"Oh, that's right. He says he killed him. Do you think he really did?" No more Vernie Wernie at least. Immy was glad of that.

"He said he did it because he loves me." Amy JoBeth shook herself like a wet dog. "Even if Rusty did kill Gretchen, he didn't deserve…well, Vern Linder is just as bad as Rusty Bucket."

Amy JoBeth waved away a fly that was intent on the trash barrel's contents and they started walking slowly toward the arena.

"Your mother whispered something to me back there when Sonny knocked my funnel cake on the ground. She said something about asking my uncle about the Squire family. Do you know what your mother was talking about?"

Amy JoBeth gave her a blank stare. Did Amy JoBeth not know or was she stonewalling?

"Do you have any idea what 'uncle' she was talking about?"

"Nope."

Now what? There was the matter of The Case of the Missing Clippings, the clippings about the Squire family. That case was still unsolved. Was she a detective or not? Well, not really. But did she want to be one?

She stared Amy JoBeth square in the eyes. The intimidation method of interrogation. "What's with you and the Squire family?"

"With me? Nothing. It's Mom. She's obsessed. What did you do to your face, Immy?"

The Cotter women were not very observant.

A male voice, distorted by a loudspeaker, floated across the grounds from the arena. A crowd swarmed around the two slow-walking women, jostling to get to the ring before the parade began. People streamed into the arena through the wide arches and Immy could see the matched palominos that would lead the parade lined up outside an entrance near the rear of the structure.

Immy faced Amy JoBeth and folded her arms, blocking her way. "I want you to give me the straight dope, Amy JoBeth. What gives with your family and the Squires?"

Amy JoBeth halted and frowned too much. "What do you mean?"

If she was trying to look puzzled, she didn't make it. Immy knew she was playing dumb.

"That won't cut it, Amy JoBeth." Immy tried to snarl like a tough interrogator. She longed for a small room and a bright light. "I know about all those newspaper notices you saved. They were all about that family."

"That's not true. Some of the things I cut out were recipes."

"But why did you save all that stuff about Tinnie's family?"

"I didn't know it *was* Tinnie's family. Until much later. I never would have sold Gretchen to her if I'd known she was a Squire." Anguish tinged Amy JoBeth's wails.

"But why not? What did Tinnie's family ever do to you? Your mom hates Sonny Squire. I'm not sure he even knows why."

"Oh, he knows why."

Wild cheering erupted from the stadium.

"The parade must be starting," said Immy. She waited for Amy JoBeth to elaborate, but Amy JoBeth turned away and walked into the arena.

It would have worked better if she'd had that small stuffy room with a bright light and an uncomfortable chair. And a locked door so the suspect couldn't walk away.

Immy hurried through the gate to catch the rest of the parade.

A quick scan showed her Hortense's formidable form in a second row seat. Being large made her easy to spot in a crowd. Drew and Ralph were sitting by Hortense. Immy made her way down the row to the empty seat they'd saved for her beside Ralph.

"Were you detained?" asked Hortense.

"I talked to Amy JoBeth for a minute."

"How is the unfortunate breeder of porcine animals faring?"

"Well, she's over Vern anyway."

"That's good," said Ralph. "He's a bad one."

"Look, clowns!" Drew stood on her seat to see the rodeo clowns better.

Immy lowered her voice to speak to Ralph. "Did he really admit he killed Rusty?"

"After you spotted the confetti on him, he did. After several hours of questioning. He finally ran out of excuses and explanations and told us the truth."

"The truth, the whole truth, and nothing but the truth?" She spied Amy JoBeth and Louise across the way, about a third of the way around the circle. They sat watching the parade, not speaking to each other.

"Probably not. But part of it. Enough to hold him and probably to get at least one conviction."

"You want more than one?"

"We want him for Poppy Jenkins, too." Ralph sucked his breath in.

"Hey, I shouldn't have told you that. Forget I said it. Okay?"

"How can I do that? I can't forget stuff I heard."

Ralph groaned. "Well, just don't tell anyone I told you."

Maybe she was better at interrogation than she thought. She'd gotten some inside dope on The Case of the Dead Poppy without even trying.

"So, Vern killed Poppy Jenkins, too?"

"Sh!" Ralph looked around, then brought his face close to hers. "Don't tell anyone, I said. Don't talk about it." He drew away. "Does your face feel okay? Look, do you want me to get you some cotton candy?"

"Are you trying to distract me?"

"Yes."

"Okay. My face feels fine and I'd like some cotton candy."

The prancing palominos led the parade out of the arena, after which the wranglers set up for the first event, barrel racing.

Drew clapped her hands, eager to watch the race while Ralph got up, climbed past Immy, and went to fetch some cotton candy.

"Pink," Immy called after him. "Not blue." She didn't care what color, but Drew would only eat pink and she'd end up sharing it with her. And Mother.

*****

The calf roping was finished and the boys and girls doing the mutton bust had been called down to the waiting area.

"We'd better get you cleaned, up," said Immy to Drew. "The Pig Scramble is next." They hurried to the restroom to dissolve some of the sticky cotton-candy sugar off Drew's face and hands.

"I hafta have clean hands to catch a pig, huh." Drew rubbed her hands vigorously under the stream of cold water, the only kind the sink put out. She managed to get a lot of water on her shirt and shorts, and on the floor. Immy swiped the puddle with some paper towels and they rushed to the back of the arena.

They were in plenty of time since there were still five more mutton busters to go, all small boys. Three girls had ridden this year, though.

They were all eight or under, the age limit for that event. Immy hoped Drew wouldn't want to mutton bust when she was a little older. She'd seen kids get hurt doing it.

The next boy put on his helmet and his dad made sure it was adjusted properly. A wrangler picked the boy up and, at almost the same moment the gate opened, set the boy onto the bare back of the adult sheep. The child had nothing but wool to hang onto and lasted about two seconds on the animal's back. As soon as the sheep and the boy were out of the ring, the next one went. The clowns kept busy during this event, plucking the boys off as they slipped sideways or grabbing them when they fell to the ground, saving them from the sharp hooves of the frightened sheep.

When the last mutton buster finished, the crowd waited for the announcement of the winner. After third and second place were announced, a boy from Wymee Falls walked to the center of the ring and got his ribbon for staying on the back of his sheep for all of five seconds, the best time in the event.

Then it was time for the Pig Scramble. When the piglet handlers released the little squealers into the chute, the children, including Drew, tucked burlap sacks into their waistbands and went to stand on the opposite end of the arena.

The announcer raised his voice. "Are you ready, kids? Here they come!"

Squealing piglets streamed across the sandy surface. The kids ran towards them. Immy climbed up the fence next to the chutes so she could see better.

The little porkers were fast. Some of the children were faster, but most ran far behind the pigs. Each kid picked out a pig to concentrate on. Drew managed to trap hers in a corner.

"One minute left," said the announcer.

"Hold on! You got it!" screamed Immy. "Grab the leg!"

Drew got it by the leg. The piglet squirmed, but Drew held tight.

"Keep it, Drew! Get the sack on it!"

Immy kept yelling and, after several tries, Drew managed to get her sack over the small head.

"Don't let go yet!"

The roar of the onlookers was deafening, further frightening the pigs and making the ones still loose run even faster. The running children were starting to pant.

"Thirty seconds," said the timekeeper.

But Drew still clung to the hind leg of her pig. Immy yelled louder to make herself heard over the din.

Drew inched the sack up the wriggling body until it was half way in. At that point, a clown showed up and finished the job. He stuffed the rest of it into the sack, tied the top, and handed it to Drew. She gave him a huge smile and tried to lift the sack.

The timekeeper started calling the last few seconds. Parents screamed at their kids even louder and the kids put on a last burst of speed, trying to catch up to the energized pigs.

In the end, about half the kids had pigs.

One of the clowns walked Drew out of the ring carrying her sack for her and handed it to Immy.

Drew saw Zack right when Immy did. He stood next to them, outside the arena, waiting for Tinnie, Immy guessed, who hadn't stayed near the chute. He burst into tears.

"Oh, Zack," Immy said, squatting down to his level. He hadn't gotten a piglet. "Your mommy will be here in a minute."

"I diddun get a pig," Zack wailed.

"It's okay," said Drew. "You can have mine."

When the children bagged a pig, it was theirs to keep, or it could be donated back to the rodeo if they didn't have a place for it. Immy had assumed they would donate this one back, since they already had Marshmallow.

Immy was impressed with her daughter's kind generosity. "That's a good thought, Drew," she said. "But we'd better see if Zack's mommy will let him keep it. Or if Zack wants it."

"Do you?" Drew asked.

Zack looked from Drew to the wiggling sack Immy held. His tears seemed to dry right up.

Tinnie arrived and Zack ran to greet her. He asked if he could keep Drew's pig.

She didn't answer for a few seconds, eyeing the animated sack with a dubious expression. "This isn't a pig like Gretchen, honey."

"I know. It's a tiny wittle pig."

"Yes, but it will get great, great big."

"I wike gweat big pigs," Zack said, "gweat, gweat big," spreading his arms to indicate a "gweat big pig".

Immy and Tinnie both chuckled.

To Immy's surprise, Tinnie said he could keep it. "But let's see if we can leave it in the pen until the rodeo's over."

"Move outta the way, ladies."

Immy looked up to see a trailer containing a bull. The four of them, with the piglet, got far out of the way. Bull riding was next.

Twenty

Immy felt awkward standing out the arena, next to Tinnie while Drew and Zack talked about his new pig. Especially since she suspected Tinnie of killing her own husband. After all, Tinnie had been right there when Rusty was killed—that gave her opportunity. She'd been spitting mad about his affairs—motive. Weapon? The drugs? What about where he ended up? She could have hauled him into the smokehouse after he was drugged, but she probably couldn't have lifted him onto the hook. Unless she was fueled by anger and adrenaline. Immy had heard they did powerful things to a person.

The breeze stirred a dust devil at her feet.

Then there was Poppy. Tinnie wasn't the one who had driven her to the motel. No, that was certainly Vern Linder. But what if Tinnie and Vern were in cahoots? Vern could have gotten the drugs, he could have helped Tinnie lift Rusty's body, and she knew he drove Poppy to Cowtail's Finest. Maybe he drove Poppy there after Tinnie had killed her.

Immy swiped at the sweat on her forehead with the back of her hand and edged a little farther away from Tinnie, who had summoned a wrangler to take the piglet.

Immy watched the handlers unload the bull into the chute and heard the first ride announced. This wasn't her favorite event. The bulls, even though the tips of their horns were wrapped, were intent on trying to kill the cowboys after they fell off and some succeeded in doing quite a bit of injury. The bull riders wore protective vests, but could still get trampled and severely injured.

"Zack, you wanna see the bulls?" said Drew. She looked at her mother. "Can we?"

The rest of the animals for the bull riding event were penned about thirty feet away. Bulls can't be all put together in a ring like a lot of other rodeo animals. They don't like each other and will start fighting when they're confined together. So they were kept in separate pens just before the rides. The pens were bigger than the chutes so the bulls could move around comfortably before they had to be squeezed into the chutes. Immy shuddered when she thought about the close quarters of the chutes.

Drew hadn't waited for an answer. Immy hurried to catch up with the youngsters. Tinnie finished talking to the wrangler about stowing her new pig and followed sedately.

By the time Immy reached them, Drew was halfway up the side of a pen, climbing the wooden slats. Zack was right behind her, a few rungs down. The bull lifted his head and watched.

"Drew, don't climb up on—"

Time slowed as Immy saw Drew balance on the top slat. Saw the bull aim his horns at Drew. Saw Drew reach a hand out to the beast. Saw the bull lower his great head and butt the fence below Drew.

Zack dropped onto the dirt.

Drew tottered, lost her balance. Fell into the pen.

Someone was screaming.

Drew was screaming. Immy was screaming.

The bull, his head lowered, turned his body sideways and swung his head back and forth. Those tiny eyes grew bigger and harder and meaner.

As Drew's body fell, nearing the ground and the bull's hooves, Immy shot forward, arms stretched toward her daughter.

She was jostled aside, caught a whiff of whiskey breath.

Sonny Squire. Sonny clambered halfway up the fence.

Immy was shoved aside again, harder this time.

Kyle Joe, Betsy's bull rider.

Kyle Joe was over the fence, scooped Drew up, and was back, setting her onto her feet, before Immy could close her mouth and lower her outstretched arms.

Sonny looked down, perplexed, and slowly climbed to the ground.

"How…what…oh my god," stammered Immy. "Thank you so much, Kyle Joe. Drew, are you all right?"

The bull pawed the dirt, gave a couple snorts, then raised his head and turned his attention elsewhere. Sonny reeled, then regained his balance. He got a hip flask from his back pocket and took a long draw.

Drew clutched Immy around the legs and wailed.

"How did you get out of there without getting gored?" Immy asked Kyle Joe.

"That bull wasn't ready to charge yet, ma'am," he said. The cowboy hadn't even lost his hat.

"How do you know?"

"He had his body sideways to your young 'un. When they're ready to charge they turn to face you."

Betsy appeared at his side. "Ain't he SOMETHIN'?" She bumped her upper arm against his.

Immy thought the bull might have been able to change directions pretty quick. But Drew was safe, along with everyone else. That was all that mattered.

"They don't make up their minds in a powerful hurry," said Kyle Joe, seeming to read her mind.

"Well, thank you for saving Drew's life."

"No problem."

Betsy put her hand, tipped with blood red talons, on Kyle Joe's thick arm. Immy felt a stirring inside. If only Betsy weren't here, she thought.

The announcer called Kyle Joe's name and he hurried away, Betsy in his wake.

Immy agreed with Betsy. Kyle Joe was somethin'.

*****

Tinnie picked Zack up and dusted him off. He joined Drew's crying chorus for the climax, then they both tapered off to gulping whimpers.

181

Sonny pocketed his flask and patted his grandson on the head. He, Tinnie, and Zack left with Tinnie carrying Zack while Sonny supported her by the elbow. Or maybe, Immy thought, he was supporting himself.

"Was that bull going to hurt me?" asked Drew.

"I think he might have," Immy answered.

"He's a bad bull."

"No, sugar, he's just a bull. They're all like that."

"They all are mean?"

"They don't much like people falling into their pens. It scares them."

"What's that?"

"Oh, you know what being scared is like, don't you?"

"No, that." Drew pointed to a dull metal object on the ground. "That gun." She moved toward it and reached her hand out.

"No! Don't touch it!" Immy thought, furiously fast. Where had it come from? Either Sonny or Kyle Joe must have dropped it climbing the fence. Probably not Kyle Joe, since he was riding a bull any minute now. Immy heard the loudspeaker announce the release and the crowd started cheering for him.

She had to retrieve the pistol. She picked it up by the barrel and tucked it into the outer compartment of her purse where she kept her sunglasses, presently resting on her nose.

So probably Sonny Squire. He did usually carry a sidearm. Immy's mind kept racing, top speed. Rusty said he killed his wife's pig. He told Vern that, according to Amy JoBeth. But Tinnie had said Rusty and her father, Sonny, had been out target shooting together that night. What if this was the gun they'd been using? Immy thought it would be worthwhile to run ballistics on it, since she had the bullets she'd dug out of Gretchen.

Now how was she going to get a ballistics test?

Her first thought, while picking it up, had been to preserve fingerprints.

Her second thought was that, since the gun belonged to Sonny, his prints were likely on it.

Her third thought was that she didn't want hers on it. So she took a tissue from the main compartment of her purse and wiped off the barrel where she'd picked up the gun.

"What is transpiring?" Hortense rushed to Drew, breathless, and wrapped her arms around the child. "I learned, from the Squire family, of a disturbance in the bovine enclosure."

"I fell in," said Drew, her voice muffled by her grandmother's upper arm. "A big, strong man got me out."

"True," said Immy. "A bull rider named Kyle Joe."

Immy heard the crowd roar and the announcer yell, "Eight seconds!" A loud buzzer sounded. Good for Kyle Joe. He'd stayed on eight seconds, which meant a complete ride. He'd be in competition for first place.

"How did she fall in from here?" asked Hortense.

"She climbed up the fence before I could stop her, Mother."

"Mommy told me, don't do that."

"Mommy is correct," said Hortense.

"I wanna go home and see Marshmallow," wailed Drew.

"That is an excellent proposal." Hortense picked Drew up and they left the rodeo early.

*****

The next day was Sunday, but, judging from all the Saltlickians Immy saw at the rodeo that morning, she'd bet Holiness Baptist Church was nearly empty. Her favorite event, saddle bronc, had started and she sat with Hortense and Drew in the stands, waiting for the chute gate to spring open for the next contender.

Drew slurped a lemonade loudly but neither Immy nor Hortense corrected her, since it was likely no one but those two could hear the child above the crowd.

The horse leapt out of the gate and the cowboy flopped back and forth as the animal tried to get the dang thing off its back. The first rider barely made two seconds. Very disappointing. But the next rider up was last year's champion. This ought to be a good ride, Immy thought, scooting forward on the bench seat.

"Mommy." Drew tugged on her arm. "I hafta go potty."

"Mother?" Immy didn't want to miss the next rider.

183

"I took her to the facility the previous time." Hortense didn't want to miss him either.

"Twenty minutes ago," muttered Immy, rising and taking Drew's hand.

Immy looked over her shoulder until they got out of sight of the arena, but the champion rider didn't appear. She led Drew to the rooms tucked under the bleachers, but there was no need. Drew knew the way. She loved the noise the hand dryers made. That was the reason Drew liked to go so often, Immy knew. She also knew that the one time she told Drew, no, they couldn't go right now, would be the time she really did have to and there would be an "accident."

The line at the restroom snaked out the door. Immy heard the crowd cheer as the rider and horse started. They had just reached the door of the room when the announcer screamed, "Fantastic ride! I've never seen anything like this! This ride that will go down in history!" He went on, but his words were drowned by the noise of the crowd.

"Great," said Immy.

"What's great, Mommy?"

"Nothing, sugar. Come on, there's an open stall."

After Drew did her business, which had amounted to about a teaspoon's worth, Immy drummed her fingers against the wall while Drew held her hands under the dryer. She tried it on her arms, then tried to make it blow on her legs. The whirr echoed in the concrete room.

"Are you finished?" Immy looked up to see Betsy Wiggins, her red-nailed fingers dripping.

"Drew, sugar, Ms. Wiggins want to use the dryer," said Immy.

Drew sadly took her hands from beneath the hot air stream.

"I'm so grateful to your friend for saving Drew from the bull yesterday," said Immy over the roar of the dryer.

"Ain't he just the cutest THANG?" Betsy showed her brilliant teeth as she flashed a smile.

"Is he married, too?" asked Immy.

Betsy's eyes narrowed. "That's a bitchy comment and you know it."

"My child is here, Betsy."

"Well then you oughta mind your manners. I only saw Rusty because he needed consoling."

"I'm sure."

"It's true. Rusty was too good for Tinnie. Why, do y'all know, he told her he shot the pig just so she wouldn't get upset with her daddy? She thinks the world of her daddy, you know."

"What?"

Betsy raised her voice. "I said she thinks—"

"No, what you said before that."

Betsy drew her hands out of the air stream and the room grew several decibels quieter. "Let's go outside."

They found a spot relatively free of people and Betsy repeated her statement. "Rusty thought Tinnie would be so upset if she knew her daddy shot that damn pig that Rusty told her he did it. And look what that got him. Amy JoBeth killed him because she thought he killed that damn pig."

"What damn pig?" piped up Drew.

"Are you sure about that?" asked Immy.

"Positive. Rusty told me everything. He said she was already mad enough to kill him, on account of he was seein' me, she couldn't be any madder, so he might as well tell her that."

"Tell her what?" said Drew.

Tinnie was angry that Rusty was banging every woman around him, and she had a right to be, Immy thought.

"Come on, sugar, we have to go."

After they were out of earshot from Betsy, Drew whispered to her mother, "That lady doesn't talk nice."

"You're right, sweetie, she doesn't."

But Immy had a feeling she talked true. At least this time. Tinnie's daddy shot Gretchen? Old, drunk Sonny Squire? Immy could see that happening.

Twenty-One

SADDLE BRONC WAS DONE WITH AND TEAM ROPING was under way when Immy and Drew returned to the stands.

"That was the most spectacular—" began Hortense.

"I don't want to hear about it," said Immy. "I heard the announcement."

She hardly paid attention to the team roping event, mulling over Betsy's revelation. How did that change things? She didn't know for sure that Rusty was killed because he murdered the pig, or said he did, but that was reasonable to assume.

So who thought he did it and would kill him for that? Amy JoBeth? Vern Linder? Louise Cotter? Tinnie? Whoever killed him had made a mistake, though.

It crossed her mind that Ophelia Jenkins might have killed him for seducing her daughter, but she dismissed that thought. For one, Ophelia didn't seem all that much bothered by the relationship. For another, Poppy seemed to have been killed in tandem with Rusty. Same method, about the same time. So probably by the same person. Why would they be killed together?

A gust of wind blew a dirt cloud from the arena in her direction, but she absently waved it away.

"Ew, gross," said Drew. "I need another lemonade." Drew made fake choking sounds to demonstrate her acute need.

Immy looked around. The roping was still in progress, but bareback would be next, another of Immy's favorites.

"Mother, your turn," she said.

"Now, Imogene, you know how much delight I take in the spectacle of man versus beast in the bareback competition."

"And you know how much I take, too, Mother. It's your turn."

Hortense gave a much-put-upon look and grunted as she pushed up from the bench. Immy felt a slight twinge of guilt. It really was much harder for Mother to navigate the bleachers than it was for her. The twinge grew to a pang.

"Sit down, Mother. I'll go. C'mon, Drew."

"Would you mind bringing me the same libation? I'm so appreciative, Imogene. You're a good daughter."

After Immy and Drew had made it through the long line at the lemonade trailer, they started back. Since Immy balanced three large flimsy cups, she decided not to hold Drew's hand for once. Immy dodged when she saw Sonny Squire coming at her from the picnic area, reeling and staggering more than usual. She wasn't going to let him knock her lemonades out of her hands.

"Hey there, Mizz Imogene. Can I ask you a queshun?" He stood before her, swaying, red-eyed. "Have you seen…did you see me…drop somethin'?"

Immy knew exactly what he was talking about. His pistol. She phrased her answer carefully. "No, I didn't see you drop anything."

"Yesserday, I mean. At the bull pens. When Drew fell in. 'Member?"

"Of course I remember. Thanks for trying to—"

"Mommy—"

"Drew, be quiet. We have to go now, Mr. Squire. I hope you find it."

"But Mommy—"

"Hush."

As they turned toward the bleachers Louise Cotter rushed up. "I heard you, you old coot. Whatever you lost, I hope you never get it back."

Louise made such a sour face Immy was afraid, for a minute, she was going to spit on Sonny.

"Like *we* never got back what you stole from *us*," Louise said, her screech turning heads toward them.

"Din steal it. Got it fair and square, you bitch."

"You call refusing a loan during a drought fair and square, you bastard? You call watching us lose the ranch for taxes fair and square? You call poisoning our herd fair and—" Louise's voice broke. She screwed up her face and, this time, she did spit. She didn't have much range though, and her spittle landed on the pointy toe of Sonny's ostrich-skin cowboy boot.

Louise turned away and almost tripped over Drew, who had been watching the exchange, ears and eyes wide open.

Drew picked that moment to be helpful. "Mr. Sonny lost his gun, Mizz Louise."

Now how in the hell did she figure out that's what he was talking about, wondered Immy.

"Yeah." Sonny swayed ominously, staring at the stained toe of his expensive boot. "The one that shot that, that…."

A strangled sound came from Louise.

"Gotta find it. It's here somewhere." Sonny staggered through the picnic tables, crashing against them and tipping a bench upside-down.

Immy looked from Louise, frozen with incomprehension, to Sonny, who had just about told her the gun killed Gretchen. How could he have said that? On the other hand, how could he be that drunk and still be standing?

Louise shook her head slowly. "Sonny Squire killed Gretchen?"

"I don't think he meant that," said Immy. "He's just, just looking for his gun." She didn't know what Louise would do to Sonny if she got any madder at him.

"The gun that shot… Gretchen."

"Mommy, you have—"

"Hush, Drew." She thrust two of the cups into her small hands.

"Take these to Grandma. Right now."

"Sonny Squire killed Gretchen," Louise repeated.

"Not necessarily," insisted Immy. "He's lost his gun. I don't think that's what he meant."

"So what did he mean?"

Immy didn't honestly know. It could be that Rusty killed the pig with that gun. But she didn't think so. "I hope he finds it," said Immy.

Louise pondered a moment. "Well, he couldn't have shot Gretchen. Rusty shot her."

Immy didn't say anything to that. She didn't know how much of what she'd learned was true, anyway. People say things. And who could believe that ditz, Betsy Wiggins?

"That man is plumb crazy," said Louise. "He's stark ravin'. I'm not sorry to see it happen, neither." She twisted her mouth into a mean sneer and took off for the stands. "Needs to be committed," she mumbled as she left.

Immy wondered if the bareback event was over yet.

*****

As Immy returned to Hortense and Drew, and to watch the last two bareback riders, she remembered one of the clippings. The headline had read "Land Dispute" and had mentioned the Squire family. Had the Cotter family been mentioned, too? Maybe Amy JoBeth had been trying to document the history of a land dispute between the two families. Probably the dispute that was the cause of her father's suicide.

Louise's accusations were serious. It sounded like the Squire family had refused them a loan when they were in trouble. Most small town banks did everything they could for the local investors. And Louise had even accused the banker, Sonny Squire, of poisoning her family's herd. Immy wondered if charges had ever been brought.

She wished she had those damn clippings. Someone must have them. She knew Mike Mallett would never bother with them. He didn't pay attention to anything but his own folders. Immy thought Amy JoBeth might have taken them back.

Think, Immy, think. Why would Amy JoBeth collect the clippings, then carelessly leave them behind when she quit the job?

If Amy JoBeth left them behind it was improbable she had then come back and taken them. Unless they had achieved an importance they didn't have before, for some reason. Something had prompted someone to remove all traces of them from Immy's desk, and from the newspaper archives. They must be all-fired important, Immy thought, but to who?

However, if Immy couldn't find them, they wouldn't help her solve any cases.

So what would?

A louder roar erupted from the crowd. Hortense jumped to her feet and lifted Drew to stand on the bench so she could see past the heads in front of them. Immy stood, too, just in time to see the excitement. The cowboy clown galloped over and snatched the bareback rider around his chest to pull him from the bucking horse. The clown dangled the rider and urged his pony farther from the sharp rear hooves that the riderless bronc was still flinging skyward.

As the excited horse calmed down and obediently trotted to the exit chute, the announcer yelled above the din. "That was the best ride of this rodeo, folks!"

And Immy had been inside her head, being a detective, for the whole thing. That proved she should be a real one.

The wranglers started getting ready for calf roping. Immy told Hortense and Drew she needed to make a pit stop. She didn't really, but she wanted to do some hard thinking. For once, Drew didn't want to tag along. She loved calf roping.

Immy sat in the shade at a picnic table and pondered her cases. Even though her files were not there with her, she remembered everything she'd written in them.

Her table was a little too close to the portable potties that were set there to handle overflow from the permanent bathrooms at the stands. A large fly population buzzed about her head.

She still had a lot of open cases, including her first one, The Case of the Slaughtered Pig. Upon further thought, she regretted the title. Most pigs were slaughtered. That pig was murdered. Probably shot with Sonny Squire's gun. Probably by Rusty, but maybe not.

She swatted at the flies and sat up straight. She had clues for The (renamed) Case of the Murdered Pig. She had the gun and she had the bullets. Now what?

Raspy whispering came from around the corner of the nearby row of potties. That harsh grate of a whisper could only be Louise. Immy sat still and strained her ears, wishing she had something to amplify the sound with.

"Yes, I know what day it is." It sounded like Amy JoBeth.

"Well, what do you think I should do about it?"

"I thought Vern said—" That was Amy JoBeth, no longer whispering.

"I don't care what your precious Vern said—" Louise was talking aloud, too. "—Sonny killed Gretchen. He almost said it."

"But, if he didn't say it, then how do you—"

"He started to say it."

A noisy sniff sounded. "Did he say *why* he killed her?"

"Here, darlin', wipe your nose. No, he didn't finish saying he *did* it."

"Mommy!" Drew called from the other side of the picnic area. She ran toward Immy, who scrambled up and ran to meet her, to get as far from the toilets as she could. Maybe, if Louise and Amy JoBeth came out from behind them, they wouldn't know how close she'd been sitting. And wouldn't know she'd overheard them. Not that they'd said anything bad, or embarrassing. It just seemed like a private, personal conversation.

"What do you need, sugar?" asked Immy.

"Geemaw sent me to find you. She's hungry."

Immy realized it was getting dark. As she and Drew left the picnic area, strings of tiny white lights that were strung in the trees above the tables twinkled to life. The stadium lights in the ring were coming on, too. Soon it would time for the closing ceremonies. She and Drew spotted the matched palominos being ridden toward the place at the far side of the arena where they would line up for the serpentine. The riders all wore white hats and matching red shirts with "Fish and Game and Wild

Things", a local sporting goods store, stenciled on the back. They would parade, single-file, weaving back and forth, making a serpentine pattern across the arena.

Immy and Drew stopped at the pizza and lemonade stands and brought back provisions for Hortense, and for themselves. The pizza was the cheapest thing Immy could find that would keep off starvation for all of them until they returned home tonight. This outing was using up a bunch of her cash. Immy would consult the want ads first thing Monday morning.

"When are the fireworks, Mommy?" asked Drew, chewing her crust vigorously.

"Do not verbalize when your orifice contains consumables, Nancy Drew," said Hortense.

"Okay," Drew answered, her mouth still full.

Immy wasn't sure if Drew knew what her Geemaw's words meant, but she'd heard them often enough. Eventually she'd figure it out. Immy had.

Hortense leaned close to Immy and lowered her voice. "Who is the military man sitting in proximity to the Cotters?"

Immy looked in the direction of Hortense's gaze. A man in Air Force uniform, captain's bars on his shoulders, sat a row behind Louise and Amy JoBeth, who were on the other side of the arena. He leaned forward, talking to Amy JoBeth. Immy couldn't read her expression, but she could read Louise's. Not happy.

Amy JoBeth's face softened as Immy watched the interplay and soon a gentle smile played on her lips and she leaned her head slightly toward the captain's.

Hortense had said Amy JoBeth's ex was a military man. Maybe she had a weakness for a man in uniform. Immy knew she herself did. Well, Immy, herself, had a weakness for a lot of men, no matter what they were wearing. Maybe a new guy would turn the tide for Amy JoBeth's mental state and keep her out of the tornado shelter. But Louise sure looked upset about him being there, talking to her daughter.

"Okay, my mouth is empty," said Drew. "When are the fireworks?"

Immy smiled at her daughter. "Pretty soon. They have to crown the queen first."

"Oh, goody! I'm going to be a rodeo queen when I grow up."

Another reason for Immy to succeed as a detective. Or at something. A rodeo queen was a better role model than a Barbie doll, but Drew probably thought of them as equivalent. At least a rodeo queen had to know how to ride well carrying a big old flag, which is more than a lot of other beauty pageant queens need to know.

"Or maybe a princess."

"A rodeo princess?" asked Immy.

"No, I wanna be a real princess."

"I think some genetic components are required for that," said Hortense with a fond smile. "But, who knows? You may meet a Prince Charming."

Hortense got that dreamy, wistful look that meant she was thinking about Dad. Immy suddenly wanted to be home and take his badge out of her dresser drawer. To run her fingers over its cool, smooth surface. To bask in memories of her big, strong dad. She reached into her purse for a tissue and her fingers met the gun. She's forgotten to take it out last night.

Ralph Sandoval's voice came from somewhere behind Immy. She spun around and tried to spot him in the stands above her. She located him when he and his friends stood up, since he was a head taller than the two guys who stood with him. They edged to the end of their row and started making their way down. Immy waved, but Ralph wasn't looking in her direction. She waved harder, but still no luck.

The guys reached the bottom and disappeared by the time Immy got to the end of her row. She ran out to scan the area and found them at the beer vendor. The line was long because the alcohol vendors were required to stop selling very soon. Immy fiddled with her hair and her purse and paced around until the three men started back.

"Oh hi, Ralph. I didn't know you were here."

"Hi Immy," he said, brightening at the sight of her. "Hey, this is Don and Phil, my buddies from bowling."

"Nice to meet you. I'm Immy." She wondered if their last name was Everly, but they didn't look like brothers. One was thin as a rail, the other pretty chunky.

"Go ahead," Ralph told them. "I'll catch up."

"Ralph," Immy whispered as they left. "I have a clue."

Ralph gave her a blank look. "That's nice."

Immy huffed out a breath of exasperation. "I have an important clue. I think I have the gun that murdered Gretchen."

Ralph scratched his head. "I don't think you can call killing a pig murder, Immy."

"But everything ties in to that. Someone killed Rusty because they thought he was the one who killed Gretchen."

"Everything? Does Poppy's murder tie to it?"

"I don't know how she figures in, but she was killed the same way. Drugged, then hanged."

Ralph sipped his beer and squinted at Immy. "You know, you might be right."

"About what?"

"Maybe we should look more closely at what happened to that pig." He shook his head. "But we can't. We don't have the body, or anything. We didn't investigate the scene except for clues to Rusty's death."

Immy gave his a wide, triumphant grin. "I have the bullets."

"Wait. You have the bullets—from the pig?"

Immy nodded.

"And the gun?"

"Maybe. If the bullets match the gun, then I have the gun."

"Okay. It won't be evidence for court, but it could help us. Bring them in tomorrow and we'll—"

A shot sounded and Immy hit the ground, covering her head with her hands. She raised up and looked around, then saw a splotch in the dirt beside her. Her elbow was bleeding.

"It's all right," she said, sitting up and examining her elbow. "It's only a flesh wound."

Ralph reached down and gave her a hand up. "You hit your elbow on a rock. That was a firecracker."

Twenty-Two

Tʜᴇ ɴᴇxᴛ sᴛʀɪɴɢ ᴏꜰ ꜰɪʀᴇᴄʀᴀᴄᴋᴇʀs sᴏᴜɴᴅᴇᴅ ʟɪᴋᴇ ᴀ ᴍᴀᴄʜɪɴᴇ ɢᴜɴ, but Immy kept herself from diving to the dirt again.

"You're sure those are firecrackers?" she asked Ralph.

"It's the Fourth of July." He took a swig of his beer. "But I think those are kids and they shouldn't be shooting them off here."

More explosions went off and Immy heard snorting and a commotion.

"Ralph, I think they're awfully close to the bull pens."

When the official rodeo fireworks went off, which they would do in a few minutes, they were fired from far outside the arena to keep from spooking the animals.

Ralph cocked an ear in the direction of the sounds. Immy heard metal clanging, like a bull was butting the sides of his pen.

"You're right. And it sounds like an animal is spooked."

The next sound was worse. A scream.

"Hold this." Ralph thrust his beer cup at Immy and took off for the pens. Some splashed onto her shirt.

She ran after him, sloshing the rest of it on her shirt, her jeans, and some on her tennies.

"Hold it!" Ralph shouted to a pair of retreating backs. They looked like the same boys who had thrown the rocks earlier, the ones chased off by Kyle Joe. Ralph started after them, but Immy stopped to look at the bull and saw what was in the pen.

This bull was even bigger than the one whose pen Drew had fallen into. A black Mexican bull with horns that gleamed white in the dim light this far from the stadium. The tips of his horns gleamed, too, but they weren't supposed to. They were supposed to be wrapped in a dark color. And they weren't supposed to drip.

"Ralph!" yelled Immy.

The bull appeared to nuzzle the form at his feet. Then he hooked a horn into it and lifted it off the ground about twelve inches.

She heard Ralph trotting back.

The form in the pen took shape. It was a man. The man moaned.

Ralph reached her and she pointed. He ran to the pen and started to climb the wall.

The bull backed off a few feet, pawed the ground a few times, then lowered his head and came at the inert man again, goring him in the torso and tossing him again.

Immy screamed.

This time, when the man landed, the bull trampled him with its front hooves.

The man moaned louder.

Immy started to whimper. She hoped it was a bull rider and he was still wearing his protective vest.

The bull pushed at him with its massive head and turned the man so Immy could see his face.

Sonny Squire. He would not be wearing a vest.

Then the pen was surrounded by men, most of them rodeo workers, probably summoned by all the clanking and commotion. Three of them climbed into the pen and distracted the bull. They taunted it and ran up the side rails when the bull charged them.

Meanwhile, a couple more wranglers snatched Sonny and handed him over the enclosure.

He wasn't making a sound. He wasn't moving. The ambulance that was always parked just outside the arena drove in and the EMTs bundled Sonny inside. He left a wide trail of blood, from the site of his goring, up and down the sides of the pen he'd been hauled over, and across the dirt to the back of the ambulance. The vehicle took off, not starting lights and siren until it reached the outskirts of the fair area.

Immy wondered if Sonny could be alive, having lost that much blood. She hated bulls.

*****

"The malt brew libation is supposed to go inside your gastrointestinal system, Imogene, not all over the exterior of your clothing."

Immy realized she reeked from Ralph's beer, now sloshed all over her clothes.

"Mother, something horrible has happened. We have to leave."

"More horrible than being too drunk to get the beer inside you?"

"It's Ralph's beer, not mine."

"What's horrible?" asked Drew.

"Mr. Squire had an…accident in the…in the bull pen." She was shaking, her whole body was shaking. Was she going into shock? "I… I have to leave."

"Is he…?" Hortense raised her plucked eyebrows to ask Immy if he was all right.

Immy shook her head. "A bull was in the pen. An angry bull."

"Did Mr. Squire fall in?" said Drew. "Like I did? Did the big, strong cowboy get him out?"

Hortense, eyebrows still raised, shook her head behind Drew's back.

"No, not like you did." Immy's teeth chattered when she spoke. "They took him away in an ambulance. Ralph is down there handling things. I have to go home now."

"Before the Queen?" Drew sounded horrified.

Immy realized the contestants were carefully riding into the arena, in their usual prescribed formation, all dressed up in silk cowgirl shirts. The girls carried fluttering pennants, which advertised rodeo sponsors, stuck on the saddle pommel. They held them upright with difficulty as the wind picked up even more than usual.

199

"Will you make it?" asked Hortense.

Maybe it would be best to keep to as normal a routine as possible, for Drew's sake.

Immy leaned her face against her mother's soft upper arm and let her tears flow. Hortense stroked Immy's hair and they got through the pageant. The girl in the purple shirt won, which displeased Drew. She'd wanted the pink-shirted contestant to win.

*****

The next morning, Monday, Immy made a quick trip into Wymee Falls to get a copy of *The Moron's Compleat Bull and Cattle Handling Guidebook*. If people were going to keep falling into bull pens, she wanted to know how to react.

Back in Saltlick, Immy brought the bullets she'd kept all this time, with Sonny's gun, into the Saltlick police station. Tabitha had returned from vacation, but, for once, called the chief as soon as she saw Immy come in. Maybe, Immy thought, she feels sorry for me because of my bruise and my elbow.

Immy's bruised cheek was a yellow-green color today and her elbow was bandaged, where she'd cut it diving to avoid firecrackers.

Immy walked down the hallway behind Chief Emmett and put her paper bag on his desk.

"What is this?" he asked, reasonably enough, settling into his chair.

"It's complicated," answered Immy as she perched on the edge of the guest chair.

Chief drew the bag toward him, opened it up and peered inside. "It looks like a gun and…what's underneath?"

"The bullets I took out of Gretchen."

His mouth dropped open and he leaned toward Immy. She flinched. Was he going for his gun?

"I had to get them. No one else would. I wanted to know who killed Gretchen."

"Gretchen was Tinnie's pet pig, right?"

"How could you forget? That's what started this whole mess."

"I well remember what started this whole mess. I just didn't pay much attention to the pig's name."

No one paid much attention to the pig, Immy thought. Her gate was carelessly left unlatched and she was shot by accident. Poor thing. Immy hoped Tinnie had given Gretchen nice treats while she was still alive.

"I think we could solve some other crimes if we could solve this one. Is there any way you can see if those bullets came from that gun?"

"Where did you get the gun?"

"Sonny Squire dropped it last night. He was drunk. I didn't think he should have it, in his condition, so I picked it up and kept it for him. Until he sobered up." That story was close enough to the truth.

"You haven't heard, I guess," said Chief. "Sonny was DOA at Wymee Falls General Hospital last night."

Immy took a wild stab. "Was he full of horse tranquilizer, too?"

Chief kept his mouth shut, but gave a start, and Immy knew she was right.

What in the hell was going on? "I know these things can't be court evidence, but Ralph says they might point to something you could use."

Chief stroked his chin, at least considering what Immy was saying. "Ralph might be onto something. If this gun killed Gretchen...."

"Then Sonny killed Gretchen."

"No. Then this gun killed Gretchen. There's a big difference."

So, Rusty could still have killed her, but Immy didn't think so. Betsy had told Immy that Rusty lied about it to protect his wife's relationship with her father. Immy wasn't sure Tinnie deserved Rusty for a husband. Then she remembered how many other women he was sleeping with. Okay, maybe they deserved each other. Neither of them deserved little Zack.

She'd just have to wait and see if the bullets matched before she could go forward with any more speculations on who deserved whom.

"Where's Ralph today?"

"He's taking the day off," said the chief, but didn't tell her where he was.

*****

When Immy got home, her heart lifted at the sight of Ralph's truck in front of her trailer. She found him in the backyard nailing boards together. Drew was feeding treats to Marshmallow, who acted like he hadn't eaten for weeks.

"Whatcha doing?" she asked.

"Marshmallow isn't going to stay that size forever. I'm making a ramp so he can get in and out of the house."

Immy and Hortense, but mostly Immy, had been carrying Marshmallow in and out, up and down the short flight of steps to the back door that led into the utility room, where Marshmallow's litter box was kept.

"Good idea," said Immy. "Your idea about the ballistics test is good, too. Chief Emersen is going to have it done."

"What's ballistics?" asked Drew from across the yard.

"It's a scientific comparison," said Ralph. "It's something the police do to solve cases."

"Oh." Drew didn't look like she believed him. She at least knew when she was being put off, even if what Ralph said *was* true.

"Imogene, dear," called Hortense from the back door. "Could you drive me in to Wymee Falls this afternoon? I nearly forgot, my Association of Retired Librarians is meeting today."

"How could you forget that?" asked Immy.

"My conjecture is that the fact that today is a holiday threw me off."

Her group usually met the first Monday of the month. But today was July 5th and therefore was the official holiday for the Fourth. "So why are they meeting today?"

"Habit, I suppose."

Immy knew librarians were meticulous, habit-plagued people, so that made sense.

"Ralph," said Hortense, "would you like to stay for lunch?"

"Sure, Mrs. Duckworthy. I might be about half finished by then. What do you say we all ride into town and Immy and Drew and I will putter around while you meet?"

"Excellent proposition." Hortense beamed at him and went inside to prepare a sumptuous, thick, roast beef sandwich with horseradish sauce, using the bread she'd baked the day before, and some potato salad made with lots of mayonnaise.

*****

"Good shot," called Ralph.

Drew had finally gotten the golf ball through the clown's mouth. "I know," she said, complacently, in spite of her five previous failed tries. "I think I'll get a good score."

"I know you will," said Ralph.

Immy frowned. Yes, Drew would get a good score with Ralph keeping it. But she wasn't sure she wanted her daughter to learn how easy cheating was while she was so young.

Ralph caught her eye and shrugged at the frown. Immy made a little grimace and accepted the fact she was outnumbered.

After their miniature golf outing (Drew had won), they stopped at the food court in the mall where Ralph indulged Drew with a smoothie. He indulged Immy, too, and the cold treat tasted good after the heat of the golf course. She marveled that people played real golf in this weather. It took even longer and required even more exertion.

A blob of smoothie dribbled down Drew's chin and Ralph reached over and gave her a tender wipe. He caught Immy's fond gaze at her daughter and returned one to her.

It occurred to her, not for the first time, that they looked just like a little family of three. Ralph doted on Immy and Drew, Drew doted on Ralph, and Immy doted on Drew. Did Immy dote on Ralph? She needed to decide about that, probably soon. She should make a list of his plusses and minuses.

It was time right now, though, to fetch Hortense from her meeting. With Drew wiped off, they bundled into the van and Ralph drove it to the Wymee Falls library, a grand edifice fronted with two story white columns flanked by large US and Texas flags.

Hortense nearly skipped to the van when she emerged. Immy

climbed into the back seat with Drew.

"I'm so delighted," Hortense said, pulling the seatbelt to enlarge the girth, since Immy had adjusted it for herself. "The Association is making a special gift to our own little Saltlick library. Some sort of national grant monies, our president said."

Ralph headed for the outskirts of Wymee Falls.

"Unca Ralphie bought me a smoothie," exclaimed Drew. "And I won at goff."

Hortense twisted in her seat to answer Drew. "Wonderful, dear."

"Was Louise there today?" asked Immy.

"Louise!" Hortense spat. "I'll tell you about Louise Cotter. That woman is a prevaricator of the worst ilk."

"What did she do?" asked Ralph. "What did she say?" Immy thought she saw Ralph's ears prick up when he jerked his head toward her.

"She said she was a librarian in Bootstrap, where she used to live. Well, we had a new member tonight, newly retired from the self-same institution, the Bootstrap Public Library. A wonderful man named Algernon. He has never heard of Louise Cotter. According to him, a twenty-year veteran of Bootstrap, she was never employed there."

"What?" said Immy. "Where was she a librarian?"

"I doubt she was."

"She's not a librarian?"

"Not even," said Hortense.

That was a peculiar sentence structure for Mother, thought Immy.

"No one has ever heard of her," continued Hortense. "I'm positive she has never been employed by a library. To think, she lied about the profession of librarian. Who would do such a thing?"

"Louise Cotter, I guess," said Ralph.

Since it was Ralph who said it, he didn't get the glare Immy would have gotten.

Twenty-Three

TUESDAY MORNING THE PHONE RANG WHILE Immy and Hortense lingered over after-breakfast coffee. Drew had scampered to the backyard where she was coaxing Marshmallow up and down the sturdy wooden ramp Ralph had made.

Immy jumped up to answer, but hesitated when she saw the caller was Mike Mallett.

"It's my old boss," she said.

"And?" asked Hortense.

"Maybe he wants to press charges after all."

"Answer the telephone, dear."

She picked it up carefully, thinking that if she didn't squeeze too hard, the call might go better.

"Hey, kiddo," he started. "How's tricks?"

"Well...." Tricks weren't all that good without the income from her job, she wanted to say. She felt her grip tightening and flexed her fingers.

"I just wanna tell ya, I've interviewed like crazy all week long. I kinda thought you'd be easy to replace."

That didn't sound like a compliment. Immy couldn't think of a reply, so she didn't make one.

"Well, you ain't that easy, it turns out. These gals waltz in here in tank tops and flip-flops, wires and tattoos hangin' out all over. I need someone in the front that looks good, kid. How'd ya like your job back?"

"Uh, really?" *Way to sound articulate, Immy.*

"Yeah, really. They're poppin' gum and answerin' cell phones while I'm talkin' to 'em. And, I'll admit, I been hearin' all the news from those people you're mixed up with out there in Saltlick and Cowtail. I guess I can't blame you for all the time you been takin' off."

"I would really like the job back, Mr. Mallett."

"Hey, it's Mike. You've never called me Mr. Mallett. We'll have to work something out about hours, though. I can't pay you for not showing up and for not working. C'mon in next Monday and we'll talk."

"Uh...."

"Deal?"

"Deal."

Dazed, Immy turned to face her mother. "I got my job back."

Hortense beamed.

"So," said Immy, "you think that's okay?"

"I am becoming inured to your proximity to the detecting profession. And, I surmise, being in private practice is significantly different from being in service to the public."

"Don't worry, Mother. I'm never going to be a police detective. Too much school involved."

Hortense frowned at that, higher education being one of her causes. But Drew distracted them by bursting through the back door into the utility room with her pet pig trotting behind.

"Marshmallow is hungry," she announced. "And so am I."

"No wonder," said Hortense. "All that running up and down your nice new incline." She rose to get both of them something to eat and Immy retreated to her bedroom.

Her PI course book lay on her dresser, seeming to admonish her for not having studied lately. She'd been leafing through the *Bull and Cattle Handling Guidebook* instead. But if she were going to resume her detective career, she'd better get back to it. She flopped onto the bed and opened her book to the topic, "Using the Internet". The test wasn't until next Friday, so she'd be able to use Mike Mallett's computer to study. Maybe she'd discuss that with him Monday. Maybe he'd even be okay with it. She'd try to get lots of work done for him, too.

*****

Ralph phoned Immy Wednesday morning to tell her the bullets she'd extracted from Gretchen's poor dead head were a match for the test bullets they'd fired from Sonny Squire's gun.

"What does that mean?" she asked. "Chief said it doesn't mean Sonny killed Gretchen."

"Right. Sonny's gun killed Gretchen. Sonny probably fired it, but there's no way to find out now that Sonny is dead."

"Betsy Wiggins told me that Rusty admitted to her he lied about being the one who killed Gretchen. That Sonny really did."

"Since they're both dead, I don't see where we're going from here."

Immy thought there must be something they could figure out from the fact. After she hung up, she made a list on the back of an old grocery list.

-Gretchen dead

-Sonny's gun

-Rusty confessed

-Betsy says Rusty lied

-Betsy says Sonny killed Gretchen

Immy crossed out what she'd written and tossed the paper in the trash. Her list told her nothing. She needed to get a notebook. It would be much more professional.

Maybe she'd approach it from the other end. She found the envelope from the phone bill in the trash and fished it out.

-Rusty murdered

-Poppy murdered

-Sonny murdered

She drew a line from Rusty to Sonny and wrote "Gretchen" on the line. Then she drew a line from Rusty to Poppy and wrote "affair" on that line. There was no connection between Poppy and Sonny that she could see, though.

Vern had confessed to killing Rusty, but he was in jail when Sonny was trampled by the bull. She crumpled the second list and pitched it into the wastebasket. Maybe her online course would help figure this stuff out if she stuck with it. She got her course book and delved into the chapter called "Internet" again.

After two pages, Immy started pacing up and down the kitchen. Hortense and Drew were out back playing with the pig, but Immy didn't think she should play when her test loomed and her cases were unsolved.

She dialed Ralph's cell phone. "Do you still think Vern killed both Rusty and Poppy?" she asked abruptly.

"Did I say that?"

"Well, I got that idea. I think."

"He says he killed both of them. I think the *Saltlick Weekly* is publishing the confession in their next issue."

"But then, what made that bull decide to kill Sonny Squire?"

"I'm on my way to make an arrest for that right now."

"Really? Who?"

"I can't say right now, Immy. Come to the station in about half an hour and you'll see me take her in."

"Her?"

"Good-bye, Immy."

Her?

What else could she do? She grabbed her purse and car keys and raced out the front door to try to follow Ralph.

He was gone by the time she got to the station. She idled the van in a parking space and thought, hard. Vern, Poppy, Rusty, Sonny, Gretchen. They formed a web, and sitting in the center was Amy JoBeth. Gretchen, the initial victim. Either Rusty or Sonny, the perpetrator, the killer of Amy JoBeth's pig. Vern, the avenger. For Amy JoBeth. Poppy, she suddenly thought, the innocent bystander who may have witnessed Rusty's death. And all the strands of the web led to Amy JoBeth, huddled in her storm cellar while death swirled around her.

Immy pointed the van toward Amy's Swine.

A little more than halfway there the wind picked up and the sky darkened. Immy peered up at the sky and scanned for funnel clouds, the automatic reaction to sudden weather changes in Texas. She also switched the radio on. The unwelcome grunt of the storm warming system issued from the dash speakers.

Immy grabbed her cell phone and called home.

"Mother, there's a tornado spotted outside Saltlick."

"I know, dear. The sirens just went off. Drew and I are under Ralph's nice new ramp, with Marshmallow. I think it's the safest place."

They usually exited the trailer for tornado warnings and lay flat in the yard, since tornadoes seemed to have a preference for picking up trailer homes and flinging them around. Immy thought that maybe under the ramp would be a good place to shelter.

She was closer to her destination than to home, so she kept going. She didn't see a funnel at the moment, but picked up her speed anyway. When she reached Amy's Swine, the wooden sign swung with such violence Immy thought it would fly off the post. She bumped down the long driveway, where she saw Ralph's vehicle at the end.

She slammed the van up next to Ralph's cop car and tried to open her door. Something large and wooden flew past her windshield, followed by a barrage of paper. She put her shoulder into the door and pushed it open. A piece of flying metal clanged against the other side of the van.

Immy ran for the tornado shelter. She tugged at the handle. It was locked.

"Let me in!" She banged on the hatch three times. It flew open.

Ralph ran up the steps, dragged her inside and slammed the door down.

"Immy, what in the goddam hell are you doing here?" Was he angry?

A sudden roar outside drowned out further conversation. Immy sank beside Amy JoBeth on the mattress, Ralph leaned on the wall, giving Immy frequent scowls, and the three of them listened to the storm rage for a good fifteen minutes.

Amy JoBeth shook so hard that Immy put her arms around her to keep the poor woman from falling apart. As the terrible din started to subside, Immy could hear Amy JoBeth's teeth rattling together. She was surprised she couldn't hear her bones, too.

"My pigs, my pigs," Amy JoBeth intoned over and over.

Immy wondered if any of the little porkers would be alive when they emerged.

Twenty-Four

THE SUN PEEKED THROUGH THE CLOUDS with an innocence unrelated to the terror that had just descended from the sky. Amy JoBeth's shaking continued, so Ralph and Immy supported her up the steps into daylight.

Immy, who had taken her purse with her, was glad to see the van intact, except for some dings where debris had hit it. Ralph's car had lost the front passenger window, but was otherwise unscathed. Immy wondered how bulletproof that car must be.

They all looked around, assessing the damage. A huge pecan tree lay across the front yard, its roots reaching upwards, but Amy JoBeth's house still stood, looking unharmed, roof and all.

Amy JoBeth broke from their grasp and ran around the house. Ralph and Immy trailed after. Immy wanted to close her eyes, but couldn't resist looking.

The pigs trotted to the fence and grunted at Amy JoBeth. She poked a forefinger at the pens, counting. "They're all here!" she shouted, then she fell backward.

Ralph caught her before she hit the ground and Immy helped him haul her to her back porch steps.

This, thought Immy, is the faintingest family.

*****

"You can't arrest her when she just fainted," Immy exclaimed.

"I can. That's exactly what I'm doing," said Ralph, turning back to Amy JoBeth. "You're under arrest for obstructing justice in the murder of Rusty Bucket."

"I didn't do it." Amy JoBeth was near tears.

"We have witnesses testifying that you planted evidence leading to a false arrest."

He read the Miranda warning and gestured for Amy JoBeth to accompany him to the police car.

It didn't sound like he was going to take any guff so Immy kept her mouth shut.

"I'll be back later for your truck, Amy JoBeth," said Ralph. "I have a warrant to impound it."

"I never should have loaned it to Vern," muttered Amy JoBeth.

This was awful, thought Immy. Her client had now been arrested twice. Some PI she was.

"Immy." Amy JoBeth twisted her head to see around Ralph, walking behind her. "Can you make sure the pigs are fed?"

"Um...."

"They get the pig chow that's in the shed."

Immy thought she should be able to find that. "How often? How much?"

"Twice a day."

Ralph had the back door open and tugged Amy JoBeth toward it.

"Five of those big scoops from the bag in the shed," Amy JoBeth continued, ducking to get into the car. "Put it in the big trough. And there's apples and carrots in my fridge. They like those, too."

Ralph slammed the door before Immy could ask Amy JoBeth how she was supposed to get into her house. But the pigs could probably go without fruits and vegetables for a few days. Immy hoped her client wouldn't be in stir longer than that.

As she watched the cop car disappear down the road, Immy had another thought. Louise had surely fed her daughter's pigs when she was in jail before. Why had she asked Immy this time? Maybe because

Immy was handy. Or maybe there'd been a falling-out?

Maybe Immy should get hold of Louise and let her know that her daughter was in jail again. That was the least she could do, considering she'd failed at finding the killer.

"Okay, Immy, think," she told herself aloud. Evidence leading to a false arrest. Well, the evidence that led to Vern's arrest was the confetti. If it was planted, who else but Amy JoBeth would have planted it? And those two were no longer a lovey-dovey couple. Maybe Vern turned against Amy JoBeth because she broke up with him, or because she fingered him.

But Immy knew she broke up with him because he was a killer. So she wasn't one. Was she?

Ralph was impounding Amy JoBeth's white truck. Something tickled the back of her brain. A white truck. Hadn't Wanda, the front desk gal at Cowtail's Finest, seen Vern arrive in a light-colored truck? His own was a dark color, usually so dirty you could hardly tell what color it was supposed to be. Amy JoBeth kept her white one spotless. But she'd loaned it to Vern. If a dead Poppy had been transported in it, Immy bet it wouldn't be exactly spotless. And wouldn't Amy JoBeth have to know he'd done that?

The truth hit Immy like a lead tumbleweed.

She sank to the damp grass. She couldn't solve her way out of a pig feed sack. She was no Detective. She wasn't even a detective with a lower case D. She was a file clerk. And her client was probably guilty.

Immy wasn't sure how much time passed, but she looked up as the sun broke through the clouds, which were abandoning the sky. Her hair fell into her face when she bowed her head. A light breeze, stirring her hair, made her realize her cheeks were wet with tears. She eyed the storm shelter.

Maybe she should retreat from life, like Amy JoBeth did. People would get all concerned about her. They would come and try to talk her into leaving the hole in the ground. They would bring her food. Drew would climb into her lap and put her hands around Immy's neck, give her a wet kiss. Hortense would bring—-no, Hortense would probably not go down those steep steps. But she would send comfort food down with Drew.

Hortense would be so disappointed, though. Maybe she wouldn't even show up. A daughter of hers, in a tornado shelter with depression—the very idea. She would remind Immy that she had a loving family, and a job to go to next week. And that she had gotten a very high score on her last test for the PI course.

Immy pushed herself to her feet and drove home to study for next Friday's test.

*****

Ralph had the gall to show up for supper that night. After they ate, Immy talked him into their usual hand-in-hand walk at dusk. Immy thought Ralph seemed reluctant to be alone with her. He must suspect, Immy thought, that she would pump him.

When they were well away from the trailer, Immy asked why he arrested Amy JoBeth.

"Don't start in on me, Immy," he said. "You know I can't tell you anything."

"But she's my client."

"Your what? You suddenly have a law degree?" His hand tightened on hers.

"No, I'm investigating on her behalf. She asked me to."

"She asked you to find out who killed her pig."

Immy kicked at a rock in the road.

"Right? And you got the bullets matched up." He gave her hand a squeeze. "Good job there."

"But you said that didn't prove anything." Was Ralph patronizing her?

"It proved which gun was used."

He was. "And there's no proof of who fired the gun. Except that Sonny Squire practically admitted it to me. And you won't take my word for it."

"But you did get that part figured out."

"Oh yes. Little Immy can figure out stuff." She stuck out her tongue at him. "Stuff that doesn't mean anything. Stuff that doesn't prove anything." She flung his hand away and headed toward home.

"Immy, please."

She kept walking.

"I could maybe tell you a few things," he called.

She turned around and came back. They were in front of Mrs. Wilson's house. Her chained Rottweiler got to its feet and took a few steps in their direction, a low growl arising from deep within his broad chest.

"Let's go someplace else," said Ralph.

They walked across Saltlick to the park. Immy hadn't been there after dark in years. It was usually a teen-age hangout this time of night, but none were here. The Fourth was officially over, this being the Tuesday after. The teens must have other things to do tonight, Immy thought.

Ralph sat on a picnic table under the shelter and put his boots on the bench. Immy took a seat beside his feet.

"What can you tell me?" she asked.

"Let me think."

"Well, what did you arrest Amy JoBeth for? She'll tell me if I go see her." She leaned against his leg.

"True." Ralph ran his hand over his jaw. His slight stubble raised a scratchy sound. "Vern decided to talk. He said he used her truck to transport Poppy to the motel."

"I knew it!"

"And he says Amy JoBeth planted the pink confetti on him and hid the drugs in her shelter."

"And you believe him?" She laid her head on his thick, hard thigh.

"Not entirely. If it weren't for the truck, I'd say he's lying all the way."

"Yeah, you figure she must have known he was using her truck to transport bodies."

"How could she not?" Ralph absently stroked Immy's hair.

"Well, she's been unwell for awhile now. Maybe she's not too perceptive." Immy looked up at his face.

Ralph narrowed his eyes. He was considering what she said.

"He could have just said he wanted to borrow it," Immy said. "She wouldn't necessarily know he was going to carry a dead body around in it." Immy did not want Amy JoBeth to be a murderer, or even an abettor. "Ralph, she was truly upset when he told her he murdered two people. She wants nothing more to do with him."

"But we have to look at the truck and consider what that means. If it turns out her truck has traces of anything from transporting Poppy, well...."

Her scalp was beginning to tingle from Ralph's touch. "This is really going to set her back, if that happens."

"Oh, hell, Immy, everything sets that woman back."

The locust clatter was louder at the playground than on the streets. Probably because the park was ringed with live oak trees, Immy thought. The first few stars were beginning to poke through the sky's violet curtain, and the moon hung low in the east tonight.

Immy wished life weren't so hard for Amy JoBeth. She couldn't imagine what was going to happen if it turned out her truck had helped Vern carry out his unspeakable act.

"What about Sonny?" she asked. "Vern couldn't have gotten that bull to kill him. He's still locked up. You haven't let him out, have you?"

"No. No, we still think he's good for Rusty and Poppy."

"But how does Sonny's death fit in?"

"You got me."

Ralph bent down and lifted Immy's head up for a long, lingering kiss.

Twenty-Five

ON THEIR WAY TO THE TRAILER, Immy had a sudden thought. She was sure Amy JoBeth didn't kill Rusty or Poppy. But what about Sonny? Could she have killed him? What about those clippings? What about Louise intimating that Sonny had swindled them out of their land, caused her husband's suicide? Maybe Amy JoBeth had decided to avenge the family honor. After all, she had been obsessed enough about the history to collect those clippings. She probably even stole the originals from the newspaper morgue.

After Ralph left, Immy realized she hadn't yet called Louise to let her know Amy JoBeth had been taken in again. She got her cell phone and took it into the front yard to call Louise, not wanting Drew to be exposed to their discussion, in case she had to say anything that tender young ears shouldn't hear.

Louise answered right away.

"Immy? What's going on? I can't find Amy JoBeth anywhere."

"She was arrested this morning. That's what I'm calling to tell you."

"Again? What for now? She hasn't done a thing."

"I know. But the police got some new testimony."

"What about?" That high decibel shriek reached an almost unbearable pitch. Immy held the phone away from her ear.

"I think the main thing is her truck."

"Her truck? That has nothing to do with Sonny's death."

Sonny's death? Why would she think that? "No, it's linked to Poppy's death."

"What?"

Immy moved the phone even farther from her battered eardrum. "Did Amy JoBeth have something to do with Sonny? Because of the family history? Did she drug him?"

Louise lowered her voice. "Immy, I need you to come to Amy JoBeth's place. There's something I have to show you."

"What is it?"

"I can't tell you on the phone. It's urgent."

Should she trust a woman who lied about being a librarian? "I don't think I can come right now."

"This can't wait. I need you to do something for Amy JoBeth."

Immy remembered that she hadn't fed the pigs. "Maybe I can stop by for a few minutes. Are the pigs fed?"

"Good. I'll be waiting."

This was kind of strange. But, if she could do something for Amy JoBeth.... after all, the woman was her client, and Immy had failed her so far.

She ran into the house to get her purse and car keys and told Hortense she was going to feed the pigs at the pig farm and would be right back.

Hortense was deep into a drama and waved goodbye without looking up. Drew was probably in the bedroom, deep into Barbies that were pretending to be rodeo queens.

Darkness was complete by the time Immy reached Amy's Swine. Her headlights picked up the fallen tree and swept across the yard as she turned the van around so it would be ready to go when she left. She didn't see Louise anywhere. Her old brown Buick was parked up close to the house, though. Maybe she was inside.

Immy cut her engine. Leaving her purse on the seat, she got out and headed around the house to the pig's enclosure to give them five scoops of chow. She would talk to Louise after she fed the cute little porkers. Well, not so little, but very cute.

It was dark behind the house. Come to think of it, it was dark inside the house, too. Where was Louise? Immy made her way to the shed in the pig's enclosure and patted around the vicinity of the door to find the latch. Luckily, there was a light switch right inside the door.

She flinched at the bright light after the darkness outside, but found a huge sack labeled "Pig Chow" beside the door. A scoop was conveniently located on the floor next to it. Now to find the trough. The open door of the shed lent enough light to show her where it was, not far away. She made four trips to the trough, carefully holding the full scoop level so she wouldn't spill the food in the dirt. Although the pigs could probably get it from there, she thought.

On her return to the shed to get the fifth scoop, she found Louise.

Immy had trouble processing what she was seeing. Louise, the non-librarian mother of Amy JoBeth, the timid and depressed pig farmer, stood in the doorway of the shed with a mean look in her eye. And a shotgun aimed at Immy's chest.

Immy let the scoop fall to the ground.

"Louise? It's me, Immy."

"Yes, it is, isn't it? Immy, first class snoop and busybody. So you figured everything out, didn't you?" Louise was dressed cowgirl style, despite the fact she didn't have a ranch, or cattle anymore. She wore a denim jacket and boots, too warm for the July weather. Immy wondered if she was wearing a jacket so that she could conceal something in the pockets. One of them bulged like it contained something.

"I don't think so," said Immy. She hadn't actually figured anything out. Had she?

"Who have you told?" Louise walked toward Immy, gun still trained on her torso.

"I haven't told anyone. Honest."

"I don't know if I can believe you. Walk that way." Louise jerked the gun toward the gate.

Immy walked woodenly out of the pen with Louise close on her heels.

"Keep going." Louise poked the barrel hard into Immy's back.

It was harder and harder to breathe. But all her senses went onto high alert. And her mind worked super fast. The culprit was Louise? She killed Sonny? Because she blamed him for her husband's death?

"Did you take Vern's stolen drugs from the shelter?" Immy asked.

"Yep, I knew you'd figured out all the details. Vern was sure upset. He didn't need 'em no more, though. He'd done his dirty work."

A double negative. This woman was definitely not a librarian.

"And I needed 'em."

"To drug Sonny. Like Vern drugged Rusty and Poppy. So Vern really killed those two? Not you?"

Louise's laugh sent icicles shooting through Immy's veins. "What an idiot! I told him to kill Gretchen's killer. My poor Amy JoBeth was so damned upset, I wanted to make her feel better. And I loved that pig, too. He's so stupid he got the wrong person. Tinnie told Amy JoBeth just the other day that Sonny was the one who shot Gretchen. Not that Rusty deserved to live, treating Amy JoBeth's pig like that, wanting to smoke her, but poor Poppy was in the wrong place at the wrong time."

"She saw Vern kill Rusty, you mean."

Louise nodded. "Don't stop. Keep going."

"But you drugged Sonny?"

"Now there's someone that should have been killed a long time ago. When he and his bank foreclosed on my husband, I should have just shot him. Poor Al committed suicide because of that sidewinder."

"But you didn't ever shoot him."

"I put him in with that bull and poked the damn thing until he trampled that son of a bitch to death."

"Why did you kill Sonny now? After all this time?"

"Breaking my daughter's heart was the last straw. I thought Vern had done my work for me when he killed Rusty, but then it turns out it was Sonny that shot Amy JoBeth's pig. So Sonny had to die. That was the last straw! And Tinnie will be next."

Immy stopped walking. Evil radiated from this woman in waves.

"Keep walking." They were headed toward the storm shelter. Was

Louise going to lock Immy inside it?

"How did you get Sonny into the bullpen?" Immy asked.

"You'll find out. I'm a lot stronger than I look."

It was then that Immy realized they were passing the steps to the shelter and heading for the fence that bordered the property. The fence with the neighboring rancher's bull on the other side.

Was Louise going to drug her? She'd fight like a bull herself to prevent that.

"Stand right there." Louise shifted the shotgun to her left hand and reached into the pocket of her jacket with her right. Immy didn't think her assailant could fire the weapon one-handed, so she ducked and rushed Louise, toppling her to the ground.

But, as Immy fell atop the larger woman, she felt a prick in her thigh.

Louise shoved Immy off her and scrambled to her feet, an evil smile on her face and a syringe in her hand.

The shotgun lay beside Immy. She grabbed for it, but Louise stomped on her hand.

"Ow!" yelled Immy. "You drugged me!" She made another try for the gun but this time Louise smashed her booted foot into Immy's face, catching her in the mouth. A metal taste sprang to her tongue. Immy spat and, even though it was dark, she knew she had just gotten rid of a mouthful of blood. She curled up in pain. Another blow landed on the back of her head.

Immy rolled away so she wouldn't get kicked again. She had to get up. She had to get away.

She struggled to her feet, dripping blood from her mouth. She wondered if she'd lost some teeth.

Immy turned and started to run. She made it to the door of her van and yanked it open. Louise was sauntering toward her, working the pump on the shotgun.

"You're not going anywhere."

"I'm getting out of here."

"Not in that condition." Louise was still grinning. Immy wanted to kick her in the mouth.

Immy swayed. She grabbed the door handle. Swayed again.

Tried to lift her foot into the van. It wouldn't move.

"See? That stuff works fast. Now, get over to that fence."

Louise poked her in the side with the shotgun barrel. Immy made a grab for it, but missed. The barrel seemed to be out of reach, even though it was touching her.

She stared at the shotgun. The barrel curved and wavered. Louise wavered. There were two Louises. No, three. Immy couldn't feel her hands. Or her feet.

When Louise pushed with her hand, Immy stumbled forward until she was at the fence.

"Now, upsy-daisy." Louise used two hands to shove Immy's slight form up the fence and over the top.

She set the gun down. I need to get the gun.

But Immy was on the other side of the fence. The fence was fifty feet high, at least. Maybe a hundred. How had those women gotten her over it? How many Louises were there?

A snort behind her got her attention.

Louise's cackle came from miles away. "I'll be leaving now. Maybe later I'll discover your body." Her car made an eerie sound when it started up.

I'm drugged. There's only one Louise. There's only one bull.

One bull was a lot, though.

Immy grasped a fence rail and managed to stay upright. A sliver of faint moon showed her the animal.

There's only one bull.

He was at least twenty feet away. Or was that twenty miles? Could she climb back up the fence? She tried to put a foot on the lowest rail. It wouldn't go there. She couldn't feel her foot, couldn't control it.

One of the many bulls floated off the ground. The moon lowered itself and spun around, generating smaller moons and stardust. Someone started singing. The cows were jumping over the moons. Immy shook her head and concentrated.

The bull walked toward her. She held perfectly still. She had read about attacking bulls in *The Moron's Compleat Bull and Cattle Handling Guidebook*. She knew she had. What had the book said?

The bull stopped about ten feet from her. He lowered his head and turned sideways to her. He shook his head slowly, side to side.

Right, that's what the book said. She remembered the illustration. Those were the first signs of threat. Closer to attack, the bull would hunch his shoulders and paw the ground.

Dirt flew from the bull's hooves.

Now she should...what was it she should do? She closed her eyes to block out the swimming, swirling world of her sight. She pictured the pages of the book.

Don't turn your back. Move away slowly.

She grabbed the fence and leaned against it. She squeezed her eyes shut, gripped the fence as hard as she could, and summoned every ounce of her strength. Her foot moved. She took a step alongside the rails.

The bull advanced two steps.

She shoved her hands along the fence. Took another step away. Another.

The bull stopped and watched, head still down, the hairs on his back standing up stiff.

Immy swayed. She couldn't go another step. She knew she had to get farther away, out of his threat zone.

She closed her eyes and grabbed the fence with both hands. Pulled herself along it with hands she couldn't feel. Hands that must have, surely, belonged to someone else.

Another step. Another.

The bull stopped swaying his head. He snorted. Stood watching her.

She took three more steps. Three more.

The bull lost interest. Turned. Walked to the other side of the pasture.

Immy slumped to the ground and let the world spin all it wanted to.

*****

Ralph and Hortense were both there. It was a nice dream. Drew stood behind them. But she looked worried. Well, so did Ralph and Hortense.

Voices came to her from the other end of a tunnel. Immy strained to make them out.

Her head started to clear and the sounds formed into words.

"One good thing, if it is ketamine," said Ralph, "it starts quick, but it goes away quick, too."

"Immy. Sweetheart. Darling." Hortense put her large, warm hand on Immy's forehead, feeling for a fever like she'd done when Immy was a child.

"I'm here, Mother." The bull. "Where's the bull?"

"We found you in his pen," said Ralph.

"Unscathed," said Hortense. "Except for your inebriated state."

"More like hallu—hallugen—hallucin—"

"Hallucinatory." Hortense finished for her.

"Where's Louise?" asked Immy, slurring slightly.

Ralph gestured to his cop car, sitting next to the van.

"When you didn't return forthwith, as you'd indicated you would, I telephoned the constabulary and told Ralph where you were."

"Louise was leaving like a bat out of hell," said Ralph.

"Language."

"Sorry, Hortense. She looked guilty, that's for sure, so I stopped her and she started screaming, trying to hit me."

"So," mumbled Immy, "what did you do?"

"I tased her."

Immy grinned, then grimaced at the pain of her split lip. She ran her tongue around her teeth and they all seemed to be there. She realized she was lying on the ground outside the bull's fence, near the cars. Tears sprang to her eyes. She wiped her face. She could feel her hands.

"Could someone feed the pigs one more scoop? I only gave them four."

Twenty-Six

IMMY AND RALPH STRILLED THE DARK, heading away from the trailer and toward the park. Immy was hoping for a repeat of the events of a few nights ago, and maybe even further developments. But she knew Ralph wasn't one to rush things.

"How was work today?" asked Ralph.

Immy gave a contented sigh. "It's so good to be back in the office. The window in the door is still boarded up, but Mike told me to call a glass company to fix it. It's kind of dark in there during the day."

"I'm glad he hired you back."

"He's letting me study for my course, but only during my lunch time and breaks."

"That's fair." Ralph stroked her knuckles with his thumb.

"And he gave me the day off for Poppy's funeral."

"I saw you talking to Ophelia. She looked ragged at the reception."

"She's decided to move away. She doesn't know where yet, maybe near her brother in Florida, but she did give Drew three pig harnesses."

"Three?"

"For when Marshmallow changes sizes. I hope he doesn't get as big as that huge one. Has Louise admitted killing Sonny?" she asked.

"She's asked for a lawyer. That's about the same thing."

"I was hoping she'd sing like a canary."

"Louise? With her vocal chords? She'd sound more like a screech owl if she sang."

"I called Mr. Bunyun and he says he remembers, all of a sudden, that Amy JoBeth was in looking at the old family articles, and he thinks she cut them out and took them."

"Did he say why?" said Ralph.

"No, but Amy JoBeth did when I called her up about it. She wanted to destroy all traces of those articles so her mother wouldn't ever find them. Louise was getting more irrational every day. Amy JoBeth was afraid that her mother would kill Tinnie if she found out Tinnie was related to Sonny."

"Because she already hated Sonny so much?"

"Exactly. Totally bonkers. But Amy JoBeth also didn't want *you* to figure out how the Squire family had underhandedly gotten the Cotter ranchland. She was afraid her mother had killed Rusty and that would lead the cops to her."

"Not totally bonkers, Immy. Just off the rails of the moral railroad."

"The Squire deal *was* underhanded. Louise is right about that. But it's too bad she had to come so unhinged. Louise is the one who took the envelope from my office."

"How did she get in?"

"With Amy JoBeth's key. That's what Amy JoBeth thinks."

"Have you seen Amy JoBeth in the last couple of days?" Ralph said. "She hasn't been in to the jail to see her mother even once."

"The last time I saw her she looked so happy. That guy I saw at the rodeo with her? That's her ex, Ernie Anderson. He got a promotion to Captain and came here to ask her to remarry him. She told me she's never speaking to her mother again. Amy JoBeth thinks her mother is part of the reason for her depression. Louise always told her daughter how sick she was and treated Amy JoBeth like an invalid."

"Louise is sick."

"Yes. Amy JoBeth is so happy with Ernie, now that her mother's not around."

"I wonder if she's going to move away?" asked Ralph.

"I guess it depends on where Ernie gets stationed next. He's still in the Army."

"Maybe someone will buy Amy's Swine."

"And Jerry's Jerky," said Immy. "I hope someone buys that, too, so it'll keep going."

"Yeah. I guess Tinnie's moving to be near her mother in Fort Worth."

"Drew will miss Zack."

They had reached the park. A necking couple occupied one of the picnic tables, so they walked to the benches near the woods at the edge of the playground. The moon was playing peek-a-boo with the soft, high clouds. A breeze stirred the leaves behind them. Katydids sang so loud their chirps echoed off the live oaks.

Immy and Ralph, oblivious to all of it, got down to business.

About the Author

Kaye George is an award-winning novelist and short-story writer. She writes cozy and traditional mysteries, a prehistory series, and has a suspense novel coming out soon, which will be her seventeenth book. Over fifty short stories have been published, mostly in anthologies and magazines. With family scattered all over the globe, she makes her home in Knoxville TN.